Candles
AND
White
Roses

REBEKAH FANNING

The Book Guild Ltd

First published in Great Britain in 2024 by
The Book Guild Ltd
Unit E2 Airfield Business Park,
Harrison Road, Market Harborough,
Leicestershire. LE16 7UL
Tel: 0116 2792299
www.bookguild.co.uk
Email: info@bookguild.co.uk
Twitter: @bookguild

Typeset in 11pt Minion Pro

Printed and bound by CPI Group (UK) Ltd, Croydon, CR0 4YY

ISBN 978 1916668 836

British Library Cataloguing in Publication Data.
A catalogue record for this book is available from the British Library.

I would like to dedicate this book to my wonderful husband, Peter, whose constant support and encouragement has helped me achieve my dream of becoming a published author.

Introduction

From seemingly humble beginnings, I now sit at the high table adjacent to our glorious new king. Edward IV, King of England. A great man, who is loved by many. He is brave and strong, courageous and true, and, unlike his predecessor, he is a born leader. A king by right. People flock to his side and his presence is unmistakable. As I survey the room, though, it is a bittersweet experience. For only a few months ago, I was in the service of his father, Richard, Duke of York. Alas, he lives no more and for that I grieve, but my grief is nothing compared to that of his wife and children.

My story begins six years ago when I left my village to go on a pilgrimage to the Holy Shrine of St Mary the Virgin at Walsingham. In those days, I was a naïve young woman with failing eyesight and a thirst for knowledge. Along the way, I changed forever and for that I am eternally grateful. During those years, I was fortunate enough to learn about many aspects of life from festivals to friendship, history to tradition, and a great deal more. As I travelled the country, I met new people, learnt secrets from my past, uncovered spies and carried news of great importance to the House of York.

But for all that I have seen, I am still an innocent. I still seek nothing more than adventure and enlightenment. I long for my old life, but that has gone forever. However, if you will allow me to recall my past adventures, I will happily describe them for you. So, let's start at the beginning.

Leaving Home

S weet singing fills the air and all of my senses are heightened. This is the moment I have dreamt of for such a long time.

I slowly rise from the floor onto my knees and immediately my body begins to feel warm again. Lying prostrate before the altar may be a goodly sign to the Lord – and I undertake my pilgrimage with the most devout of intentions – but, in reality, it is cold and uncomfortable. Fully standing now, I quickly survey the congregation. I can see smiles and tears.

The priest begins to speak, "The almighty and everlasting God, who is the way, the truth and the light; dispose of your journey accordingly to His good pleasure. May He send His Archangel Raphael to watch over you, protect you and guide you along the way. Then, at the end, when you have finished, may He return you home safely to us."

With this, he blesses me and my mind begins to race. All of a sudden, everything is real and I question myself. Have I remembered to do everything that is expected of me? Settled any debts, yes. Attended confession, yes. Healed any rifts, yes. Gained my lord's written permission, yes. Without thinking, I look down at the long leather pouch hanging from

1

my girdle that contains my letter of commendation. I pat it gently, like a dear friend – this is my passport to safety. On presentation of this testimonial, officials will let me pass on my way. It is proof that I am not a common wanderer. I am a pilgrim. It also affords me the pilgrim's privilege of access to alms and lodgings. This is not to say that I am a beggar, as that would be untrue. I have means enough. From my girdle also hangs a small leather pouch, which contains a collection of half-pennies, which were given to me by the local guild.

The priest is now sprinkling holy water all over me and my possessions. This is for protection.

As I stand, I am dressed in a pale-yellow kirtle – the colour of which I am very proud of, as I dyed it myself using onion skins. Underneath, I wear a much thinner linen kirtle and on my head is a linen coif. Oh, and I forgot to mention that my eating knife and spoon also hang from my girdle. In my left hand, I hold my staff and over my right shoulder hangs a beautiful soft brown leather satchel. It was a present from my father. It has two long leather straps that can be used to tie it about my body, which will come in very handy when travelling. The front is embossed with white roses and on the back it is plain. Inside, I carry my wooden cup and bowl. In truth, I have known this satchel all my life as it has taken pride of place in our home for years. I think it may have belonged to my mother, but I'm not too sure.

The mass is drawing to a close and the priest is quoting passages from the Book of Matthew. At the end of the reading comes the most painful part of the journey so far. I shake with a mixture of fear and anticipation. Now, I must prepare to leave everyone. Few have ever left my village on pilgrimage, but the ones that have now surround me at the door of the church. One hands me a wide-brimmed hat to protect my head and face from the elements. Another ties their cherished Canterbury Bell to my girdle, but I am overwhelmed when I am presented with a pair of sturdy new leather boots. How kind. I immediately remove my old ones and place them in my satchel. I am most grateful to have two pairs. Leaving the church, we walk downhill towards the stream, for it is here where we must part.

Before I leave, I pull my long woollen cloak about my shoulders. Then, after a flurry of kisses, I am on my way. Once across the stream, I turn to wave before wrapping my cloak tightly about my person – this is not just for comfort, but it hides my sobbing body. I so wish that my father had come to see me off, to wish me well and to bid me a safe return, but he chose to remain at home. I do not know or understand why.

Towards London

For the first part of my journey, I will travel with the baggage
train of Sir John Flegge. He is the keeper of this manor
and our lord's loyal retainer, who I have met just once in my
adult life. I am to meet the train just beyond the crossroads
at the farthest point of the track. My instructions are quite
clear. I am to stand by the large oak tree and wait until I am
approached by a lady called Alice. I must talk to no one else.

The baggage train now rumbles into view. It is much
larger than I expected and it comprises of a great many carts,
most of which appear to be full to the brim with wooden
boxes. Men walk alongside the carts, carrying all manner of
birds that squawk in unison. I can hear hawks, falcons and
rooks. How strange to be carrying rooks? I cannot think why
they would do so. Behind them, I can see even more carts,
but these are filled with fine ladies in fashionable dress. Their
veils are fluttering in the breeze like butterflies.

When the train comes to a halt, I notice an elderly lady
rise up and stretch before tentatively climbing down. She
is muttering loudly. Embarrassed to be the focal point of
everyone's attention, I let my eyes drop to the floor. I can hear

the old lady shuffling through the long grass and across the gravel. Her breathing is laboured and coming in great gasps.

"Hello there, hello. Are you Mistress Bethany of Stratfield Mortimer?"

I look up and nod in agreement.

"Excellent. We meet at last. I understand that you are to travel with us to Watling Street."

Smiling, I nod once more, unable to find my voice.

"Oh, well, we have a quiet one here, don't we?" she announces to one and all.

My embarrassment grows as I follow her. I cannot be sure, but some of the ladies appear to be whispering about me. I am sure that I heard one of them say, "From a traitorous family, that one. I'd keep a distance, if I were you."

Surely, they cannot be speaking about me in those terms. They must have the wrong person.

"Budge up. Come on, let us in." Alice sits none too gently between the two gossiping ladies and points to a small space next to her.

To my surprise, it is very comfortable and unlike any cart I have ever travelled in. The seats are cushioned and there is even a rug to cover my legs. Slowly, the train begins to move off. From this viewpoint, I can see that we are guarded by a large retinue of men-at-arms. All of whom carry swords, which can be drawn at a moment's notice. They are interspersed between the men carrying the birds. It feels like they are hiding in plain sight, but I wonder why so many are needed.

As the light begins to fade and we roll forever onwards, I wonder where we will spend the night. Maybe at an inn or perhaps we will be guests at another manor where Sir John

Flegge has influence. Shortly, I realise that it is neither of these options as Alice nudges me in the ribs.

"Mistress Bethany, tonight we will rest within the grounds of Chertsey Abbey. They have prepared an encampment for us. We will spend the night beneath the stars." I can see that this amuses her, as she cackles uncontrollably to herself and rolls from cheek to cheek. I look into the distance and try not to stare at her. She frightens me a little and makes me think of witchcraft. "When we arrive, the brothers will have laid out all the refreshments. They usually put on a good spread." With this, Alice appears to go into a trance, before licking her lips and gulping down imaginary food and drink. "And then, my dear, once we have had our fill, we will be shown to our tents. I suggest that you get as much rest as possible as we set off for London tomorrow just before dawn. Now, listen good, when we arrive, I'll give you further instructions. I don't want to overload you now."

Intentional or not, Alice's manner has offended me and I stew for the remainder of the journey. However, this soon passes when Chertsey Abbey comes into sight.

On arrival, I am pleasantly surprised to find that the encampment is far grander than I expected it to be. It is located well within the stone walls of the Benedictine monastery and heavily protected from the outside world by a deep ditch that surrounds it. As the gates are fully opened, I can see row upon row of tents nestling tightly alongside each other. I never knew that tents could come in all different shapes and sizes, and I certainly never knew that they could come in different colours. Some are plain, while others are blue, green and gold. One even has a crest painted onto its opening flap. Opposite the tents, canopies have been erected to provide shelter for those who tend the fires and cook the food. Caldrons and skillets litter the ground. Their contents smouldering and spitting. At the back of each canopy, I can see wooden buckets, huge piles of charcoal and faggots of wood.

Once the entire baggage train is safely inside, the great door of the abbey is closed and barred with sturdy beams. As instructed, I wait for Alice to tell me what to do.

"Now, come on, Mistress Bethany, don't be tardy. Let's get our skates on and head for the refreshments. Or would you prefer to be shown to your tent first? You could always leave your things there and be unencumbered if that suits you?"

"No, I should like to keep everything with me, if that's alright."

Alice smiles and nods vigorously before climbing down from the cart. I smile as I watch Alice touch the ground and then spin around with great vigour, before heading off towards the canopy where the tables groan under the weight of food. When I eventually catch up with Alice, she begins again.

"Now, Mistress Bethany, just help yourself to whatever takes your fancy. Once the others descend, everything will disappear."

With this in mind, I take two pieces of bread and place one of them in my satchel before filling my bowl to the brim with pottage from the largest caldron. To my delight, there are large pieces of meat and plenty of vegetables. After deciding to sit at the furthest end of the canopy, I place my bowl and bread next to my satchel before returning to the fire once more. This time I take a green glazed bowl from the stack and help myself to a ladle of hawthorn pudding. It is thick and milky, just the way I like it. I can hear the others approaching, so I take my rest.

True to Alice's word, the others make short shrift of the food. Many taking far more than they can possibly eat and then leaving it. In a way, I am glad of this, as I felt guilty for taking an extra piece of bread. Seeing that I have finished, Alice beckons to me to join her.

"Mistress Bethany, shall we retire? I am tired and I expect that you feel the same."

Touched that Alice has noticed, I follow her gladly until we stop by a small round tent, the canopy of which has been drawn to one side. Inside, it has been divided into two sections with curtains looping over the top pole.

"Now, mistress, if you should need to use the latrines in the night, please be careful. The ground is rather uneven around here. There's no need for me to tell you where they are, just follow your nose and you'll find them."

Pulling the curtain back, I notice that I have been provided with a sheepskin to lie upon. This, together with my cloak, will ensure that I have a comfortable night. As I lay down, I watch as shadows pass by.

The morning arrives far quicker than I expected. In fact, it feels like I have hardly slept at all. The sunlight streams in and I am reluctant to move, but time is of the essence and I must break my fast before we leave. Perhaps it is wise to eat now before the others wake and yet again devour everything in sight. Outside, I am surprised to meet Alice, who is up and about already.

"Good morrow, mistress. I hope I did not wake you, but I always rise just before dawn. I like to make good use of my time. Now that I am old, I no longer need a great deal of sleep. As you can see, I have been busy preparing the fire and the eggs for breakfast. Will you join me?"

Grateful, I take two more pieces of bread and a large bowl of buttered eggs. "Thank you, Alice, the eggs are delicious."

"Well, you eat up and take more if you are hungry. I expect the others will take far more than they need when they arrive. It's a disgrace how they act. It is really. Greedy, the lot of them, but I have been told to say nothing and that's what I'll do." Before I can answer, Alice continues, "However, that doesn't really matter anymore as the chattering ladies are leaving us today. They are on their way to King Henry's court at Westminster and they are welcome to it as far as I'm concerned. All that they will find there is intrigue and falseness. We, on the other hand, are set for the city of London and by the setting of the sun, we will be safely ensconced in our lodgings."

Something in Alice's manner makes me uncomfortable. After my second bowl of eggs, I politely take my leave and make my way to the cart. I am determined to observe as much as possible on my journey, therefore I ask the reins man if I can sit next to him in the front of the cart.

To my delight, he agrees. "You're more than welcome, my dear, but you'll find it nowhere near as comfortable as back there. That being said, I'll be glad of the company. It'll be nice to have someone to talk to. I've made this journey every quarter for as long as I can remember, but this is the first time that anyone's ever wanted to sit with me." With this, he smiles. "My name is Morris and if you'll grab my hand, I'll help you up."

Carefully, I place my left foot on a wooden rung before taking Morris's hand. "Thank you, Morris, I am Bethany."

Travelling in the same formation as yesterday, the carts trundle along at barely more than walking pace. The two horses that pull us are obviously used to the journey and know how to avoid the larger stones, making the ride far smoother.

"Have you ever been to London before, Bethany?"

"No, Morris, this is my first time. In truth, I have never even left my village. Recently, my father decided that I was no longer needed on the farm and as my mother died last year, I am all alone now."

"That is sad news indeed."

"Yes, it hurts, but – even worse – the shock of both events has affected my sight. Sometimes I can see clearly, while other times everything is misty. I pray to God daily, asking him for guidance. That's why I'm here. I am on my way to the Shrine of Our Lady in Walsingham."

All of a sudden, Morris looks sad. "I was a pilgrim in my youth," he says, "but I travelled northwards to York and the Shrine of Archbishop Richard Scrope."

On hearing the archbishop's name, I cross myself.

"Ah well, let's not dwell on that, shall we? Let's concentrate on happier times. You certainly have an adventure ahead of you and you're starting at the right place. Can you see that stone chapel over there? The building on the hill. It's dedicated to St Anne and reputation has it that the holy waters within it are healing, especially to the eyes. I suggest that we stop when we get there. You could make a quick visit before we leave. Don't worry about the others. I'll tell them why we're stopping. No one apart from old Alice will think it strange and I can deal with her." Morris' eyes dance with devilment.

True to his word, Morris holds his left hand aloft and halts the horses as we draw close. Shouting loudly, he calls out, "If there's anyone who wants to say a quick pray for a safe journey, you can do so now."

Looking around, I can tell from the blank faces that stare back at me that no one else is interested. I appear to be the only one who wants to take up the offer. So, with Morris' help, I climb down from the cart and cross quickly to the chapel. Once inside, I fall to my knees before the statue of St Anne and pray fervently. Before leaving, I fill my ampulla with holy water and quickly return to the cart. I will use this holy water to help soothe my eyes before I go to sleep tonight.

Once I am settled, Morris picks up the horses' reins and instructs them to move on. "Would you like me to point out places of interest to you as we pass? There's a lot to see on the way, you know, and I wouldn't want you to miss out."

"Oh, yes please, Morris, that would be wonderful—"

Alas, our conversation is rudely cut short by Alice, who begins shouting loudly. "Morris, why did you stop? How dare you inconvenience everyone! I have plans, you know. I am due to meet an acquaintance at dusk." With this, she fidgets uncontrollably.

Shocked by Morris' reply, I momentarily hold my breath.

"Stop your beefing, Alice, we'll make it to the city in plenty of time."

Obviously not one to let Alice's mood affect him, Morris carries on, seemingly oblivious to Alice's simmering anger. "I love this area, especially when the water meadows are in flood. The flowers appear to float on the water and the birds, well, they dance in the air and swoop from side to side. My whole life, I have been fascinated by just how quickly the landscape changes around here. Just a few miles upstream, these water meadows join the mighty River Thames and when they do… ahh… they play tricks on the eye, that's for certain. At high tide, if you look quickly, you could be forgiven for thinking that the abbey stands alone on an island. I suspect that the monks add to this impression by clearing back the surrounding forests. Perhaps it makes them feel safer, for attackers would surely think twice about invading an island – especially if they thought that they were going to get stuck in the mud."

My first real view of the River Thames is when we reach a rickety old wooden bridge. Noticing a look of alarm on my face, Morris reassures me. "There's no need to fret, Bethany, this bridge may look old, but it's perfectly solid. The monks take great care to keep it that way. As soon as they see a damaged piece of wood, they cut it out immediately and replace it with new. They make a great deal of money at this crossing, you see, and it's no wonder – there's not another crossing this side of Baynard's Castle."

Alice, obviously still smarting, cannot help herself. "Can't you speed those horses up? I've told you, I have an appointment to keep."

Morris's answer is terse and confrontational. "I'm in charge of this baggage train, not you, and it's my job to make sure that we arrive safely. So, I suggest that you pipe down or I'll report you to Sir John – and you don't want another scolding, do you?"

Apart from the obvious, sitting at the front has many advantages and one of them is to note the smile on Morris' face. I suspect that he enjoys winding Alice up and that he'll take any opportunity to do so.

Crossing the bridge is far more comfortable than I imagined it would be. To my surprise, the wooden slats barely move as we pass over them.

Once we descend the bridge, Morris calls out to the furthest cart. "With your permission, I'll carry on, but remember: keep following me until I say otherwise." Turning back to face the front, Morris explains that the baggage train will split very soon. "Those for Westminster and the court will travel on the North Road, whereas we will follow the river all the way to Ludgate Hill. On a sunny day like today, it will lift our spirits. I love the way it ripples gently as the tide comes and goes, and I'm sure that you will, too. Have you ever heard folks say that the river is the life-blood of the city?" I shake my head. "Well, you will at some point. Londoners tend to live their lives around it. Some days, its bright and uplifting, while on others its dark and menacing. Either way, one thing's for certain, it must always be respected. For the river can give life, but it can also take it away."

I ponder on this until we stop. It would seem that only three carts are continuing onto the city. All the rest have turned right and are now disappearing into the forest. I notice that Alice is fast asleep. Determined to make the most of every moment, I face forwards once more, wriggle until I am comfortable and then listen to the birds and the water lapping against the shore. It is blissful. In no time at all, I catch my first glimpse of the city walls. They are glistening in the sunshine. So much so that they appear white in colour. High above the walls, I can just about see the church towers that peep over them. My excitement grows.

"Morris, how far are we from the city?"

"Alas, we still have quite a way to go. The sun will be lowering by the time we enter Ludgate."

Never before have I felt such anticipation. I am so excited! My heart races and my chest pounds. I notice how the landscape is ever changing and that as we pass through village after village, we are joined on the road by more people. I find myself looking at their clothes. Some are fine, while others are barely more than rags. I have heard that certain colours can only be worn by those of a certain status, so it's pretty easy to work out who is who.

"Bethany, see him over there. The one in fancy clothes. The one with a bitter face and a stoop. Well, that's the only son of William de la Pole, the late Duke of Suffolk. His name is John and he's a nasty bit of work. Just like his father. Always looking for advancement at court. Let me tell you now, be careful in the city. Speak no evil and guard your thoughts. Gossip spreads like wildfire and words become mangled. There are spies everywhere. Our lord is luckier than most. He's a good man and his actions are genuine and forthright. So, you always know where you stand with him. He expects high standards and he gets them. This and the fact that he has a tight grip on the reins, knowing exactly what is happening in each of his manors. He inspires loyalty from all who serve him, so it is rare that a spy ever makes their way into Baynard's Castle. Like the good duke who lived there before him, he's a champion of the common folk."

"Thank you for warning me, Morris. I'll be very careful."

We fall quiet again, so quiet that I can hear Alice snoring. With a very cheery look upon his face, I notice how Morris asks the horses to swerve a little. Looking ahead, I can see no obvious reason for him to do this, but then I realise that he did it to startle Alice.

Waking, she shouts, "What's happening? Can't you control those beasts?"

"I've told you before, Alice, stop your chuntering. How was I to know that you were sleeping?"

"I wasn't asleep, I was just resting my eyes. This journey is taking far too long. I have an appointment, you know."

"Yes, yes, we all know. You've told us a hundred times. Don't worry, we'll be at Ludgate by the chiming of the next hour."

These words are overheard by all and cause considerable excitement.

"Well, Bethany, we are nearly there now. Once we reach the top of the hill, the whole of the city will be laid out before you and, let me tell you, what you'll see will amaze you. For even though I have done this journey hundreds of times, I always marvel at the sight. Then, there's the noise. You must be prepared for the noise. You'll have heard nothing like it in your life. There's always shouting and cussing at the gate. If only people would keep to the correct side of the road, many of the problems would disappear."

At the top of the hill, I catch my breath. Before us stands the most amazing gatehouse. It is constructed by layer upon layer of large stones. It stands some four storeys high – each storey standing slightly proud of the other. It has at least six windows, four arrow splits and two sturdy wooden gates. Just inside, I can see the spikes of a terrifying portcullis, which is neither up nor down. The spikes are absolutely terrifying. As we pass, I lower my head for fear of touching them.

"Don't you worry about hitting your head, Bethany, the portcullis is higher than you imagine."

Once inside, the road widens considerably. "Well, by my reckoning, we have made it right on time. The light should last for a few more hours and old Alice will be happy."

Almost instantly, Alice splutters a reply, "I heard that, you old rascal, you. If I'm old, you're ancient."

Morris smiles once more. "Oh, how I enjoy riling her. It makes my day."

As the road descends gently, we weave our way through a myriad of lanes. It would seem that all of life has appeared before us. "Now, if you look to your left, you'll see the magnificent Baynard's Castle."

On seeing it, I am at a loss for words. How can I possibly describe it?

"I said you'd be amazed and I was right, eh?"

Still startled, I take in the walls, the towers, the windows and the battlements. I am rudely jolted back to life when Morris promptly raises his left hand and brings all three carts to a shuddering halt.

"Well, Bethany, we have arrived. This is Watling Street and, alas, this is where we must part. It has been a pleasure to travel with you and I wish you a safe journey. Remember to light a candle for me at Walsingham."

As I step down from the cart, Alice snorts loudly. "You'll need more than a candle lit for you."

"Stop your carry-on, you're holding everyone up."

Walking away, Alice just cannot help herself. "That man drives me mad. He's always carrying on. I swear that one day I will refuse to travel with him." Alice leads me further away from the cart towards the side of the road. "Now, Bethany, listen carefully. You must make your own way to The Falcon Inn. It's not far. It's located on the corner of Pilgrim Street and

Hay Lane. The innkeeper is expecting you. From here, all you have to do is to walk in a straight line and then turn a sharp right when you reach the river. Now, have a safe journey and please don't deviate from the directions I have just given." Then, as a parting gesture, she turns to me. "Perhaps you could light a candle for me, too."

"Come on, Alice, we must go. You have an appointment or have you forgotten?" Morris says.

As the carts trundle away, I smile and wave. I shall miss Morris and Alice.

The Sparkling City

The city is buzzing with life and the noise is almost overwhelming. Curiosity takes over and I decide to ignore Alice's warnings and explore a little before making my way to The Falcon Inn.

There is so much to see, even at this time of the day. Cooks are selling the last of their wares. They cry, "Hot roast beef, pies and ribs!" over and over again. As I pass by, I can see row upon row of puddings. They look and smell amazing, but, somehow, I manage to resist. Further along the passage, I can see lambskins that are hanging from hooks. Some have been dyed with madder, while others are natural. As I walk further down the narrow passageway, I notice that there is a lot of jostling and commotion. Mindful of the advice that I have been given, I am careful to hide my satchel and purse beneath my cloak. At the end, I turn left – only to find two men sitting on stools outside a merchant's house. Both are attended by beard-cutters. Fascinated, I join the small crowd who look on. The beard-cutters' skill with a blade is terrifying. I can imagine how they can cut a man's throat as easily as shave him.

I promise myself that I will explore just one more passageway. Unfortunately, this time, I walk straight into chaos. Instantly, I realise that I am now in the infamous Hoggenelane, where all of the hogs are kept. The squealing is so loud that it pierces my ears, but the noise is nothing compared to the smell. It's absolutely awful. I pinch my nose and try to hold my breath, but each time I have to breathe, the fumes appear worse. Oh no, I dance from foot to foot as a river of muck heads my way. Phew, that was a close shave. Perhaps I should change into my old boots again or perhaps it's time to make my way to Pilgrims Lane. I decide upon the latter and say a silent thank you to the Lord for saving me from the wretched muck.

Carefully retracing my footsteps, I am once again at the place where I was dropped off. Remembering Alice's instructions, I walk straight ahead and then turn a sharp right. I am relieved to have made it in time as the light is beginning to fade. On the corner of Pilgrim Street, I can see crowds of pilgrims disembarking from boats. They are all walking towards the inn. Looking up, I can now see the sign of The Falcon. It's magnificent! Set against a pale-blue and white backdrop, a golden falcon sits inside a decorated fetterlock. It has a look of determination upon its face and it appears ready to fly into action at a moment's notice. My heart pounds once more as I fumble in my long leather pouch for my letter of commendation.

Stepping across the threshold, I am greeted by the innkeeper. He smiles and welcomes me. "If I'm not mistaken, you must be Bethany of Stratfield Mortimer."

Nodding proudly, I hand over my letter.

"My name's Bill and my wife, who you'll meet later, is

Isabel. We're happy to accommodate you. Now, put that away safely and I'll take you to your room. You must be exhausted. We were starting to worry about where you'd got to. Morris should have arrived long ago. Did the baggage train get held up?"

Acutely aware that dusk had fallen, I bow my head and apologise. "I am very sorry to have caused concern. I could not help myself. The urge to explore was too great. Alice told me not to deviate, but I just couldn't help myself."

"Well, there's no need to worry. There's no harm done and you're here now – safe and sound. Come on, let me show you to your room."

As we climb the spiral staircase, Bill continues, "Sir William Oldhall has requested that we give you our best room. He has asked that you rest in comfort. He is concerned that your journey may prove difficult. I understand that your eyes do not see too well?"

"Yes, that's correct, but I'm happy to sleep anywhere."

Bill looks directly into my eyes and smiles. He has a kind face and deep-green eyes. "Be that as it may, everything has been prepared as per Sir William's wishes. Isabel takes great pride in preparing all of our rooms and we are sure that you will be overjoyed when you see it."

Bill is not wrong. On opening the door, I am astounded to see that the floor comprises of blue and yellow glazed tiles. The design mirrors that of the Mortimer family. In front of me are the waves of the sea and the sand of the Holy Land.

"Tiles are much better than rushes, don't you think? They are far less slippery and we don't want you to fall."

"But how can I ever repay you for such kindness?"

"Now, don't you go worrying about that. Your family has given sterling service over many a year and now it's our pleasure to look after you. Did you know that I served alongside your grandfather at Agincourt?" My face obviously betrays my surprise. "No, I didn't think that you would. He was my friend. A true comrade in arms."

"Really?"

"Yes, my dear. He was the bravest man I ever knew."

"Oh, Bill, how I wish I knew more about my past. Now that my mother is dead, I have no one to talk to."

"Well, let's see about that. I'm sure I can answer some of your questions later – but first you need to rest. Tomorrow, you have a great deal to do. I'll take my leave for now, but if you need me, I'll be downstairs."

I am in awe of my room. It's the most beautiful room that I have ever seen in my life. The walls have been limewashed a gentle shade of green and then decorated with white irises and ivy. In the corner, there is a small bed topped with a fine-looking mattress. I walk over and squeeze it gently. As expected, it is deep and soft. Then, I run my hand over the linen sheet that covers it. It feels cool beneath my fingers. How I long to undress and climb inside, but I am stopped by a knock at the door. I open it to find a large, chubby woman standing with what looks like a cup of watered wine in one hand and a wooden trencher covered with linen in the other.

"Hello, Bethany, I am Isabel, Bill's wife. It's a pleasure to meet you. I expect that you are tired. I have often journeyed from London to Reading via Stratfield Mortimer and I remember all too well the aches and pains from the cart journey. Therefore, I have brought you some refreshments." With this, Isabel bustles in and lays down her load on a low table by the fireplace. Turning, she begins again, "Have you ever tried losynge before?"

"No never."

"Well, you're in for a treat, then, my girl. It's an ancient dish and one of my specialities – even if I do say so myself. I hear that the recipe was favoured many years ago by King Richard II." We both stop for a second to cross ourselves in remembrance of the murdered king. "The recipe I use has been passed down by word of mouth from the time of the Crusaders, but I have made it my own with a secret ingredient." Isabel pauses to take a breath. "I make mine with a blend of creamy dough, which is layered with butter, cheese and my secret ingredient." Isabel stops once more. This time, she looks extremely smug. I sense that she wants me to ask what her secret ingredient is, but before I can speak, she starts again. "At the end, I bake it in my own bread oven just to make sure that it bubbles and browns. Bill loves it that way." Nodding, I try once more to get a word in, but to no avail. "Now, I can't stop and chatter all night. I've got things to do." With that, Isabel smiles and bustles out.

I cannot say that I am sad at her departure. In fact, I am rather relieved as my ears are ringing.

By the fireplace sits a stool. I drag it to the table and prepare to eat. Fortunately, a napkin has been left for my use. I place it carefully around my neck and remove my spoon from my belt. As I remove the linen from the Losynge, I get a waft of herbs. Careful to eat from the side and not to burn my mouth, I relish the heavy sauce. It is silky smooth and extremely tasty. If I'm not mistaken, I think Isabel's secret ingredient is ginger as my mouth begins to tingle.

Once I am finished, sleep overwhelms me. In addition, the wine was far stronger than I had expected. Standing to close the shutters, I am relieved to feel a cool breeze upon my face. In the distance, I can hear the *couvre-feu* bell chiming. It rings out to warn everyone that the city gates are about to be closed. I understand that no one goes about once the bell has tolled and that the wisest course of action is to return home as soon as possible. The city echoes with tales of robberies, murders and all manner of violence. Grateful to be safe and comfortable, I make my way over to the bed and undress as far as my under-kirtle. Laying my possessions upon a small wooden box, I slip into bed. The cool linen is soothing and I relax immediately. My aches and pains ease as I sink into the mattress. The beeswax candles spit and crackle as they burn down. I close my eyes and drift off into sleep immediately.

***

The morning sunlight steams in through the shutters, making patterns on the walls. I cannot remember anything of the night, as my sleep was uninterrupted by dreams. Today, I feel refreshed and raring to go. Jumping up, I dress as quickly as possible. Excitement courses through my body. I have a great many things to do today. Firstly, I am set for the mighty St Paul's Cathedral. For it is well known throughout the land that a blessing is given every day in the open-air pulpit and, oh, how I long to take part. Then, more importantly, I am to travel to Holborn to see my lord's attorney, as I must make my last will and testament before I travel to Walsingham.

Downstairs, I am relieved to see that Bill is on his own. My ears have only just recovered from Isabel's visit.

"Good day, Bethany, did you sleep well?"

"Oh yes. It was wonderful! The bed was so comfortable and the linen so soothing. I have never known such luxury."

"Well, make the most of it. Pilgrimages can be hard and tiresome." With that, he laughs, obviously remembering his own adventures. "Now, there are just a couple of things that I must say before you go. Please be very careful. Danger lurks everywhere. The Duke of Somerset's residence is not too far away and his retainers are everywhere. Confusingly, they also wear blue and white livery – the only difference being that their shade of blue is far deeper. Trust no one apart from myself and our attorney. Even Isabel's counsel is to be avoided wherever possible. I love her dearly, but her tongue is loose and sometimes she is so desperate to impress others that she blurts out far too much information. This is not usually a problem, but – as you will be aware – these are disturbing times. And one more thing, if you ever feel that you are being followed, you must make your way back here immediately. Though, with that being said, please don't let me put you off. I only mean to protect you. Have a pleasurable day and I will see you later."

Walking away, I feel a little unsettled, but determined to enjoy my stay in the city. Retracing my footsteps, I am soon back at the spot where Morris and Alice dropped me off. St Paul's Cathedral looms over the area. I could never have imagined how large or tall the building would be. Gazing at it, I feel protected, almost as if St Paul the Apostle is watching over me.

Then I remember stories of how newsmongers and locals frequent the cathedral – how they speak of current affairs and the intrigues of the court. Although, I must not allow myself to get seduced. Turning the corner, I encounter a group of fine ladies, who are parading around in their fashionable clothes. None appear to be happy. Instead, they are all wearing fixed expressions of either glee or ill-concealed jealousy. Further on, mercers are completing deals and exchanging money. I walk on by, uninterested by such things.

As I make my way to the north-east side of the churchyard and to St Paul's cross, I find it increasingly difficult to walk in a straight line as the churchyard is crammed with hundreds of pilgrims. All are jostling for a good position. Some, like me, are obviously new to pilgrimage, while others appear to be hardened adventurers, who are decorated by an inordinate number of pilgrim badges. I decide not to go forward, but to stay where I am. If I stand on my tiptoes, I can just about see the wooden cross with its covered pulpit. Anyway, it's probably safer to stay at this distance – I've often heard how thieves mingle with the crowd. I wait for the blessing to begin!

In what seems like no time at all, a priest emerges from the north door of the cathedral. He is accompanied by four servers and a verger. One of the servers carries an open Bible upright before the priest. All are chanting rhythmically. Strangely, the priest's appearance is not how I imagined it to be at all. He is wearing a red vestment over a white linen garment. The vestment is elaborately embroidered with a large golden cross and encrusted with precious stones. Such wealth cannot be right. Silence descends, as he climbs the stone steps and enters the large pulpit alone. He begins by reciting the Lord's Prayer before the Lamb of God is sung. To my astonishment, I can hear every word, as clear as day. The crowd is almost silent. Next, the priest recites a prayer to

St James the Apostle. Fortunately, it is read in English and, for this, I am grateful. I have spent many months trying to memorise it and now I can join in.

"O God. Be for us our companion on the walk. Our guide at the crossroads. Our breath in our weariness. Our protection in danger. Our home. Our shade in the heat. Our light in the darkness. Our consolation in our discouragements and our strength in our intentions. So that with your guidance, we may arrive safe and sound at the end of the road. Enriched with grace and virtue when we return safely to our homes filled with joy. In the name of Jesus Christ, our Lord, Amen."

Surprisingly, I remember most of the words and participate fully. At the end, the priest makes the sign of the cross and bids us a safe journey, before descending the steps and disappearing once more into the cathedral. I decide to wait for a little while, just to let the rush past. As I stand, I consider St Erkenwald's Shrine. I am a little sad that I cannot visit it, but as the court is in residence, I fear that St Paul's will be far too busy. Anyway, the city is buzzing with talk of war and I wish to hear none of it. So, I am set for Holborn.

Leaving the cathedral precinct, I head off in the direction of Paternoster Row. To my surprise, there is a vast amount of construction taking place in the row. Looking around, I can count at least eight small stone houses that are being built. There are tradesmen and stalls everywhere. All vying for position. Curiosity gets the better of me and I decide to stop and look, browsing each stall in turn. I can see various types of jugs, pots and bowls. Some items are familiar to me, but others are not. The seller announces that they are all new in this morning – direct from Rouen. My favourite piece is a beaker made from bright-blue glass. I cannot imagine how expensive it must be. If it were mine, I would be far too frightened to drink from it. The glass is extremely thin and has fine air bubbles trapped within.

I decide to carry on and explore a little further. As I walk, I am passed by clergy, who hold their rosary beads tightly in their hands. I can hear them mumble as they walk. I think that they are reciting the Pater Noster, but I'm not too sure.

Leaving the row, I head for Fetter Lane, but as I turn the corner, I encounter a large group of men. Immediately, I am frightened. One is urinating against a low wall; another is swiping the air with his dagger and shouting, "Die, man, die. Choke on your blood." The rest are laughing coarsely at his antics. From their livery, I realise that they are the Duke of Somerset's men. Their voices are strange. Nasal and base. I find them hard to understand. Their intended malice makes me freeze with terror. I want to turn and run, but my legs quiver. I have no option, but to hold my head high and walk past. Their livery is torn and dirty. One is stained with dark blood and all appear dishevelled. I can sense that they are looking at me. Thank God that others are about.

When Fetter Lane comes into view, I breathe a sigh of relief. As instructed, I look for the sign of The Falcon. At last, I have made it. Knocking on the door, my nerves get the better of me and I begin to shake uncontrollably.

The door is opened by a young boy. "Have you an appointment?"

Surprised by his sharpness, I begin to cry. "Yes, I am Bethany Mortimer and I have been instructed to make my last will and testament with Sir Robert."

"Oh, please forgive me. I never meant to make you cry. I should not have snapped. Each knock of the door makes me nervous nowadays." With this, he smiles and bows respectfully. "Please let me introduce myself. My name is Joeb. I am Sir Robert's apprentice. Part of my job is to protect him and to make sure that only those who have been invited enter this building." Bethany enters, then Joeb shuts the door quickly and secures it with an iron bar.

"I understand. I am sorry, too. I rarely cry, but I encountered a group of Somerset's men as I left Paternoster Row and their words have chilled me to the bone. I can't stop shaking."

Joeb's face turns red with rage. "They are a menace. They are everywhere. No one is safe. They have returned from France and are baying for blood. The blood of our Lord of York and his adherents in the main."

Sickness consumes me. I notice that Sir Robert's house is very grand. I follow Joeb up a finely carved wooden staircase to a galleried hall.

"If you would like to take a seat, I will let Sir Robert know that you are here."

Grateful for time alone, I decide not to sit, but to gaze down upon the great hall below. I have never seen anything like it before. The walls are adorned with green and red silk hangings. Each is decorated with Sir Robert's initials and a golden fetterlock. Two long tables mirror each other on either side of the room. All are dressed with pewter plates, tankards and enamelled cups. At the opposite end of the room, there is a low cupboard. This, too, has Sir Robert's initials engraved into it. On this are displayed even finer goods. Mainly silver and glass.

Joeb returns. "Here you go. This will calm you."

To my delight, Joeb offers me a cup of warm spiced cider.

Grateful for such kindness, I take a seat and begin to relax. "Thank you very much." Joeb leaves once more, allowing me to enjoy my drink and the surroundings.

When I am finished, Joeb reappears. "My master is ready for you now."

Leaving my cup, I follow Joeb through a steeply arched doorway. Inside, the room is quite dark, so I stand and wait for my eyes to adjust. It takes but a moment.

"Good day, Mistress Mortimer. I am pleased to meet you. I am Sir Robert. Please, come with me and take a seat." I am directed to a very fine chair. It has green and red velvet cushions. Again, these are embroidered with his initials and a fetterlock. Sir Robert has a kindly face and a broad smile. Dark curls escape from beneath his green velvet cap. I feel like I am sitting on air. "Now, make yourself comfortable. I understand from Joeb that you encountered a group of Somerset's thugs on the way here. Would you like another cup of cider to calm you?"

"Thank you, but no. I am recovered now. The shaking has stopped."

"Well, do not worry. When we are finished, Joeb will escort you back to The Falcon. In hindsight, I was remiss. I should have sent him to fetch you. On the way back, Joeb can take you to the Greyfriars Monastery. I expect that you would like to visit Sir Roger Mortimer's resting place. He has a splendid tomb there."

"Oh yes, please. I had hoped to visit both Sir Roger and Queen Isabella's tomb before I left. I even bought a small wooden cross from home with me, just in case I had the opportunity to pray at their tomb." Producing the cross from my satchel, I hand it to Sir Robert. "Did you carve this yourself?"

"Yes, it took me hours to get it right. I kept chipping away. Taking off too much wood and then having to start again. That's why it is so fine."

I am warmed by his smile. "Well, let's get to work." Sir Robert seats himself at his desk. On it stands a quill, a bottle of ink and a long piece of narrow parchment. "Now, if you could tell me, one item at a time, what you own and who you would like to bequeath it to, I will make notes. At the end, we will both sign our names. I understand that you can read and write with great skill."

"Yes, I am most fortunate to have been taught by my mother." I think for a moment before beginning – alas, I have very little of my own to leave. "I have two brown woollen kirtles that I would like to leave to Betty Wheeler of Mortimer's Common. Then, I have an embroidered cushion and a heavy wooden trunk, which I would like to leave to my cousin, Lucy de Fanning, who lives in York. The only trouble is that I do not know her address."

"Please do not worry about such things. If the worst was to happen, I have my ways of finding out."

"The only item remaining is my heron broach."

"Ah, yes, I will need to make a special provision for that. You do understand that I cannot mention this in your will?"

"Of course, but I thought it wise to tell you."

"Yes, but please tell no other. Joeb must know nothing of it. He is extremely loyal to me, but I do not wish to tempt fate. There are some things that must remain a secret."

At the end, Joeb is summoned into the room by a small bronze handbell.

"Now, if you can sign here, Bethany, I will sign below. Then, Joeb, please can you apply a small amount of heated wax as normal, so that I can seal the document with my ring." The sealing takes but a moment. "Well, Joeb, can I take it that no one has called for me since you showed Mistress Bethany in?"

"No, Master, no one."

"Good. I have decided on a change of plan. Bethany, if you would allow me, I should like to accompany you to the Greyfriars Monastery and then The Falcon Inn. I haven't seen Bill for a while and it will be good to catch up."

Leaving Sir Robert's house, we must appear a strange pair. Sir Robert, so fine and proud, whereas I am dressed in simple pilgrim garb. The streets are emptier now and I can see no sign of Somerset's men.

"It's not too far to Greyfriars. I often visit twice a year with financial provision, as our Lord of York provides for the upkeep of the tombs."

As we turn the corner, I can see the monastery clearly. It sits in the shadow of St Paul's and is of modest size. It appears far smaller than the abbey at Chertsey. Plain but demure. Flowers line the edge of the path and not a weed can be seen. As we approach the main gate, a small door within opens. "Sir Robert, it's a delight to see you, as always, but Father Prior, unaware of your visit, is not here."

"Brother Samuel, please do not look so worried. I was also unaware of my visit until an hour ago. I have no business with Father Prior today. I am here on personal business. Please may I introduce Mistress Bethany Mortimer of Stratfield Mortimer."

Brother Samuel smiles. "Welcome, I expect you wish to visit Sir Roger's tomb?"

"Oh, yes please."

As we approach the chapel, I can hear the monks chanting within. Once inside, I can see the two white tombs standing proud. They are surrounded by four large white candles and white flowers. Incense hangs heavy in the air. It creates a swirling mist. At the farthest end of each tomb, a monk kneels. Brother Samuel explains that prayers are said continually both night and day. Sir Robert's look is one of great reverence.

"Bethany, shall we pray? There are cushions, if you would like one."

I shake my head. "No, thank you. I would like to kneel on the floor."

In silence, all three of us cross ourselves before kneeling. Never had I imagined that I would be so close to the remains of my mother's kinsman. Before leaving, I take out my handmade wooden cross and place it on top of Sir Roger's tomb. While doing so, my hand begins to shake. Outside, evening has fallen and a rosy glow lights the sky. Sir Robert and I say farewell to Brother Samuel and leave for The Falcon Inn. Sir Robert, with his local knowledge, directs me through a series of narrow alleys. Some are so tiny that we have to walk in single file, one behind the other. To my astonishment, the buildings above us almost meet in the middle.

When we arrive at The Falcon Inn, we are greeted by Bill, who is standing by the door. "Well, look who we have here. Sir Robert, it's been far too long. It's good to see you. How are you?"

"Very well, my friend, and you?"

"Yes, life has been kind to Isabel and myself."

"Excellent. That's what I like to hear. Time passes by so quickly, don't you think?"

"Indeed, I do, so let's not waste any more. Come on, let's go inside and eat, drink and be merry."

"I'll second that."

We follow Bill to a large table by the fireplace, before he calls loudly for his serving boy. "Jacob, please find the mistress and ask her to bring us wine, ale and a selection of her best fare – and ask her to be quick about it."

"Yes Master."

With that, Jacob scurries off. When he returns, he is accompanied by Isabel. Both are laden with food and drink.

"Thank you, my dear. You have done us proud. What could be better than your roast pork and liver pies?"

Jacob fills our tankards with ale and Bill immediately rises from his seat. "Before we start, let's stand and toast our late commander. Here's to the good Duke Humphrey." To this, everyone in the vicinity rises to join the toast. "Ah, he was a good soul." Then, sitting down, Bill begins to reminisce about the good old days. "He was a fine commander, you know. He always led from the front. He was one of us."

Sir Robert agrees. "Yes, he was slow to get the hang of campaigning at first, but he soon got the hang of things. Can you remember when he fell at the Battle of Agincourt?"

A laughing Bill remembers. "That's right! He had to be protected by his brother, the king."

"And can you remember the king's rage when he had to stand over him and wait for reinforcements?"

"Ah, that I can. Gloucester had to be carried from the field after fighting magnificently."

"Yes, but the king was furious with him and sent him home after a good earbashing. He was warned to listen to orders next time. Fortunately for us, there was no next time."

"Yes, those were the days."

"Shall we eat? While the pies are still hot?"

To my mind, Isabel's pies are the best that I have ever eaten. Therefore, I am delighted when Bill requests that Jacob fetch some more. Not just for us, but for everyone in the inn.

"Tonight, the pies are on us and there's a tankard of ale for everyone, too." A merry Bill then continues, "Now, Bethany, let us tell you about your grandfather. Did you know that he was at Agincourt and fought beside us? He was an amazing man with a mighty spirit. You remind me of him."

"Do I?"

"Oh, yes. Don't you agree, Robert?"

Looking into my eyes, he smiles.

"Yes, your eyes are exactly the same. And your determination – well, that's the same as his. Not many would go on a pilgrimage alone and even fewer would have the inclination to learn to read and write as you have done. I have no doubt that he would be proud of you."

With such kind words, I blush a little. To be thought of in the same mould as my mother's family is an honour. Relaxed and happy, I allow sleep to wash over me. Now seems as good a time as any to retire for the night. I also expect that the men would like to be alone to enjoy their memories of the past.

"You are both so kind. Today has surpassed all of my expectations. Thank you both for everything. I hope that you do not mind, but I must retire now."

Standing, Sir Robert takes my hands in his. "Bethany Mortimer, it has been a joy to meet you. I hope that we will meet again. Whenever you are in London, there's always a place for you at my home in Fetter Lane." A little unsteady from the strong ale, he kisses my hand and returns to his seat. "May God protect you and keep you safe."

Once in my room, I am delighted to note that everything is as perfect as when I first arrived. The linen on my bed has been smoothed and the floor sparkles once more. All evidence of my muddy boots has been cleared away. Determined to make the most of my last night, I undress quickly and say my prayers before replaying the events of the day in my head.

***

Morning breaks. Today, I must leave The Falcon Inn and make my way to the Inn of the Bleeding Heart. Here, I will meet my fellow pilgrims. I wonder who I will be travelling with and how many will be in our party? Will they be pious or simply escaping the tedium of everyday life? I expect that I am more fortunate than most as I have no time limits on my pilgrimage. I am not needed at home. There are plenty of others to tend to the land and to look after the animals.

There is a knock at the door. "Are you awake, Bethany? Please can I enter? I have refreshments for you."

Without waiting for an answer, Isabel enters the room. "I knew you'd be awake. Bill said to leave you and let you rest, but I knew you would be up and about. Excited for the day ahead. Well, I can't have you leaving the city without a good meal in your stomach. I have bought you some hot roast meat, some cheese and some bread. Whatever you can't eat can be wrapped and taken with you. It's always a good idea to have something stashed away for later." Again, without taking breath, she continued, "Oh, how I envy you. I have often longed to go on pilgrimage. Mainly to

Canterbury or York, but Bill couldn't do without me here. The place needs a woman's touch, don't you think? Men only see the bigger picture. They never notice the smaller details, whereas I pride myself on the details. Then there's Jacob, you see. I'm needed to look after him. His mother died a few months ago. I'm not too sure what carried her off, but getting soaked can't have helped. Her lungs suffered terribly at the end. I know that I can never replace her, but I can show him kindness and give him a home. Well, that's enough of me. I'll let you get ready."

With that, Isabel turns and leaves. Her comely figure sways from side to side as she closes the door behind her. Perching on the side of my bed, I tuck into the meat and cheese. Bread is much easier to carry in my satchel, so I wrap it carefully in a clean piece of linen before putting it away. After breaking my fast, sadness overwhelms me. How strange to think that I arrived as a stranger, but I leave as a friend. Before closing the door, I take one final look around the room, trying to remember every detail before I descend the stairs.

The inn is empty apart from Jacob, who is cleaning the tables. He appears to be lost in a world of his own and I'm not too sure that he has seen me. I cough to make my presence known.

With a startled look, he gazes up. "Hello, mistress. Are you leaving us so soon?"

"Yes, Jacob. Today, I leave for Walsingham. In a short while, I am to meet my travelling companions."

"Are you excited?"

"Yes, very, but a little nervous at the same time."

"Please, mistress, could you help me? When you get to

Walsingham, could you pray for my mother? She died a short while ago and I miss her so much."

"Yes, of course. Would you like me to pray for you at the same time?"

"Oh no, there's no need for that. I'm safe now. Bill and Isabel have promised to take care of me and I am determined to work hard for them."

We smile. I understand both his grief and his joy.

Outside, it's time to say goodbye to Bill and Isabel. Tears fill my eyes as I thank them for their kindness. "This is for you." I reach out my hand to Isabel. "I bought this for you yesterday." Isabel's eyes begin to dance. "It's nothing really, just a very small thank you for taking care of me."

Obviously intrigued, Isabel unwraps the package carefully. "Why, it's beautiful!" Turning to Bill, she holds out the small horn bowl, before turning back to me. "Bethany, thank you so much. I will treasure this and the memories of your visit for a long time. Please return safe and sound. I long to hear of your adventures at Walsingham."

Walking away, I am surprised when Bill begins to follow me. Laughing, he says, "You don't get rid of me that easily. Last night, Sir Robert and myself decided that someone should escort you to Cheapside. As he has an appointment this morning, I have the honour of escorting you."

Relieved not to be travelling alone, I relax. "Thank you Bill, that's very kind of you. In truth, I was rather nervous about making my way to the Cheapside Cross all alone."

"I can understand that. It can get awfully busy down there at the best of times. It's a melting pot, you see. People are always coming and going, and we couldn't be sure that you would be able to find Owain on your own – and God knows what would have befallen you if you had met the wrong person." For a second, I freeze in terror. "Well, we don't have to worry about that now do we. Shall we go." Smiling once more I wave to Isabel and Jacob before turning the corner.

"There's quite a few ways to get to the cross, but I think that the wisest way would be via Bread Street. Then, we will be able to avoid the main marketplace entirely. It seems such a shame to pass it by, but time marches on and, in reality, it's a strange place. One where both rich and poor come together. Unlike anywhere else that I know of. Every day, it's thronged with huge numbers of people. Some on their way to court; others off to Westminster. Then there's the soldiers on their way to France and the criminals on their way to trial."

Inside I am more grateful than ever for Bill's company.

As we continue, Bill explains that the cross is being rebuilt at the moment. "The works have been going on for years. Our king, not content with the old wooden cross, is having it replaced with a carved stone one. The dust and mess gets everywhere. I expect that you know the story of the Eleanor crosses?"

"Oh yes, they commemorate where Queen Eleanor's funeral cortege rested overnight, don't they?"

"That's right. You'll see another one when you get to Waltham Cross and – let me tell you – the original ones are far more beautiful than this modern monstrosity."

When we arrive at the cross, all I can see is wave upon wave of people. Pilgrims are everywhere. "I said that it would be busy, didn't I, but I never expected this many people. I wonder why there are so many?"

"Bill, do you know what Owain looks like?"

"Yes, he's a very handsome lad. He has short blond hair and chubby red cheeks." Bill scans the crowd. "There he is. I can see him." Bill clasps my hand and leads me through the crowds. "Owain, we're over here."

Owain, having spotted Bill, waves enthusiastically and comes forward to greet us. "Hello, Bill, it's good to see you. You must be Mistress Bethany. It's very good to meet you. I'm Owain Weaver and I'll be travelling with you all the way to Walsingham."

Taken aback by Owain's good looks and sweet nature, I blush uncontrollably. "It's good to meet you, too, Owain. Have you been to Walsingham before?"

"Yes, many times. My family live nearby and I regularly accompany special travellers on their journey."

"Oh dear, there must be some mistake. I am not a special traveller, I am just a plain country girl – a pilgrim."

With a delightful smile, Owain replies, "I think not."

Before I can reply, Bill begins, "Owain, why are there so many travellers about today?"

"Oh, I think there are two reasons. One being that the court is holding session at St Paul's again and everyone has come to catch a glimpse of our queen." Then, in a hushed voice, "It is said that she is vengeful and unpredictable, and it is wise to be seen revering her."

"Ah… and what is the other reason?"

"Well, that's much easier to explain. Two pilgrimages – one to Canterbury and the other to Winchester – have been arranged far too close together. Whoever decided it was a good idea to meet at the same place and at the same time obviously had not realised the court would be in session this week."

"Well, I must get back, lad," Bill interjected. "Isabel will be wondering where I have got to."

"Send my love to Isabel and let her know that I'll see her when I'm next in the city."

"That'll keep her more than happy, my lad."

With that, Bill kissed my hand and leaves.

"We should go too." After escaping the crush, Owain explains that we will be travelling with seven others. Three men and four women. "We will meet them in the grounds of St Helen's Nunnery in Bishopsgate. Unfortunately, we're not permitted to enter any of the buildings there as the nuns have been banned from entertaining visitors."

"Really, who has banned them?"

"Well, it's a rather amusing story." Owain chuckles. "The archbishop, that's who. By all accounts, he's not a happy man. When the old prioress died, a new one was installed and what she found broke nearly every rule in the book. The nunnery was being used as a boarding house by rich city families, who wanted to dispose of their unmarried daughters. Some were even paying vast sums of money to the prioress in an attempt to create an illusion of respectability for the family. As it is unlikely that any of them had a calling, God was most probably not the first thing on their minds. Stories abound of much coming and going in the early hours. Then, there's the dancing and the frolicking. It seems that both men and women were entertained after dark!" With an even cheekier grin, he laughs. "Now, the nuns are forbidden from even looking out into the street. My, oh my, how things have changed for them."

Words escape me and I cannot help but laugh at their antics, even though they are extremely shameful.

"Ah… I can see our party. They are over there. Sitting on the boundary wall by the main entrance." Owain waves enthusiastically.

As we approach, the men stand to greet us. "Owain, you made it then. News reached us that the cross is even busier than usual and we were concerned that something had happened."

"You can say that again. I've never seen so many there since we left for France ten years ago – but, please, let me introduce you to Mistress Bethany of Stratfield Mortimer."

Making our way from one to another, Owain begins, "This is Alard, this is Davy and, last but not least, this is Ned."

Their manners are impeccable and I instantly take a liking to all three, especially Ned, who appears to be a free spirit. His clothes are unconventional, particoloured and patched. He appears to be a seasoned campaigner and, more interestingly, one who travels with a well-worn shawm hanging from his belt. Seeing this, I doubt that the journey will be dull.

Moving on, Owain askes Alard to introduce the women. "Of course. Here we have Ethel, Agnes, Anne and Cecily. Ursula and Bernadette will be joining us at Cheshunt Park."

Turning to face Owain, he immediately apologises. "I'm very sorry, Owain, but we must be on our way as soon as possible. I fear that the evening will be upon us early tonight. The clouds are low today and I need to gauge how quickly our party can walk."

"Of course, I hadn't thought of that. Let's be on our way. There will be plenty of time for us to get to know each other along the way."

Leaving the City Behind

W alking two by two, we head away from St Helen's Nunnery in the direction of Bishopsgate. As we approach the gate, the street widens considerably. This area of the city is completely different to Ludgate or Cheapside. From what I can see, it consists mainly of monastic foundations and markets.

Owain leans over. "I love this part of the city. I'm always at my happiest here. The religious houses and the markets give me a sense of security. Somehow, the people seem different, too."

Smiling, I agree. "The air feels much fresher here. It's almost like being in a village."

"You know, I'd never thought of that, but you're right. A village with lots to see and do. If you don't mind, I would love to point out some of my favourite places as we pass, but I promise not to bore you. It's just so nice to have a companion to share my thoughts with."

"I agree. We can learn together."

"The church that we are just about to pass is dedicated to St Ethelburga. A rare dedication. By all accounts, she was a very strong woman. A natural leader. I wonder if her namesake within our party shares the same values?" Laughing, he continues, "I always think the stones of the church sparkle brightly in the sunshine. Mirroring the bright light that St Ethelburga witnessed when she was blessed with a vision at Barking Priory, where she was the abbess. Jesus Christ appeared to her and requested that she dedicate her life to caring for others. This she did to her dying day. I have often prayed to her for guidance when I have faced difficult situations and I know that she hears me and guides me."

I find it strange that Owain should mention a vision, as this is what I pray for night and day. I wonder if that was a sign from God? Turning the corner, Bishopsgate comes into view. Completely different to Ludgate, it's crenelated to look like a castle with rounded towers flanking both sides of the actual gate. The tower to the right is topped by a small wooden building. I expect that it's used as a lookout, but I decide not to ask, as Owain is now enthusiastically pointing to the House of St John & St Charity.

"Here, the brothers mourn continuously for the souls of the departed. Their services are well rewarded, especially at times of war." We cross ourselves. No doubt remembering our loved ones and dreading what should happen if our lord's protectorship should end. I am relieved to have this thought banished from my mind by Owain, who has moved on already and is pointing with an outstretched arm. "Now, this street is very interesting. It leads to the Augustine Priory of the Begging Friars. It's well known that the brothers who reside within are the most pious in the city. They're often seen in the streets, speaking to people and spreading the Word of God. Although, I'm embarrassed to say that I try to avoid them as much as possible, as they have such strict beliefs and are a little frightening."

Changing the subject, I ask Owain about the many markets that we have just passed.

"Well, some are formal and have charters, but for the most part people just sell what they grow, where they grow it. Why pay for a plot when you can sell it for nothing on your own piece of ground? Bartering is also commonplace in these parts. I often return with items, just so that I can sample the fruit here. The plums are the tastiest I've ever had."

In the distance, I can see ridge and furrow everywhere. They abut the city walls and stretch for as far as the eye can see. On reflection, I can well understand Owain's enthusiasm for this area. Alard halts our group just in front of the gate. Standing slightly to the left of the road, we are surrounded by a moat of camomile flowers and wild herbs. The smell is amazing!

Owain leans over, before whispering in my ear, "Alard will be happy. We've made it in good time."

Nodding, I make no mention of my thoughts. I'm also surprised by just how quickly we have travelled, especially as both Ethel and Agnes appear to be of a great age. Sadly, their backs are bent. That being said, however, they are far more sprightly than Anne, who puffs as she waddles. The gate is a wonder to behold and must be the depth of at least two carts. If only all defences could be so beautiful. I can clearly see the metal hinges, which secure the wooden gates to the stone wall. They shine brightly and are in good order. I can see no sign of rust or deterioration.

Owain explains that the gates are maintained by the Bishop of London and that it's in his interest to keep the gates in pristine condition. "For every cart that passes through this gate, the bishop is given one stick of wood in payment. I hear that his household is bright and cheerful, and that they never know the cold."

Alard, raising his right hand to get our attention, calls out, "The formalities are now complete and we can leave the city. All that remains is for us to visit St Botolph's church. Here, we will join with other wayfarers. Some are praying for a safe journey, while others are giving thanks for their safe arrival. When we leave, all I ask is that we walk together. If anyone needs to stop, please just call out and we will move to the side of the road and rest. Davy, please can you walk at the back? And Ned, please can you walk in the middle? I will lead all the way to Cheshunt."

Everyone nods in agreement. Looking around, I notice that Ned has a wry smile on his face. "I'll play a tune as we walk."

Once through the gate, I peer down into the deep ditch that runs the entire length of the wall. I fear for anyone who falls into it as the sides are extremely steep and there is stagnant water at the bottom. Looking up, I am taken aback by the number of people in front of me. The quiet calm of the monasteries and markets has been replaced by a wall of noise.

"Stay close, Bethany. In fact, why don't you take my arm?"

Gratefully, I hold onto Owain. The queue of people waiting to enter the city is orderly in comparison to the crowd that swirls around St Botolph's church. As we get closer, I notice that there are tramps everywhere. Most are wearing little more than dirty rags. Alarmingly, some are nearly naked. A few are standing, while others are lying down under hedges. All are filthy and some appear to be stained with what looks like dried blood. I try not to stare, but I find it almost impossible to avert my eyes.

Ahead of me, Alard looks concerned and raises his hand sharply. "Please, everyone, come close. I just cannot understand what is afoot. I have never known such a scene. It's not safe. I tell you, it's just not safe. Ned, did you see those beggars in the ditch back there? Well, I'm sure that I recognised two of them as Somerset's men. I fear a trap or even worse. It's far too dangerous to enter the church. We must walk on by as quickly as possible. Ned, Davy, Owain, unsheathe your daggers. A drawn blade will act as a deterrent."

Looking from one face to another, I can't help but think that Anne and Cecily seem unaffected, whereas Agnes, Ethel and myself are visibly shaking.

"Try not to worry, Bethany. Alard is right; we need to get out of this place as soon as possible."

"Owain, what did Alard mean when he said that it could be a trap or even worse?"

"Ah, well, you see that building over there? The one that's setback and guarded. It's a hospital for those whose minds have been damaged in ways that aren't fully understood. It's rumoured that some may be violent murderers, but no one knows for sure. Word has it that the Duke of Somerset's men have been trying to free those who are imprisoned within. The duke will then use the ensuing pandemonium to blacken the protectorship of our lord."

As we begin to walk away, I decide to sing quietly to myself. This will divert my thoughts. My fear begins to subside the further we travel, but I am still concerned about Anne and Cecily. I wonder if I should mention it to Owain tonight when we are alone. To everyone's relief, the road begins to widen out and the crush disappears. Ned, Davy and Owain put away their daggers and we all begin to relax.

Owain once more begins to comment on our surroundings, "This road will take us all the way to Cheshunt. It's called Ermine Street and it was built by the Roman invaders hundreds of years ago. Straight as a die, it is. I like to think of it as the backbone of our country. It runs all the way from London to York."

I ponder silently on the latter city, which shares its name with our lord. "Owain, have you been to York?"

"Yes, many times. Mostly walking, but once on horseback. I had to run an urgent errand. It was all very exciting! Such a fine city."

With this thought, I let the beauty of the day wash over me. The clear blue sky is uninterrupted by clouds and the hedgerows are snowed under with late blossom. New green leaves continue to unfurl themselves and the earth waits patiently for the full force of the sun. Looking over my shoulder, I realise that the city has disappeared.

Along the way, we pass through manor after manor, all of which appear to be very similar to my own. To the right of the road, flooded fields stretch into infinity as pools of mud mix with the river. They create the illusion of a very large mirror. In this mirror, I can see all manner of wildlife. Birds swoop high in the air and then dive straight down to the ground, singing loudly to announce their presence and to attract potential mates. Such is the time of year.

Owain breaks the silence to tell a tale. "It's beautiful, isn't it? I always think that the River Lea looks magnificent at this time of the year. Although, you have to be very careful and stick to the road. Even though the ground can appear quite solid, its often marshy underfoot. When I was young, I ignored the advice of my elders to my peril and I nearly sunk. Luckily, Ned was on hand to pull me out." Chuckling loudly, he continues, "And he's never let me forget it either. I'm sure that tonight, after a couple of tankards of ale, he'll tell the story again and embellish it, as he always does."

We laugh in unison. "I'll look forward to it and act surprised when he mentions it. I wouldn't want to ruin his enjoyment."

"That's very kind of you, Bethany, but don't be too kind or he'll tell his tales all day long – and he'll keep playing that blessed shawm. I'm sure that he likens himself to one of Chaucer's pilgrims in his mind."

"I wonder which one?"

"The miller, no doubt."

We laugh at the very thought it.

Further down the road, Alard announces that we are nearing Cheshunt. "Not far now. When we arrive at the next junction, all we have to do is to turn right and the abbey will be directly in front of us."

True to his word, once we turn right, the abbey stands before us.

Alard rubs his hands and smiles. "It's magnificent, isn't it, and tonight we'll be staying in the great hall. We'll also be joined by the last two of our party, Bernadette and Ursula. In fact, I think I can see them now, standing just to the left of the gatehouse."

Ned cranes his neck and then calls out, "That looks like Bernadette and Ursula to me."

On arrival, Alard and Ned greet them in turn. Ursula is

noteworthy for her warty nose and lopsided mouth. I try my hardest not to stare, but I find myself drawn to Ursula's nose and protruding hair. Bernadette, on the other hand, is very beautiful, with skin as white as milk. Alard knocks loudly on the abbey door.

Cautiously, it opens. "The Lord be praised. Alard, my dear friend, you have made good time. We were not expecting you so soon."

Alard bows. "Brother David, it's good to see you. It's been too long. We made good time as we travelled direct and avoided St Botolph's."

Brother David's face momentarily crumples. "So, the rumours that I have heard are true. Somerset's men have flooded the area?"

"Yes, it looks that way."

Regaining his composure, Brother David's smile returns. "Well, let's not dwell on that. Please come in and we'll get you all settled."

Inside the hall, I survey the scene before me. No fine linen or soft mattress for me tonight, but the floor will suffice. I have my cloak for warmth and there is a hearth. The light inside the hall fades faster than I had expected. Alard was right to be concerned about the clouds this morning. I shiver a little, but this is more to do with my nerves than the cold. In truth, I am a little worried about the sleeping arrangements. However, this soon fades when I realise that the men have made their encampment at the farthest end of the hall by the door and us ladies are positioned at the kitchen end. Fortunately, I am nowhere near Anne and Cecily, for they still concern me. I have managed to position myself between Agnes and Ethel.

Suddenly, and quite by surprise, Ned strides purposefully into the middle of the room. Clapping loudly to get everyone's attention, he announces, "Let the entertainment begin. Yes, now is the time that you have all been waiting for. I am going to play my shawm. Tonight, we will eat, drink and be merry." With this, Ned notices that an embarrassed Davy has retreated into the furthest corner. "Why, Davy, are you shy? Do you not want to dance to the tune of my shawm?" Silently, Davy shakes his head.

Owain, who now stands beside me, explains what is about to happen, "Here we go. I told you this would happen. As soon as he has an audience, especially one as bewitched as Agnes and Ethel, he begins to play his shawm manically. Then, he'll dance and prance around, jumping in the air, before tumbling to the ground. After our meal, he'll drink two or three cups of ale and then the storytelling will begin. Then, who knows how he'll finish the night?"

"Oh, Owain, what fun! It's just like April Fool's Day all over again."

"Yes, I'll give you that."

Ned, who has assumed the position of the 'Lord of Misrule' is now wearing a long floppy, pointed hat, which he produced from his satchel. It's rather worn and adorned with a great deal of small silver bells. This means that his every movement will be accompanied by jingling. Everyone – apart from Davy – is either clapping or stamping their feet until the door at the farthest end of the hall opens.

Two surprised brothers enter. Both are carrying food and both seem bemused by the sight before their eyes. For a split second, the music stops, before starting again, but this time as a fanfare. I sense that the brothers are enjoying their part in the entertainment a little too much and I wonder whether this is not an entirely new situation. Maybe this is a tried-and-tested ritual? Eating, on the other hand, is a rather more sedate affair. The exertions of the day seemingly affecting everyone, even Ned.

Owain nudges me gently. "Bethany, I think that we may be saved from the storytelling tonight. Ned's audience has fallen asleep." Laughing silently to ourselves, we gaze around the hall. "Well, I think that now's as good a time as ever to settle down for the night. Goodnight, Bethany."

"Yes, goodnight, Owain – and thank you, I've had a marvellous day. I cannot wait until the morning."

***

First light brings with it cheery faces. Alard, as organised as ever, announces that we should leave by the striking of the hour. "Waltham Cross awaits us. It's not very far and it will provide us with an interesting day. We will be staying at The Falcon Inn, which is right next to the cross. The rooms are very comfortable and will serve us well, as tomorrow we have a long walk ahead of us. When we arrive, the innkeeper and his sons will show us where to go. I think that most of us will have to share, but, rest assured, the innkeeper will let us know."

On the road again, we walk in the same pairs as yesterday. Our pattern is now set for the pilgrimage I expect. Time passes quickly today and before we know it, we have arrived at Waltham Cross. I am surprised by its size, as it has two main crossroads and I have already passed three large inns: The Lion, The Four Swannes and The Welsh Harp. I play with the names in my head. They appear to be linked, but are they? Royalty, could this be the key? The Lion – well, that could be King Richard, *Coeur de Lion*. The Four Swannes – again, swans are a sign of royalty and are linked to our lord's father, Richard of Conisbrough, the late Earl of Cambridge. The Welsh Harp – well, that's more difficult. I know that King Henry V was of Welsh decent, so it could relate to him. How strange! Usually, it's very easy to read the signs, to discover whether people are friend or foe, but not this time. I wonder why.

When we arrive at the cross, I remember Bill's comments and silently nod my head in agreement. The original cross that stands before me is far more beautiful than the one being constructed in the city. The stone is aging gracefully and its hard edges are softening with time. The base consists of three layers, which in itself is intricately carved. I cannot say exactly how high the cross stands. All I know for sure is that it stands higher that the roof of the neighbouring Falcon Inn. I long to investigate further, but we are being called to enter the inn. Inside, a huge fire burns within the hearth.

"Welcome to my inn. I am Samuel and these are my sons, Jon and Robert." My attention wavers slightly, as I am surprised to see that both Anne and Cecily have pushed their way to the front. "Your rooms are ready and in a moment, we will take you to them—"

Rudely, Cecily interrupts, "I want to share with Anne."

Shocked by her tone of voice and rudeness, Ned turns abruptly to face her. His jovial manner is completely banished. "You will sleep where Samuel has put you and if you don't like it, there's a hedge outside. You can sleep under that."

An obviously annoyed Davy strides forward. "Apologise now, Cecily."

Reeling with annoyance, Cecily blurts out an insincere, "Sorry," before stomping out of the inn.

Having regained his composure, Samuel picks up a handful of keys, all of which have large leather fobs. Some are green, while others are red. "Jon, please can you handout the green ones? And Robert, please can you handout the red ones?"

Owain, who has been silent throughout, tugs at my arm and draws me to one side. "The green fobs relate to the rooms inside the inn, while the red ones relate to the rooms in the courtyard. The red rooms are maintained for travellers whose backgrounds are unknown. It's a way of ensuring that those lodged outside are only able to access their room and the downstairs area of the inn. Their ability to spy is severely curtailed."

"Surely, we do not have to worry about such things on this pilgrimage?"

"Oh, yes. We must be on our guard at all times. Allegiances can change."

Relief floods over me as I am given a key with a green fob.

"You never thought that you'd be given a red one, did you?" Owain laughs before continuing, "Come on, let's explore our rooms."

It turns out that our rooms are next to each other on the first floor. Surprised to have a room to myself, I decide to explore it thoroughly. Although, in reality, there is very little to explore. It is small and cosy. New rushes have been strewn across the floor and I sense that they have been sprinkled with rosemary, as each footstep releases a burst of fragrance. The window is quite small and seems to be in the shade. Looking out, I am surprised to see that I am within touching distance of the cross. Fancy crockets and statues are but an arm's length away. The temptation to reach out is almost unbearable, but I am stopped by a knocking on the wall.

"Bethany, can you hear me?"

Walking over, I put my face as close to the wall as possible and answer, "Yes, Owain."

"Good, are you ready to explore?"

Excited at this unexpected invitation, I reply, "Oh, yes. I'll meet you on the landing." I lay my cloak on the bed and change into my new boots.

***

Outside, we make our way to the bottom of the cross. Looking up makes me feel quite dizzy. Owain's excitement is palpable and infectious.

"It's amazing, isn't it? The craftsmen certainly didn't cut any corners. The leaves and berries are so real, and then there's the heraldic shields. Can you see the one closest to us? That's the arms of England – and the one over there, that's the arms of Castile and Leon."

I gaze in awe, unable to speak.

"Please excuse me for asking, but can you see the buttresses?" Owain asks.

"Yes, just about."

A sad-looking Owain drops his eyes to the floor.

"What's wrong?" I ask.

"I shouldn't have asked you that, I'm sorry."

Without thinking, I take hold of Owain's hand and squeeze it tightly. "Please, don't be sorry. I'm not offended. In fact, I would be very grateful if you could describe the bits that I cannot see."

A smiling Owain looks into my face. His cheeks are rosy and his eyes are happy once more. "That would be a pleasure."

The rest of our day flies by in a haze of discovery. Surprisingly, we only saw Bernadette on our adventures. Strangely, she was loitering by one of the outside rooms! After a late meal, we pass the evening by the fire. Beeswax candles splutter and flicker. The smell reminds me of home. Inside, I feel a sense of contentment and peace. Ethel is reciting a passage from the Bible. I listen intently, as it's a strange passage and one that I have not heard before. Looking around, I quickly realise that no one appears to recognise it. Agnes, however, is the first to speak.

"Ethel, what on earth does it mean?"

With a kind smile, Ethel replies, "I'm very sorry, my dear, but I have never understood it either."

Laughter rings out and continues to do so until we retire.

The Road to Ware

At first light, I pack up my belongings and change into my old boots once more. Downstairs, we prepare to leave for Ware.

Agnes, full of jollity, askes Alard, "What way do we travel? I mean, do we head north or south?"

Scratching his head, Alard seems perplexed. "Why, north, but how did you guess that?"

"Oh, no reason." Then, with a giggle, Agnes nudges Ethel so hard that she nearly topples off her bench. "I wonder if there's a gate to enter through?"

Again, Alard stares blankly at Agnes, before the penny finally falls into place. "Ah, now I understand, you're referring to the Bible passage from last night."

Laughter erupts and we start another day full of joy.

Before we leave, we take it in turns to thank Samuel, Jon and Robert. I should imagine that their life is a hard one. No doubt another group of pilgrims will arrive later today, meaning that the rooms will need to be cleaned and the barrels of ale replenished. Speaking of such, I think that Ned may have drunk a barrel of ale all by himself last night, judging by the redness of his eyes!

The road ahead appears very quiet and I happily retreat into my thoughts, until I am woken a short while later by a very large commotion directly in front of us. All of a sudden, the air has become dry and is filled with a fine brown dust.

Alard's words shock me into action. "Mind yourselves; quick, quick, move out of the way."

These are the only words that I fully understand, as the men ahead of us are speaking a strange language. One that I have never heard before. The ground is shaking. I open my eyes fully and see a herd of cows bearing down on us. Ten, fifteen, maybe twenty. There are too many to count. The screaming gets louder and louder. A heavy weight lands on top of me and darkness descends.

I fear opening my eyes, but when I do, I realise that I am in one piece and have come to no harm. My back aches slightly, but it could have been far worse.

"God be praised you are safe." A dishevelled Owain sighs with relief. "I had feared the worst when I saw the cows running in our direction. I tried to grab your arm to pull you to safety, but I missed, so I flung myself on top of you as a last resort. I hope that I haven't hurt you too much?"

"I'm a little sore, that's all – and, anyway, that's nothing. I cannot believe that you risked your life for me. Never in my wildest dreams could I have ever imagined anyone doing that."

Standing up, I brush myself down and straighten my coif, before looking around. I am alarmed at what I see. There is chaos everywhere. Men are running in all directions. Some are waving their arms, while others are waving leather whips. It takes me a few moments before I realise that they are trying to trap the marauding cows. It seems an age before they are surrounded and when they are, I cannot bear to look. The men are cruelly hitting them, even though it is not their fault. I turn my head away as I cannot help but cry for the poor animals.

Then, all of a sudden, I remember the others. "Owain, the others, are they safe?"

"Well, yes." Owain hesitates. "Apart from Ethel and Agnes."

I wrench my hands. "Owain, please, tell me what happened?"

"Well, both managed to get to the side of the road, but when the cows rushed past, they lost their footings and fell into the ditch. Ned and Davy managed to pull them free. They could easily have drowned. Fortunately, they didn't and neither appear to have broken any bones, which is a miracle at their age. Alard is furious and has returned to Waltham Cross to get a couple of mules. He wants them to ride to Ware. He's afraid the shock may affect them. Let's go and join the others while we wait for him to return."

When Alard returns with the mules, Ethel and Agnes are lifted onto them. Neither appear to be suffering from any shock. In fact, they are both smiling. Alard, however, is not. His face is angry and contorted with rage.

Unable to control himself any longer, he confronts the drovers, "You arrogant fools. I don't know what you have to laugh about. You could have killed two of my party. Why don't you control your cattle? There're a menace."

Fearing that the situation is spiralling out of control, Owain walks over to Alard. "Come on, let's leave. There are only four of us. We are outnumbered."

"Yes, I know, but those Welsh drovers are nothing but trouble. They think that they own the road. I have had run-ins with them before. Someone should teach them a lesson." Sulkily, he turns his back and returns to the mules. Taking the reins, he asks them to walk on. Unable to keep his thoughts to himself, Alard announces that he has witnessed such a commotion before. "We must be grateful that we saw them on their way to The Welsh Harp Inn and not after. Troublemakers, the lot of them."

As we walk on, I can hear their taunts fade into the background. Well, it's certainly an eventful start to the day. I hope that the remainder of the journey is quieter. Uneventful hours pass. The sound of birdsong mixes with the rhythm of our feet.

Owain, as attentive as ever, announces that we are not far now. "We have made good time and will arrive well before the sun goes down, which is amazing considering what happened earlier. We will lodge at Ware for a couple of days. Happily, our visit coincides with the first fayre of the year. Surely, you cannot have forgotten that it is soon to be May Day?"

Clasping my face in my hands, I blurt out the words, "Oh no! How could I have forgotten. May Day is my favourite day of the year!"

As we enter Ware, I can feel excitement in the air. At last, winter can thoroughly be put to bed and we can all look forward to long summer days with plenty of warmth and an abundance of fresh food. At this time of year, how I long for the new crop of butter and soft cheeses. In fact, I long for anything that has not been dried or salted, and I expect that's the same for all of us. We are greeted by smiling faces all around. The old no doubt remembering times of old and the young, full of expectation.

On the green, a group of men are busy erecting the maypole. It's hard work, you know. First, the pole has to be dressed in long multicoloured ribbons, before it is carefully topped with a crown of ivy, then finally lifted into place and secured to the ground by study ropes.

Turning my thoughts back to our party, I am amused to see Agnes swaying around on the back of the mule and singing a carol. "The moon shines brightly and the stars give a light. A little before this day. Our Heavenly Father, he called to us. And bid us awake and pray. Awake, awake, oh, pretty, pretty maid. Out of your drowsy dream. And step into your dairy below. And fetch me a bowl of cream. If not a bowl of thy sweet cream. A cup to bring me cheer. For the Lord knows when we shall meet again. To go Maying another year."

I chuckle to myself, before looking around once more. I cannot help myself; I feel compelled to take everything in. On another part of the green, I can see four groups of men erecting brightly coloured tents. In fact, the tents remind me of Ned's clothing. I giggle to myself at the very thought of it. I am woken from my thoughts once more by Owain, who is now rather excitable.

"We are in for a real treat, Bethany. Ware is renowned for its celebrations."

"Not only Ware, my dear friends!"

Stopping for a moment, we look around before laughing heartily. Ned is now imitating a horse and is dancing past us at great speed. He is prancing to the rhythm of Agnes's singing.

"He's mad, isn't he?" Owain says with a beaming smile.

As we turn the corner, I am astonished by the view before my eyes. For as far as the eye can see, May Day preparations are in full swing. Banners are being hung from every vantage point and just beyond the half-timbered houses, groups of men are erecting even more tents.

The high street is heaving. Merchants and pilgrims are everywhere, vying for space. The area is buzzing. I have never seen so many people in one place before. Ware makes Cheapside appear quiet. I note with particular interest the grand burgage plots, which stretch right down from the roadside to the river. I consider the people who own them and wonder how they became so wealthy. A low bridge comes into view. It appears to separate a small port from the river. If I squint, I can just about see the boats bobbing around and the toll hut sitting to one side. To my surprise, the river is almost as busy as the streets. Men climb from boat to boat, poking at sacks before burying their heads inside them to inspect the goods.

My mind changes direction briefly as I consider our lodgings. I wonder where we will be staying. At an inn in the very heart of the town, or maybe somewhere further afield? I don't have to wait very long, though, as an obviously relieved Alard soon announces to everyone that we have arrived.

"Welcome to Water Row and The White Hart Inn, which will be our home for the next few days. I know that we will all be very comfortable here. The innkeeper is a fine man, by the name of Gurdy. He prides himself on his cellar and his pies. I can guarantee that we will not go hungry or thirsty here." Alard chuckles and rolls his eyes.

As we draw near, Gurdy comes into view. He is a wiry man with the appearance of a stick. His hair is wild and matted and protrudes in every direction. From first impression, it would appear that he does not eat too many of his own pies, as I can see his bones sticking out of his skin. I note that his frame is small, but his smile is large and it lights up his haunted face. Gurdy bids that we step inside and come together.

"Welcome, everyone, welcome. Friends old and new alike. I hope that your stay will be a comfortable one. If you need anything at all, please just say so. All I request in return is your cooperation. Please let me explain. This inn sits on a royal highway. It's known as the Walsingham Way. We are always busy, but especially so at the moment. The May Day festivities have attracted far more visitors than normal and this has worried our lord. He fears that not everyone is here for the right reasons. Therefore, he has asked Sir William Oldhall to provide a contingent of men from his nearby manor of Hunsdon to ensure that the peace is kept. He has also sent a missive and asked me to read it aloud at the earliest possible convenience. Now seems as good a time as ever, but as it's a rather long document, I suggest that you fill your tankards with ale before I begin."

Never one to miss a cup of ale, Ned bounds forwards with his leather tankard at the ready, closely followed by the rest of us. Then, true to his word, Gurdy read the missive, which was very long indeed. So long that I cannot remember everything that was said. However, the overriding message is that our lord forbids any female from going into town alone, as the town's population has swollen beyond belief and every inn is now full to capacity. Rumour has it that people are sleeping under hedges, all the way from Water Row to Priory Street. May Day is always popular, but our lord suspects that something is afoot.

After sitting for such a long time, it's quite a relief to stretch my legs. Outside, the air has cooled and become fresher. A sharp breeze is now blowing-up from the direction of the river. I pull my cloak tightly around my shoulders. Owain appears from seemingly nowhere.

"Bethany, I hope that you weren't going to explore Ware on your own?"

"Oh no, Owain, I just wanted to get a closer look at the blossoming trees before supper. I have no intention of walking anywhere by myself."

"Good – anyway, I like your company and its much more fun exploring together. I asked Agnes and Ethel if they wanted to join us, but they declined. I think that their bruises must be coming out now. I also extended the invitation to Ursula and Bernadette, but they want to rest for tomorrow. That only leaves Cecily and Anne, but as I don't like them, I hid from their view."

Feigning shock, I clasp my hands to my face. "Owain, that's terrible."

"I know, but I just cannot warm to their company."

"I know what you mean, but they might just be shy?"

"Huh... really."

I quickly change the subject. "What are Davy, Ned and Alard doing?"

"Well, Ned has accosted the men of Sir William Oldhall and has challenged them to a few games of dice. Alard is making plans for the return of the mules and Davy is sulking. Don't ask why, as I don't know. He's a strange one. Let's not waste any more time. Shall we take in the sights? Why don't we start with the priory?"

Walking around, I'm amazed at the number of women and children begging. Babes in arms, clinging to their mothers.

Owain, noticing my sadness, explains, "Don't be fooled by them, Bethany. They may look harmless and poor, but they are ruthless manipulators. First, they make friends with you, then they let you play with their babes, then they demand money and if you don't give them any, they tear at your clothing and scratch you. I made the mistake of befriending one many years ago. Never again. If they smile at you, just ignore them and make sure that you always keep your purse out of view."

"How terrible, women using their babes to get money."

"Unfortunately, that's the way of the towns and cities nowadays. Things aren't always what they seem."

After walking for a short while, the Franciscan Priory comes into view and it's a sight to behold. The stonework has a pinkish tinge and it casts shadows in all directions. All along the periphery wall, holy men dressed in robes and sandals are reading scriptures to passers-by.

"God forgive me, Bethany, but make sure to keep your purse shut tight. These so-called holy men are also frauds. Look closely at their hoods. Underneath, they have hair. No monk has such."

Shocked, I ask, "But how do they get away with such pretence? Can't they be stopped?"

"It's an age-old problem. Whenever they see a monk approaching, they just slide their hoods down and act dumb, and who's going to argue with them when they draw their blades?"

Stunned by such charlatans, I wonder what's actually real in life and what's false. After our exploration, we return to the inn. The night brings much joy and laughter. There is drinking, singing and dancing aplenty. The mood is slightly dampened though by Gurdy, who is now walking among everyone.

"Here, these are for tomorrow." As he passes, he hands out a pale-blue baldric to everyone. "Wear them with pride and remember to keep them on all day. Apart from decoration, they will make you visible to Sir William's men – and remember, ladies, do not wander off on your own. Not even for one moment. Let us men make your day special!"

Looking at Davy's face, I cannot believe that he will ever make anyone's day special. I wish I knew what he was sulking about.

**

Morning breaks and May Day has arrived. I dress myself quickly and tidy my belongings. I must say my prayers straightaway while the others are asleep or I fear that I will have no peace. I start with the Lord's Prayer and finish with a message to my mother.

"I miss you with all my heart. How I long to hear your voice, kiss your cheek and hold you close. Please be by my side and guide me now and always. Keep me safe and pure."

Smiling, I recount a little rhyme that we always said together on May Day. "Wake me up in the morning, Mother dear, for I be Queen of the May."

As I speak the words, I wonder if she can hear me. When I'm finished, I place the pale-blue baldric that Gurdy gave me over my head and drape it carefully across my body. To my astonishment, it hangs beautifully from left to right. The fabric is heavy and of good quality. Stroking it, I feel special. I notice that the others are now starting to wake.

"Good day, my lady. Are you ready to dance the day away?"

I laugh before responding. "Oh, Ned, yes, I think that I am. However, before I dance the day away, I must wash my face in the morning dew."

"Well, let's go then. I could do with a wash, too. I need every bit of help if I'm going to win at the tug of war."

Outside, the day is perfect and the sun is shining brightly. Ribbons and banners float gently in the breeze and the ladies of the manor have already started to dance barefoot on the green.

"Would you like to join them, Bethany?"

"Yes, I think that I would."

"Right, well, let's remove our boots and leave them by that old oak tree over there."

"Why are you taking your boots off, Ned?"

"Why, to dance, of course! I don't want to get my boots soaked with dew. I need to keep them as dry as possible for the contest later." How everyone roars with laughter at Ned's antics. Holding hands, we create a circle and dance around him. "Surely I must be the King of the May; would anyone like to kiss me?" Ned's invitation causes a great deal of interest. "Bethany, would you like to be first?" A beaming Ned rubs his cheeks viperously with both hands. "Now, don't be shy, you know you want to."

Owain and Alard, who, unbeknown to us, have been watching all of the time, laugh out loud.

"You wish, Ned. Bethany is keeping herself for later, when the real King of the May is crowned," says Owain.

I feel a warm glow of contentment and ponder on who I would kiss, as I have never kissed anyone before. 'For I be Queen of the May, Mother, for I be Queen of the May, Mother dear' is being sung. Turning, I watch as Agnes and Ursula, along with Bernadette and Ethel, skip down the road hand in hand.

Agnes calls out as she passes, "Bethany, why don't you come with us?"

I look at Owain and he nods. "Go on, Bethany, poor Davy has no one to hold his hand or to skip with."

Davy's face is not quite as sulky as yesterday, so I agree. To my surprise, Davy extends his hand and smiles. "My lady."

As I take hold, I feel his soft fingers wrap around mine. It feels good! Dancing down the street, we pass home after home that has been decorated. It would seem that the locals have used anything that they have to hand. Strips of old fabric have been sewed together to create bunting and St Brigit's crosses have been hung from the windows and the doors. Music fills the air, along with laughter. Barrels have become drums and wooden sticks have become rattles. Troubles and chores have been left behind for this most revered day. Some are wearing new clothes, but the majority are just like us. They are wearing baldrics, which proudly display their lord's colours. I have never seen so many different colours all in one place before, but that seems to be a true reflection of Ware. A place of such importance that everyone wants a piece of it.

Tired from dancing, we wait, seated on a wall, for Anne and Cecily to join us.

Alard sighs loudly. "We'll give them a just little while longer and then if they do not show, I will instruct Sir William's men to find them. Davy, are you sure that they were not in the inn?"

"Very certain. I checked everywhere. All the rooms and the garden, too."

"Ah well, let's not lose any more time. Why don't you all go off and enjoy yourselves and I'll meet you later."

"There's no need for that, Alard, I can see them heading this way."

"Come on, you two, I need to break my fast," says Ned.

They smile weakly at Ned, but neither appear very happy. Ignoring this, we all set off to explore the fayre. As expected, Ned excels at every activity – bashing the rat, sword-fighting and even maypole dancing. Not once did he become entangled in the ribbons or take a wrong step!

"Tug of war beckons; who is brave enough to take me on then?" Ned says.

"Ned, tug of war is a team sport. You can't partake on your own. You know the rules. Two teams of six."

"You watch me Davy, I'll take on the world and win. I'm stronger than anyone."

Davy shakes his head in despair. "Whatever you say."

A laughing Ned looks around. "Come on!" he shouts. "Who is brave enough to take me on? Are there any takers?"

"OK, if you think that you're up to it, I'll take you on. Just us two, mind. No cheating. I'll not pull against a team on my own. One against the other, that's the deal. Take it or leave it."

"Owain, I knew that I could rely on you. Get ready to be beaten, for I am King of the May."

"In your mind, maybe, but let's make the competition more interesting. If I win, you have to buy me as many pies as I can eat today."

"OK, and if I win, you'll have to buy me as much ale as I can sup tonight."

"That seems a fair deal. Let's get ready."

Watching them, it crosses my mind that they are akin to two rutting deers. Preening themselves, they wrap the long rope about their waists and kick the soil beneath their feet. They are trying to make ruts in the ground to push against in battle.

Ned loudly announces to all in the vicinity that he will soon be the victor. "Prepare to open your purse, Owain. I will drink until midnight at your expense."

A crowd draws around.

"We'll see about that, Ned. I beat you last year, remember."

"Oh, that. I let you win. My head was still sore from the night before and I thought that more ale was unwise."

"Really. Why did I see you buying more then?"

"Me? Surely not." Ned's face is a picture of innocence.

The spectacle was set. Alard becomes the caller. "Now, you both know the rules. It's the best of three and I don't want to see any foul play. Ned, that applies especially to you. Hold the rope taught and prepare for battle."

Silence descends as both men stare at each other.

Raising his hand, Alard waves a piece of linen aloft, before dropping it sharply. The contest begins. Pulling back and forth, they sway in time to the crowds chanting. Pretty girls shout and encourage both men.

Davy leans over and whispers in my ear, "Owain will win. He always does. Ned will soon lose interest. He is easily distracted and the draw of a pretty girl is much more desirable to him than winning against his best friend. Anyway, if he loses, the women tend to love him even more. They will mother him and tend to his every need."

"What about the pies?"

"Oh… no doubt he'll treat Owain either way."

In a few minutes, Davy's theory is proved right as Ned falls flat on his stomach. After visibly catching his breath, he looks up and smiles. "You win, my friend."

Thunderous clapping breaks out and is accompanied by comments such as, "How valorous in defeat!"

A petite blonde, with tumbling curls, runs to Ned's side. "Here, take my kerchief to wipe your hands and face."

Davy is smiling broadly. "Now you see what I mean. He has lost the battle, but won the war."

Owain stands up, disentangles himself from the rope and laughs. "Let me help you."

Clapping breaks out once more. Alard announces that both men are indeed Kings of the May and should be crowned as the bravest and the stupidest in Christendom. "Their rule will last until to midnight. God have mercy on us. Just keep your rules clean."

I have never heard such laughter.

A thoughtful Ned is the first to speak. "As joint King of the May, I declare that everyone should walk backwards and dance like chickens."

The crowd duly obeys, causing much hilarity.

Then, Owain speaks, "As joint King of the May, I request that Bethany Mortimer becomes my queen."

Before I realise what is happening, he has dropped to his knee and is begging my acceptance. The crowd chants, "Do it, do it!" Flustered, I accept. Flowers are then thrust into my hand by a woman in the crowd.

"Come, Bethany," says Owain. "Let's go in search of wine and brie."

As I walk away, I realise that Davy has walked away and

his shoulders have dropped. For a moment, I am saddened. However, I quickly bounce back to feeling normal. Indeed, I am happier now than I have ever been in my life. I am soon sitting by the mill, being fed wine and brie by Owain, and I allow myself to relax. If only life could always be like this. Alas, normality will return tomorrow – as it always does. So, I will revel in this moment and capture every detail.

Our party sits on the grassy bank, telling tales and laughing. Ursula has removed her boots and is paddling in the crystal-clear waters of the stream, while Bernadette is counting her brightly coloured glass beads. Agnes is sound asleep and snoring gently, while Anne is weaving wool around her fingers. I can see everyone apart from Davy. Then, to everyone's surprise, a loud horn is heard.

Agnes sits bolt upright and rubs her eyes. "I was only resting them, you know. I wasn't sleeping. What's happening?"

Owain stands to survey the horizon. "It's St George. See, over there. He's made an appearance at last. A little late in the day, by my reckoning, but better late than never. Where is the dragon? Can anyone see him?"

"I can!" shouts Cecily. "But something's wrong. Oh no… the dragon is chasing St George. Look!"

After much chasing, St George is pulled to the ground and they roll around for what seems like an eternity. St George eventually stands up and is as victorious as ever. He lifts his helm before bowing low. The dragon, on the other hand, lies drunken in a heap. Again, laughter fills the air.

"We had better carry him back to the inn. We can't leave him here in that costume."

The sight before me will stay in my memory forever. The dragon is, in fact, Ned, who is dressed in a see-through green outfit. To mine, and everyone else's astonishment, he is wearing nothing else but a smile! Transporting Ned back to the inn is far easier said than done.

"Stop wriggling, Ned, you drunken sop. I'm supposed to be the King of the May and exempt from anything other than pleasure." Ned, being far too drunk to care, attempts to opens one eye, but quickly closes it again. "I think that we should dunk him in the stream. That'll wake him."

"Maybe, but that's not really in the spirit of May Day, is it, Owain?"

"I suppose not, but it would be hilarious."

Back at the inn, Davy finds Ned's clothes in a bundle by his shawm. "I think that we ought to dress him, Alard. It's not right that the ladies have to see him naked."

"I agree. We'll start at the bottom and work our way up, but just his linen undergarments, that's all. He can finish the rest when he wakes."

"I agree."

Watching Ned being dressed is even more amusing than seeing him naked on the ground. He either has no idea where he is or he is playing to the crowd. He keeps clinging to Davy's arm and saying, "Thank you, Mother dear," and if that wasn't bad enough, he keeps trying to cuddle him.

A none-too-pleased Davy finishes his task, before turning to face everyone. With a cheeky smile, he announces, "As St George, I'm sure you will all agree that I am superior to the King of the May. Therefore, Owain, I claim your queen for the rest of the day."

Owain, deep in thought, does not answer immediately. Instead, he turns his face this way and that, gauging the mood of our party. Finally, he speaks. "Of course, my friend. I'll dine with the Princesses of the May instead. Ladies, would you all like to come with me?"

Davy's pleasure is obvious, as is everyone else's. With this, we all head off in search of food. The meal does not disappoint. Roasted meats are accompanied by brightly coloured jellies and numerous cups of watered wine. Finally, the day draws to an end with a Mummers' Play outside the priory. St George and the Dragon, of course – but this version is unlike any that I have ever witnessed before. I stand with the others, gazing in astonishment as the dragon returns to life and starts breathing fire into the air. Great plumes of orange flames are accompanied by golden sparks. How we all roar with approval, especially when we realise that the dragon is a recovered Ned!

Standon Beckons

The revelries of yesterday are over and today we have a long walk ahead of us. Sore heads and sulky faces surround me. Although, this is nothing new. It's always the same on the second of May. The only difference now is that we are on a pilgrimage and we do not have to return to our daily tasks. There are no animals to feed or pens to be cleaned. For this, I am eternally grateful, as I ate and drank far too much yesterday and I fear that my stomach will hurt for quite a while. I also doubt that I could deal with the smell of dung without being sick. So, to take my mind off such thoughts, I pack my belongings and make my way to the front porch. As usual, I am the first to arrive, closely followed by Owain.

"Hello, Bethany, how are you this fine morning?"

"Very well, considering. Yesterday was an amazing day, but I fear that I overate."

"Ah, well, didn't we all? It would be rude not to, especially as there were so many delicacies on offer. Anyway, I always think that it does us good to indulge at the start of a pilgrimage. It raises the spirits and helps us bond as a family. Speaking of such, I wonder where everyone is?"

"Yes, it's strange that no one else has appeared, especially as most were packed and ready to go when I left."

"Oh, well, we need ponder no more. Here they come and don't they look a miserable bunch? I'll certainly have my work cut out cheering them up today." Rubbing his hands together, Owain announces that a real treat awaits us. "Before we leave Ware, we have been invited to celebrate mass at the Church of St Mary. Not just as pilgrims, but as special guests of the Benedictines. We have also been invited to break our fast with them in the refectory afterwards. There will be sausages, bacon and their speciality, homemade oat bread, which I hear they are famous for."

Looking around, we both realise it will take far more than this to make anyone happy today. As we approach the church, plainchant can be heard. Sweet voices are preparing to worship the Lord. They rise and fall in harmony. Nearer still, I can see clouds of incense hanging in the air. The smell transports me to another place and time. Inside, I realise just how beautiful St Mary's church is. Owain's words are ringing in my ears. I remember nearly every word of his explanation. Areas of the church were rebuilt at great cost over seventy years ago by Joan, the Fair Maid of Kent. Not only was she the widow of the greatest knight of all time, Edward, Black Prince of Wales, she was mother to King Richard II.

Taking my seat, I am amazed. The nave of the church resembles a great ship, like Noah's Ark, and we are the passengers learning about other worlds. The Doom painting over the chancel arch depicts Christ on the Day of Judgement. He is separating the saints from the sinners. The sinners are being cast into the flames of hell below, while the saints are rising to heaven. How appropriate then that the church's roof is richly decorated with paintings of stars and saints. The arches and pillars of the church are adorned with corbels. Most are made from finely carved stone, but strangely two are made of wood and have been nailed to the wall. The designs are varied and range from people to dogs and monkeys. I find it strange that monkeys are depicted. I have never heard of such before. Perhaps the stonemason encountered monkeys when visiting the Holy Land? My head is spinning as I try to take in all the chantry chapels and the small altars.

Oh no, the priest is beckoning us forward to receive the host. I have missed nearly all of the service. In my trance-like state, I have heard nothing. I am deeply ashamed. I have allowed the beauty of the church to seduce me and I have not paid attention how I ought. Standing, I walk forward to the altar, cross myself and kneel down on the worn-out cushions. God forgive me. I have failed. As the priest approaches, I open my mouth in readiness to receive Christ's body. The bread melts on my tongue and I try to concentrate on Jesus's sacrifices. Once melted, I drink the wine from the chalice. His blood tingles on my lips and heats my body. I rise and return to my seat. Still annoyed at myself, I vow to repent for my behaviour. The priest delivers his final blessing and turns to leave. This is the sign for the congregation to file out. I take my place and follow.

As we leave, I stop for a few minutes by the stone font, which I passed in haste this morning. It has eight sides and is now bathed in sunlight. Facing me, I can see St James, the patron saint of pilgrims. He is dressed in garb such as ours. In one hand, he is carrying a staff and in the other, he is holding a book. I am deeply humbled as many have trodden the path that I now follow. I am left wondering if they also lost focus of the priest's words.

Outside, the day has broken fully. Birds are singing and flowers continue to bloom. It seems that the Church of St Mary has lifted everyone's spirits. Smiles have returned, as has the laughter. The priest now joins us and shakes Owain's hand. Owain greets him enthusiastically.

"Good morrow, Father Bramble. Thank you for inviting us to be your guests. It was a wonderful service."

"You are more than welcome, my child. How I love preaching to pilgrims. It's the only time that anyone listens to me." With these words, Father Bramble laughs loudly and rubs his extremely large tummy, before announcing, "Now, come on, follow me. It's time for the most important part of the day. Our refreshments have been laid out in the refectory and, I don't know about you, but I am ravenous."

Relieved to remove his robes, Father Bramble soon stands at the head of the table in a simple black linen shift. Rolling up his sleeves, he prepares to serve us. Noticing the look of shock on our faces, he explains, "I follow Jesus in all respects. Now, my dear children, let me serve you. It's my duty and one that I truly enjoy."

With these words, we all relax and pass platters up and down both sides of the table until everyone is ready to eat. After a short grace, we begin. The bread is warm and oozes with butter – so much so that it trickles down my arm as I try to eat it. Now I understand why Father Bramble rolled his sleeves up. I decide to do the same, before helping myself to sausages and bacon. The food is succulent and satisfying.

"Don't stand on ceremony; help yourself to as much as you need," says Father Bramble. "You have quite a walk ahead of you."

Once we are all sated and every crumb has been consumed, Owain stands to thank Father Bramble and the brothers. "Thank you for your kindness. We are very grateful for your hospitality, but alas the time has come for us to depart."

"Yes, you must make good use of the daylight hours. Go in peace, my children. May God protect you along the way." Then, as an endnote. "When you arrive at Standon, please could you say hello to Brother Thomas for me? I haven't seen him for quite some time, but I think of him often."

"Of course, I will pass on your good wishes. I know Brother Thomas well and such a message will cheer his heart."

Content with Owain's reassurance, Father Bramble blesses us. "May God bless you all with a safe journey. May the saints and angels travel with you, and may you live every day in justice and joy. Now, go into the world and spread the Word of God as you go."

Uplifted by our experience, we form an orderly procession and set out at a leisurely place. Glancing back, I gaze upon the new stone tower. It's unlike any other that I have ever seen before. It has turrets and arrow slits and, to my mind, it resembles a battlement far more than a church. Even its very height sets it apart. I wonder? Could the rumours be true? Has it has been built as a lookout?

The hours pass and with them I still cannot shake the thought of impending war. Are there spies among our party? Are we being watched? Who can be trusted and who cannot? I still have my doubts about Anne and Cecily, but what can I do? I know. I'll watch them and make a note of any strange behaviour. If I notice any, I will confide in Owain, who is at this very moment trying to engage with them – unfortunately, without much success.

"Ladies, have you ever been on a pilgrimage before?"

"No."

"Really, Cecily, I am sure that I have seen you on my travels. I think Ely, maybe?"

"No never."

"Why do you snap so? I am only trying to be friendly."

"Well, I don't want to talk to you. Go away."

"What about you, Anne? I'm sure that our paths have crossed on the Fens?"

Anne, not as guarded, answers politely, "No, not a pilgrimage, but I have visited Ely in the past. Perhaps you saw me in one of the inns?"

Owain, content to have ruffled their feathers, announces that we are nearing Standon Priory. "Not long now. If you look straight ahead, you can just about see the priory on the horizon."

But rather than look to the horizon, I examine Anne's face. She is sweating profusely and waving away an agitated Cecily. "Be quiet or you'll give us away."

"What do you mean, I'll 'give us away'?. I'm not the one who has just blurted out about Ely. And while I'm at it, beware of that Bethany Mortimer. Traitor by name, traitor by nature. She's far too friendly with everyone."

Hurt by such an accusation, it's all I can do not to cry. I'm not a traitor and I have never been. Then, as if by divine intervention, the sky darkens and the sun disappears. Raindrops as big as chestnuts begin to fall at an alarming rate, soaking us all to the skin and making the ground heavy and slippery. The clay sticks to my boots and I begin to slide around uncontrollably. Fortunately, Owain is close by and clasps an arm about my waist to steady me. Ned, Alard and

Davy do the same for Ursula, Ethel, Agnes and Bernadette. Anne and Cecily, on the other hand, have fallen to the ground and are covered in mud.

When we arrive at the priory, we must appear a sorry sight, bedraggled and soaking wet. Alard knocks loudly to announce our arrival. I can hear the door hinges creak from within and, to my surprise, the doors are opened by a man in very fine robes.

"Welcome all. Welcome. Come in quickly. You're soaking wet. We must get you dry as soon as possible. I have sent word to the brothers of the apothecary. They will be here in a few minutes with linen towels and shifts, but please let me introduce myself in the meantime. I am Richard Sadlier."

While waiting, I play with that name in my head. I think it must relate to saddle-makers, but I'm not entirely sure. I wonder who he is. All of a sudden, a concealed door opens and three brothers appear. As promised, they are laden down with bundles of dry linen.

"Hello, I am Brother Thomas and these are Brothers Andrew and Patrick." All three appear concerned by our appearance. "There will be time to get to know each other later, but first we must get you dry. Please come this way to the fire." Gratefully, we follow Brother Thomas. "Please make yourselves as comfortable as possible. There are benches and stools for you to sit upon, although the stools may be a little better as you can draw them closer to the hearth. We also have bowls of steaming water to sooth your feet. Once you have used the towels to dry yourself, there are shifts for you to wear, while your belongings dry."

Owain, true to his word, immediately passes on Father Bramble's kind wishes. "Brother Thomas, Father Bramble wishes to be remembered to you. He says that it's been a long time since you last saw each other."

Brother Thomas' eyes mist over. "Yes, it's been far too long, but matters of this house seem to have overtaken every waking hour. Long gone are the days of stability. Ever since the Knights Hospitallers left, our lease has been passed back and forth between the crown and Buckland Priory. Indeed, Richard Sadlier has bought even more changes." I can see sadness in Brother Thomas' eyes. "Well, let's not dwell on that. Ladies, as you are now in the house of God, you are free to remove your coifs. It's unwise to keep them on and invites ill health by encouraging a chill."

Relieved, I remove the brass pins that hold my coif in place. The sodden linen slides from my head and releases my hair, which hangs heavy about my shoulders.

Grateful for the invitation to move nearer to the hearth, we all move a touch closer. All apart from Ursula, who – to everyone's surprise – has removed her coif and is completely bald. Far from being embarrassed, she laughs. "Well, at least I don't have to dry my hair."

Once we are dry, Brother Thomas requests that food is brought to us. Bread, cheese and ale. Such simple pleasures, but pleasures none the less. The light has now faded and the candles splutter. Pallets have been prepared for us, so I bid goodnight and retire. Warm and dry, I lie down and let my mind wander. In the distance, I can hear foxes calling to each other. They are screaming and barking. I think that they must be patrolling their territory. This is something that I plan to do in the morning. I will rise early and meet Owain in the courtyard. We will then go and explore together. The prospect excites me as I know that this manor belongs to our lord.

***

As soon as the sunlight begins to flood in through the shutters, I dress quickly. Relieved to be back in my own clothes, I pick my way across the room, trying not to wake the others. Outside, the morning dew clings to my skin. I rub my eyes to clear the mist and then look around for Owain. I see him almost immediately. He is standing by a very large barn, waving enthusiastically.

"Morning, Bethany. Did you sleep well?"

"Oh, yes. Did you?"

"Sort of. Ned and Davy, both drunk, took it in turns to snore loudly. I let it carry on for a while, but it was just too much. So, I took matters into my own hands. My plan worked beautifully and they both shut up when I splashed cold water on their faces." Laughing, we walk through the barn. "Are you ready to explore?"

"Oh yes."

"Well, there's plenty to see. Firstly, we are going to leave by the back gate and then we'll walk in the direction of the church. Finally, we will explore the high street before returning in time to break our fast."

"Owain, before we go, I have something to tell you. Yesterday, I overheard Cecily being beastly about me. She said that I was a traitor. Traitor by name, traitor by nature. She also said that I'm far too friendly with everyone."

Owain's face reddens momentarily. "Holy Lord, she's spiteful that one, but please don't worry, Bethany. I'll deal with her."

Inside the barn, the brothers are already hard at work. Some are sorting dried beans and peas ready for sowing, while others are mending the plough. From what I can see, they are removing the rotten beams and replacing them with new ones. Further on, piles of hay are being turned, creating a shower of grain and plumes of dust.

"I have never seen a barn as grand as this, Owain."

"That's because it's unique. Well, almost unique. There's another one, but it's miles away. It was built by the Knights of St John of Jerusalem, on land that was granted to them by Gilbert de Clare. If you look closely at the beams, you'll see ancient symbols scored into the wood. Their meanings are lost to us, but they must have meant something to them. This manor has always been highly prized because of its location – you'll understand why when you see the view. Feuds and battles have been fought over it, but the de Clare family have always managed to hang on and it has remained in their hands since the time of the Crusades. They have passed it down through the generations and that's how it came to be in the hands of our lord. It was part of his inheritance. However, our lord has kindly granted it to Sir William Oldhall for his lifetime, as recognition of his good service and unfailing loyalty. This means that he can keep all of the rents and profits from the manor."

I smile at our lord's kindness and feel a warmth inside. Walking on, I am perplexed. "Owain, I thought that we were on our way to the back gate?"

"We are. Can't you see it?"

"What do you mean? Of course I can't see it; we are still in the barn."

"Look around, Bethany, it's nearer than you think."

"Sorry, Owain, I'm confused. What do you mean?"

With a chuckle, Owain answers, "Let me assist you."

With these words, Owain draws back a curtain made of heavy sackcloth. I still can't see anything but a tool store. There are axe handles nailed to the wall and scythes hanging from metal hooks, but no door.

"Sorry, I'm still confused."

Owain is obviously enjoying teasing me, as he begins to chuckle. "Well, you see that axe handle? The one on its own? Why don't you pull it as hard as you can?"

I tug at the handle with as much vigour as possible and am surprised when a concealed door opens. Owain continues to chuckle.

"Well, I said that it was nearer to you than you thought."

"You can say that again. I never even saw it."

"That's the idea. It's a fail-safe. If ever the hospital is attacked, the brothers can escape, and when the door is closed behind them, no one will ever know how. It will ensure that they have enough time to escape to safety."

Outside, the fields slope down sharply to the flat ground by the River Rib, which snakes off into the distance, glinting as it goes. I follow Owain down to the river. I'm glad that I put my old boots on this morning as the ground is rather heavy after yesterday's downpour. At the river, we turn left until we reach the crossroads of Ermine Street and Stane Street. Turning left again, we climb to the top of the hill, leaving the heavy terrain behind us. The view at the top is simply breathtaking. I feel like I'm standing on top of the world.

Owain is the first to break the silence. "It's a prize worth fighting for, don't you think? Friends and foe can be seen for miles."

"Oh yes. I could sit here all day and watch life pass by."

"How I wish we could, but we must get back to break our fast with the others. They will be wondering where we are."

We head back via the high street and past the church. Sadly, both are a disappointment. After such beauty, it's sad to see the high street in such decay. Life seems to have passed Standon by and, to make matters worse, when we turn into the marketplace, I gag immediately. Pinching my nose, I try to hold my breath. The smell of fish is overwhelming. There are fish heads and rotting skin everywhere. The gullies are full to overflowing and piles of fish bones littler the ground. My stomach heaves and I am relieved to escape back to the priory where the air is fresh and sweet.

As we approach, I can see Brother Thomas bending over in the garden, carefully picking nettles before placing them in a large wooden bowl. On hearing us, he straightens up gingerly and waves a chubby hand. We wave back enthusiastically. I like Brother Thomas. He is kind and thoughtful and when he smiles, his whole face lights up.

"Good day, both, I wondered where you were."

"I took Bethany to see the view from Stony Hill."

"Did you enjoy it?"

"Yes, Brother, it was glorious."

"Well, another treat awaits you inside. We are to break our fast in the hall. I think that everything should be ready by now. Shall we go and take a look?"

Inside, it takes a while for my eyes to adjust to the gloom, such is the light outside. My sense, however, needs no such adjustment. I can immediately smell strong fish. To my horror, Brother Thomas' feast comprises of salt fish pottage and nettle soup. I count my blessings and eat as much as possible, grateful for the hospitality.

I cannot say that I am sad to leave Standon. Newmarket beckons and I am excited at the prospect. Owain has warned me that today will be the longest walk so far, but even this does not dampen my spirits. Turning back one last time, I can see Brother Thomas standing proudly in his brown robes. He is waving enthusiastically, his silver hair glinting in the sunlight. I shall miss him.

Newmarket Beckons

On my own, with my thoughts once more, I recall the events of the last few days. Ware was magnificent. I have never known a May Day like it and I doubt I ever will again. Standon, on the other hand, was very interesting. The barn with its concealed door has taught me to question everything. I silently vow to be more alert in the future. Now, though, is the time to return to my spiritual journey. Hence, I grasp the small leather cross, which I bought at Ware in my left hand, and silently recite my prayers – all the time focusing on the life of Jesus. After what seems an eternity, I look up and notice a small bridge with a chapel attached to it. God has answered my prayers.

Alard steps to one side and we stop, grateful for the rest. "Welcome to the Chapel of Lady Bridge. Would anyone like to go in and pray?"

Surprisingly, I am the only one who wishes to enter. The others decide that they would prefer to rest on the riverbank. Agnes announces loudly that her feet are hurting and Ethel appears to be a little breathless. I do hope that they can make it to Walsingham.

As I approach the chapel, I notice that the door is rather low and narrow. I immediately bend down and try to make myself as small as possible. Inside, I am astounded by its beauty. The ceiling is vaulted and has an intricately carved boss in the middle. It depicts warrior monks. Their swords are held high in the air, ready for action. At the back of the chapel, there is an image of the Blessed Virgin Mary and an altar from the Holy Land. The altar is plain and simple, with only a cross for decoration. It is surrounded by burning candles and offerings. To these, I add a penny and leave, crossing myself before I go.

Outside, I can't wait to tell Agnes and Ethel all about the chapel. After a short rest, we pack up our things and leave. The miles pass pleasantly and I take delight in listening to the birdsong. The flat fields gradually descend into a well-wooded area, the branches of the trees creating an arch for us to walk under. Springs bubble up on either side of the path. Looking around, I realise that this whole area is a labyrinth of water. Pools, streams and ponds are everywhere. All are buzzing with wildlife and insects. As we leave the wood, we continue to cross bridge after bridge and wade through ford after ford. The cool water is very welcome as it numbs my aching feet, but, unfortunately, there is no time to rest.

When we reach the small village of Braughing, there is much amusement and laughter. A group of men are huddled around a shallow section of the river. On the bank, sheep are bleating furiously. Some are loose while others are being held in wattle pens, awaiting their fate. The bleating gets even louder as the men wash them thoroughly in the flowing water. The sheep wriggle and fight until they are turned on their backs. We laugh at the sight of their legs waving in the air and how they attempt to impart revenge upon their tormentors when the washing is over. Some attempt to bite the men before being shooed away.

I am still laughing internally when we approach another sight of great beauty. I have heard of Hay Street many times. Our lord, in his kindness, even presented our church with a beautiful hart skin from this very area. It has become a treasured possession and one that demonstrates the high status of our manor. The skin of a hart cannot be bought; it has to be earned by the hunter and I hear that hunting a stag is by no means easy. It is elusive, lithe and strong. When it enters its prime, it develops a vicious rack of antlers. I shudder at the thought of being impaled upon such things. Many have spoken of hunting the hart, but the words that sum it up best are those of our lord's ancestor, Edward, Duke of York "… after the boar, the leech, and after the hart, the bier." Who would have thought that a hart could be more dangerous than a boar?

As we follow the ditch and bank that encloses the deer park, I scan the horizon, trying to catch a glimpse of the elusive stag. Along the top of the bank is a wooden fence. The stakes look fierce and I fear for anyone who is foolish enough to try and enter without permission. Not far from where I am standing, a herd of young deer are frolicking in the long grass and dining on twigs and ivy. Surely their parents are not too far away. I'm glad to be joined by Owain.

"Are you enjoying the day?"

"Oh, yes. It's beautiful, isn't it? I keep looking for a stag, but I haven't found one yet."

"Um, I doubt you will. They are masters of disguise. They hide as soon as they sense people are in the area. Anyway, the yeomen of the forest have probably scared them all away. See, over there, they are mending the nets."

"What a shame."

"Never mind. Maybe we'll see them when we return."

Nodding, I agree, but the return journey is not something I want to think about at the moment. "Owain, I am really hungry and I have run out of bread. Have we got very far to go?"

"No not very. Alard has arranged for us to be fed and watered in the next village."

Relief floods over me.

Agnes, having heard this news, announces that she is famished and close to dropping. "We could do with a rest, if possible."

Leaving the main road behind us, we walk the last part of the journey across the newly ploughed fields. I can see where others have passed this way before, as their footprints are imprinted into the damp clay. When we reach the village of Barkway, Alard directs us through the narrow lanes and then back out into open fields. Confused to be leaving the village, loud groans fill the air.

"Do not despair," Alard says. "You don't think that I'd be so cruel as to make you carry on, do you? You see that motte and bailey over there? Well, that's where we will be staying tonight. We are to lodge at the castle on Periwinkle Hill. It's rather run-down these days, but it's warm, safe and dry."

A sense of relief floods over me as I can't wait to take my boots off. Others noisily express what I'm thinking. As we approach, I realise that the incline isn't half as steep as I'd first expected. Instead of climbing rapidly, the land rises gently and it's not very long until we reach the thick and sturdy curtain wall. We enter through a steeply arched stone doorway to find ourselves standing in the outer bailey, surrounded by hundreds of sheep. They appear reticent to move and impede our journey to the inner bailey. I have trouble negotiating the clumps of sheep dung – every footstep seems to bring with it a squelching sensation. At last, we reach the inner bailey. Inside, there is a large single-storey building. Alard was right when he said that it was run-down. It's certainly seen better days. Heavy wooden shutters hang from rusted metal fittings and there are piles of stone everywhere.

Alard tries to explain, "I'm so sorry. I can see the look of disappointment on all of your faces, but this castle has long been the subject of feuding between the local nobles. So much so that no one's ever really looked after it, but please don't let that worry you. Inside, provision has been made for us. We will be more than comfortable."

Stepping inside, we realise that Alard is correct. In the middle of the hall, two elderly men are stooped over a large fire. They are preparing our meal. Pots and skillets litter the floor. One is making meatballs, while the other is preparing a pottage. Sheepskins have been fashioned into makeshift beds and are lined around the walls.

"My dearest Alard. I'm so sorry, I did not hear you enter. Welcome, my son, welcome." The elderly man stands up and kisses Alard on the cheek before addressing us. "Welcome, my dear friends, welcome. Please come in; your meal is nearly ready. I am Philip and this is Morris. If you need anything at all, please just ask. Your beds have been prepared and so have the latrines. You will find scented water and fresh linen cloths within. Try to rest as much as possible. I understand that today's walk has been testing and I fear that tomorrow's will be no different. Between here and Newmarket, there are many challenges." I sense that Alard is annoyed at the last part of the sentence, as he tries but fails to supress a scowl. Philip continues, "Never mind tomorrow. Morris, is that food ready yet?"

I stand to the side and wait for everyone to choose their beds. As usual, everyone sticks to their walking pairs and the only bed left is located between Owain and Davy. This pleases me and I begin unpacking. I place my leather cross beneath my rolled-up cloak, all the time wondering what Philip meant by 'challenges'.

Joining the others who have already started eating, I am handed a bowl of steaming pottage. The meatballs float between chunks of purple and white carrots. I have never eaten the latter as I thought that they were only meant for cattle, but surprisingly they taste just the same. If anything, they are slightly less chewy. I am offered another bowl, which I gratefully accept. Again, I keep my bread for the journey and I fill up on what is being offered.

When I am finished, I say goodnight and retire immediately, before drifting off into a dreamless sleep.

***

I wake up to the aroma of pancakes being cooked on the hearth. Sweetness fills the air. Sitting up, I can see Morris carefully ladling the thick mixture into the hot fat. It sizzles and spits, indicating that they need to be turned. Next to the fire is a bowl of what looks like apples. I do hope so, as this is my favourite combination. Sitting up, I also notice that all of the men are missing. How strange, but I decide not to go off in search of them. Instead, I join Morris by the fire.

"They look lovely. Can I help?"

"Thank you, Miss. I could do with some help. You see those apples over there? Well, they need to be peeled, cored and added to the pot. I must have them ready for when Philip returns. Otherwise, I'll get it in the ear."

Innocently, I ask where the men have gone. "They've gone scouting." I decide to ask no more and concentrate on preparing the apples, all the while fearing what lies ahead.

When the men return, we break our fast on pancakes and stewed apples before preparing to set off. I sense tension in the air between Alard and Philip and I can't help but wonder what they found on their scouting mission. Moving a touch nearer, I listen intently to their conversation until Davy approaches.

"It was good of you to help Morris with the cooking this morning. He's terribly slow and Philip gets tetchy if his meals are late."

"How long have you known Philip and Morris?"

"All my life. They are kinsmen of my mother."

Our conversation is cut short by Alard, who is trying to chivvy everyone up. "I would like to leave shortly. We are set for the House of the Crutched Friars at Barham. The prior there is a miserable old soul and if we're late, he'll moan, but, even worse, if another group of pilgrims arrive before us, they'll get the best beds."

Such words were almost guaranteed to spur everyone into action. Outside, we gather and wait for the off. Leaving through the outer bailey, I return to my thoughts. However hard I try, I find it impossible to shake off my concerns. Since we now travel at the back of the group, I decide to ask Owain outright.

Quietly, I lean over and enquire, "Owain, are we in danger?"

A shocked Owain stops and looks at me, "What gives you that idea, Bethany?"

"Well, it was something that Morris said while I was helping him with the cooking. He told me that you had all gone on a scouting mission."

"That man. He's an idiot. An out-and-out village idiot. Philip and Alard both told him not to say a word. When will he ever listen?"

"Sorry, Owain, please don't be annoyed with me."

"I'm not annoyed with you. How could I be? It's Morris and his big mouth. You haven't mentioned this to anyone else, have you?"

"No, just you."

A grateful Owain sighs. "Alard would explode if he knew and poor Davy would take the brunt of his temper once more."

"Well, are we in danger?"

To my surprise, Owain laughs. "Maybe, but Morris has it all wrong. Yes, we were on a scouting mission, but not for armed enemies, we were scouting for information. Yesterday, news reached us that the queen had given birth to a son some months ago and it seemed strange that we had only just heard. Edward of Westminster is his name." Then, in a whisper, "I'm surprised he's not called Edward of Somerset."

Trying but failing to look shocked, I nod in agreement.

Owain continues, "The latest news from the court is that the Duke of Somerset was actually found in the queen's private bedchamber recently."

I am astounded by the queen's lack of judgement. How could she? I silently consider whether the rumours of her unfaithfulness are true. Realising that we have fallen behind, Owain takes my arm and we stride out until we catch the others. In just a short while, we approach a very busy crossroads. At the front, Alard waves his left hand in the air and indicates that we must continue in a straight line.

"Owain, where do these roads lead?"

"Well, the left one goes to Cambridge and the right one goes to Sudbury."

I consider the place names. "Owain, I have heard of Cambridge. People say that it's a fine place to visit. Am I right in thinking that King Henry is building a chapel there?"

"Yes, Bethany, I have heard of the building work, too, although I rarely visit Cambridge these days, so I cannot say for certain."

As we approach Barham Priory, I can understand why Alard wanted to arrive sooner rather than later. The last part of the road descends into a heavily wooded area, so much so that the sun is now shielded from our view. I shiver as the air is cold and damp.

"Owain, have we got far to go?"

"No, not very, but don't get your hopes up. We have to pass Linton Priory first."

"Isn't it strange to have two priories so close together?"

"No, not really. All of the land in this area is owned by one religious house or another, and over the years many have been formed and supressed. The local lords are constantly arguing about who owns which piece of land. That's how the lawyers in Cambridge grow richer each day. They prosper on the constant complaints."

As we pass Linton Priory, I am surprised by how small it appears. It's hardly like a priory at all, for it comprises of little more than a boundary wall with a small cell in the middle. Leaving Linton behind us, we are once more plunged into the gloom of the wood.

Even from the back of the party, I can hear Cecily complaining, "I don't like this. Alard, why did you bring us here? I'm frightened."

I strain my ears to hear his reply, but I'm unable to do so.

"Answer me, Alard. Why did you bring us here?"

This time, though, I have no problem in hearing him. "I ask you to mind your manners, Cecily. I am in charge of this pilgrimage and therefore everyone's safety is in my hands. It's up to me where we go and – let me remind you – if you don't like it, you're very welcome to leave and make your own way back to London, but be assured you will travel on your own."

A blanket of silence descends until we emerge from the woods into a clearing where hundreds of piglets greet us with their squealing. No doubt they are hopeful for food. Barham Priory now stands before us and, to my surprise, the central door opens immediately.

A very fat prior emerges and shouts, "So, you've decided to arrive after all then, Alard. We've been waiting for hours. I sent strict instructions that you were to arrive early this time."

Biting his lip, Alard responds, respectfully and calmly, "Prior Heartsease, please accept our apologies, but we came as quickly as possible. Four of our group are of a great age and their legs do not move as fast as the younger ones."

Surveying the group, Prior Heartsease shrugs his shoulders and turns around before departing.

Alard momentarily holds his head in his hands, before speaking, "I said that he was a miserable soul, didn't I? Let's just hope that we're the first group of pilgrims to arrive or we'll have to suffer the lumpy beds."

To everyone's relief, we are the only pilgrims present. A slightly happier Alard suggests that we all choose our beds as quickly as possible before going through to the hall. After choosing my bed, I decide to lay my cloak over it. This will ensure that it's cosy and warm when I retire. While doing so, I am surprised to notice a small roll of parchment fall from Cecily's cloak. She retrieves it quickly and hides it inside a concealed pocket. I scan the room to see if anyone else has noticed. I don't think so. Cecily's face is now as white as a sheet. She has sweat on her cheeks and her hair is escaping from her coif. Mindful of her earlier accusations, I carry on as normal and return to Owain's side, but I have a plan.

Inside the hall, two frightened brothers dole out pottage under the prior's steely gaze. It doesn't smell very inviting, but I take it none the less.

"Thank you, Brothers."

Disturbed by their silence, I ask Owain, "This is not a silent order, is it?"

"No, what makes you think that?"

"Oh, well, when I thanked the brothers, they just ignored me. They never even looked up."

"They will not speak in the prior's presence. As you have seen, he has a sharp tongue and they fear retribution. He is a spiteful man and his displeasure can take many forms. They may be chastised, frozen out or even beaten. They have no one to protect them."

"But that's terrible. Do you mean that they are only allowed to speak when he approves?"

"Unfortunately, so."

"Can't something be done to help them?"

"I doubt it, even Alard has given up lodging complaints."

After eating my pottage, I decide to retire. I do not wish to look at the prior's face for a moment longer than I have to. Leaving the hall, I return to an empty bedchamber. No doubt it will fill up soon, but before it does, I decide to take a quick peak inside Cecily's cloak. On my knees, I crawl across the floor. I fear being caught, but I fear treachery even more. In the moonlight, I can just about see it. It's rolled up neatly and placed at the top of Cecily's bed. I try not to disturb the fabric too much, as she may have folded it in a specific way. I carefully slide my hand inside the folds of material. I can feel the lining, soft and heavy, but no pocket. I know that it must be here somewhere, so I stretch out my fingers and keep searching. All the while my breathing becomes more laboured. I am frightened.

At last, my fingers feel the concealed pocket. Delving deeper, I locate the parchment. I can feel a wax seal. Oh no, this is not a good sign. In a moment of madness, I am compelled to take the letter. Crawling back to my bed, I am consumed by fear. What have I done? Cecily will go mad when she realises that the parchment has gone. She will scream and demand that everyone is searched. What if Prior Heartsease is her accomplice? I begin to shake uncontrollably. The door latch rises and falls. I can hear soft footsteps approach. I recognise them as belonging to Davy. I pretend to be asleep, while watching his movements. It seems that I was not the only one to have witnessed the parchment falling from her cloak, after all. Davy is now searching her cloak. I can bear it no longer.

"Davy, come quick – over here." On hearing my words, I'm unsure who jumped the most. "Davy, please come here."

"Bethany, I thought that you were asleep."

"No, I also saw Cecily drop the parchment. I have it here." In a flash, Davy is by my side. "You do?"

"Yes, here it is. Take it. I know that I shouldn't have, but I took it."

In the moonlight, I can see relief flood over Davy's face, before he bends downs and very tenderly kisses me on the cheek.

"Thank you, sweet Bethany. Now, go to sleep and – for God's sake – say nothing. I will deal with this. Cecily will know nothing about the missing parchment tonight as Ned has dropped a strong sleeping draft into her ale, but she will remember and, by Christ, she will be angry when she finds out. Let's just hope that she doesn't find out until well after our departure."

With this, Davy is gone and I'm alone once more. Too frightened to sleep, I wait for Owain to return. Only in his presence do I feel safe.

***

A crowing cock wakes us all just before dawn. Outside the rain has stopped, but a feeling of gloom still hangs in the air. Today, we will not break our fast at Barham. This is the first time that we have ventured out without eating first and my stomach aches with hunger, but last night's pottage was the worst that I have ever eaten. I listen as the others mirror my sentiments. Ursula, not known to complain, states that she cannot wait to leave, as does Bernadette, who is scratching furiously. "My bed was absolutely crawling with bugs last night."

Fortunately, Alard enters and directs us to gather our belongings and to make our way to the porch immediately. Standing together, Alard bids farewell to the prior and thanks him for his hospitality.

Even now, the prior displays no kindness. "We must pray. Drop to your knees, all of you. Come on, I command that you all kneel."

Fearful of annoying the prior, we all do as we are told. I, for one, find it impossible to concentrate. How dare he speak to us in such a manner. Ethel, Ursula and Agnes are old, and kneeling will hurt them. I can see pain in their eyes already. I long to curse him, but I stop short of doing so. I will not descend to his level, but equally I will not pray in such a frame of mind. Looking about, I notice the small ring on his index finger. It's a seal and, if I'm not mistaken, it's the same as the one on Cecily's parchment. Long and oval, it depicts St Margaret standing on a dragon. In her right hand, she holds a long cross and in her left hand, she holds a book. How I wish Prior Heartsease could be trodden on and defeated like the dragon. After the short prayer, we are instructed to leave. Happily, we do so, and the feeling of gloom begins to lift.

Once we are out of the prior's earshot, Alard apologies profusely for our stay. "I am so sorry to have put you all through that, but I had little choice. This area is unpredictable at the best of times, but please do not worry – for in a short while, we will break our fast properly. Until then, we have bread and cheese to see us through."

Relieved to have something tasty to eat, we sit by the side of the road to enjoy it. I cannot help but notice that Cecily appears rather floppy. Her head is lolling from one side to the other, and her words are slurred.

Agnes, finding this amusing, laughs. "That one must have drunk far too much ale last night. Probably to wash away the taste of that awful pottage."

The laughter continues as stories of last night's awful stay are told.

Once we are rested, Alard gets to his feet. "Come on then. Newmarket beckons and, with it, hot sausage pasties." With these words, Alard once more leads our party.

Almost immediately, a speeding horse can be heard and we all freeze in terror. I'm unsure of its exact location, but I sense that it's somewhere behind me. The noise stops abruptly and I hear the rider dismount with a hollow thud. Alard can be heard to shout, "Friend or foe?"

Turning around, I am relieved to see that the herald is clad from head to toe in pale-blue and white. "Forgive me for frightening you. My name is Edmund and I come with a warning from our lord. There has been trouble in Newmarket. Arson, we fear, and to make matters worse, the queen's men have been seen in town. Please guard yourselves, stay close, do not separate, keep your allegiances secret and be especially careful when passing through the heath. Recently, it has become a dangerous place for felons and evildoers roam freely. Large parts of the town have become unsafe and we have received numerous reports of robberies and abuse. The king's subjects live in fear of the queen's men. Hence, our lord now fears for his tenants and supporters. Ambushes have become commonplace and tensions have risen. Allegiances are changing quickly and our lord wishes to protect those who are loyal to him. Beyond Newmarket, you will be safe, but, in the meantime, take care." With those words, the herald remounts and disappears off into the distance, leaving us in disarray.

Alard, quick to act, instructs Ned to lead. "I will protect our flank alongside Owain and Davy. We must make haste. There is no time to waste."

Entering Newmarket feels like descending into a valley of fear. The road dips down sharply and within minutes, a wave of noise hits us. There are tenements and inns on both sides of the high street. We are to stay at The Griffin, an inn aligned to the Dukes of Clarence and our lord's family. The innkeeper, Arthur Greysson, and his wife, Margery, are to be our hosts. Although I doubt that we will see much of them, as I hear that they are also the keepers of The Sword, The Bull and The Saracen's Head.

Owain, who has linked his arm with mine, explains that we are nearly there. "We just have to cross the tollbooth and then our safety is guaranteed."

I survey the scene in front of us and wonder how so many traders can share such a small space. There are stalls akin to workshops everywhere. Certainly far too many for me to count. In a split second, madness descends. Two men have appeared from nowhere and are dragging me away from Owain. I can smell their foul breath and see their brown decaying teeth. One has a small dagger in his hand and he is thrusting it straight at my stomach. His accomplice tries to snatch my leather purse. My mind begins to race. Sweat is pouring from my body. I can see the knife blade glinting in the sunlight. I retch and can feel the contents of my stomach gurgle upwards. People continue to swarm around. Surely they must be able to see what's happening? It seems that people are averting their eyes. I begin to sob uncontrollably. Then, as quickly as they appeared, they are gone. Owain, having regained his balance, is once again by my side, holding me close. My head is spinning and my mouth is dry. Blackness descends.

Mother Mary, please help me. My body aches and my head is throbbing. Where am I? I can smell warm beeswax and sense a gentle heat wafting in the air, but I just cannot think straight. Gingerly, I open my eyes and look around. Everything is out of focus. I close my eyes again and, in that moment, I remember what happened. I vividly recall the two men and I begin to sob uncontrollably.

"Bethany, please do not cry. You are safe."

Owain holds my hand and an unknown priest smiles down at me. The priest repeats Owain's words with the emphasis on 'You are safe'.

"Owain has told me of your terrible experience and it pains me," the priest says. "Alas, Newmarket is not safe nowadays. By the very nature of the town, people come and go, but it's made worse at the moment by the presence of a great many strangers. They have made their way here in readiness for the fair on the heath. Myself and many others have petitioned that mass events should be outlawed. Unfortunately, the powers that be do not want to hear us. They quote history in their defence. They say that King Edward II granted permission for markets, fairs and tournaments to be held on the heath. In turn, we argue that there are so many fairs nowadays and surely it would be better to keep to just the three main ones. We are sure that these would suffice. The town has a problem with illegal supplies as it is. Ale is the main problem. There is just not enough to go around. Recently, by-laws have been passed stating that residents should be given preference over travellers, but it's obviously more profitable to sell to travellers as the price can be raised and they are none the wiser. Unfortunately, it's not only the amount of ale on offer that's the problem. The local alewife's employ some very underhand ways. The supply short measures aplenty, especially when the men have been at their cups too long and are hazy of mind. Sorry, I should not go on like this, you must rest. The trouble is that I care so much for all the souls and I am distressed at the un-Godly behaviour taking place on a regular basis. Today, we have cuts and bruises, but I hate to think of what tomorrow may bring."

The father crosses himself. Owain and I immediately do the same. Sitting up, I smile and tell Owain that I am well enough to leave. The shock has passed. Turning to the father, I thank him for looking after me.

"Praise the Lord," he replies. "I had feared the worst when you arrived. You were so pale and lifeless when Owain carried you in. Let's pray in the Old Chapel before you leave."

Walking down the centre aisle, we enter the Old Chapel through a very small doorway.

"Did you know that pilgrims flock here from all over the country to pay their respects in this chapel? They honour the memories of St Simon Theobald and St Thomas Becket. St Simon's skull rests not far away in St Gregory's Church at Sudbury. He's known to perform miracles and protect the innocent, and that's just what we need here."

Outside, we make our way along the high street. I have never felt so nervous. I'm aware that I'm acting like a madwoman, turning this way and that, but I just can't help myself. Owain calls out, "Bethany, wait!" but it's too late. I curse and then immediately feel remorseful, for it's my own fault. If only I had stopped when Owain called out to me. Now I have hit my head on the low-hanging sign of The Swan Inn and I have no one to blame but myself, as we had been warned about the sign when we entered Newmarket. Apparently, the innkeeper, John Kyrkeby, is forever being fined for displaying his sign too low and a great many others have suffered the same fate. Why, oh why, did we choose to rest in this terrible town? I would prefer to sleep in a dry ditch. I can see bystanders laughing at my fate. I can hear them, too. They are saying, "Poor soul; she'll be black and blue on the morrow."

Safe inside The Griffin Inn, I sit by the fire. Ursula and Agnes are by my side. At last, I can relax. Davy hands me a cup of ale, which I gratefully accept, while Bernadette holds a cold compress to my head.

"Thank you, the throbbing has nearly stopped."

A smiling Davy announces, "Well, let's hope it stays that way."

A joyful Ned shrugs his shoulders. "I'll keep the noise down if that's what you mean, Davy? For I have no plans on being raucous tonight. Instead, I am going to treat everyone to a sweet lament – a love song that I learnt in France. It tells the story of Tristan and Iseult."

To everyone's amazement, Ned has the most beautifully pitched singing voice. Sitting transfixed, we let the cares of the day wash away.

As morning breaks, we are treated to a beautiful pink sky. Everything bodes well for a pleasant day. Today, we are set for Ely. It's a slight detour, but one that Owain says is well worth the while. It seems that none of us will be sad to leave Newmarket behind. For unbeknown to me, Ethel witnessed a robbery and Cecily was subjected to lewd behaviour. I will not go into detail – suffice to say that men should keep their private parts to themselves. Alard had his soft brown leather belt stolen and is really quite distraught. Walking ahead of us, his shoulders are hunched and we can all hear him huffing and puffing loudly.

Over the Horizon to Ely

As we near the Fens, the fields begin to flatten out. Thick black soil now replaces the white chalky fields of Newmarket. To our surprise, the fields are a hive of activity. Men and boys are cutting large lumps of peat, while the women and girls are stacking it into piles. Those pour souls – what a terrible job! They are completely covered in muck and water. Speaking of water, I fear that we will also be wet through very soon, as the water in these parts behaves very oddly. One minute it's lapping against the left-hand side of the track, before it disappears, only to re-emerge on the right-hand side.

"Owain, have you noticed how the water seems to come and go?"

"Yes, it's very strange, isn't it? I've never met anyone who understands why, not even the locals. I hear that they also get caught out sometimes. I fear for anyone who passes this way unaccompanied."

As we continue, I become increasingly concerned as the water is now coming at us from both sides. The track is narrowing and I can feel my feet slip and slide beneath me.

Alard calls out, "Please take care. From here, we must walk in single file for a short while, but there's nothing to be alarmed about. Just keep to the track and you'll be safe."

The great swathes of water make my head sway, so I keep my eyes downcast, fixed firmly on the track. I must take care not to fall over. Shortly, I notice that the track begins to widen. Gravel and stones now glisten as the water washes over them. At last, I feel safe enough to look up and, to my relief, everyone is safe. But my relief is short-lived, as ahead of us stands a cloaked man and he is occupying the only piece of dry land. How on earth will we pass him? My mind is racing.

Alard raises his hand and bids that we stop. We watch and wait in anticipation as Alard walks towards the figure. To everyone's relief, it appears that they know each other. After a short exchange of words, they shake hands and embrace warmly. The cloaked figure then pushes back his hood to reveal a man of means. Everything about him appears expensive. Not only is his hooded cloak lined with fur, but it's fastened with a beautifully enamelled broach.

"Hello, one and all," he says, before smiling handsomely, bowing low and opening his arms wide in a very grand gesture. "Please let me introduce myself. My name is Oxherd Thresshere. Our liege lord, with care for your safety and comfort, has employed me as your guide and host. I will lead you from this place to the Shrine of Our Lady at Walsingham. Have not a care or a worry, as my family have lived within sight of this great isle for many generations – if anyone can cross safely, it's me. I take great pride in my abilities."

Oxherd, moving to the side, reveals the beginnings of a raised causeway. Constructed of wooden posts and planks, it rises above the natural track. "Please be careful, the wood can be very slippery at this time of the year," he says.

When it comes to my turn to step onto the causeway, I am surprised by just how sturdy it is and how wide. Those in front of me now walk side by side once more. I am mesmerised by the experience. I recall the miracle of Jesus walking on the water and his message: 'Take courage!'. Steeled with these words, I am determined to enjoy the experience. Much later, I am woken from my thoughts by gasps of pleasure. I look up to see what's causing all the excitement and I'm astonished. The view ahead of me is breathtaking. The causeway, after much twisting and turning, has bought us to our destination.

"I said the detour was well worth the while, didn't I?"

"Oh, Owain. Yes, you did, but you never mentioned just how amazing it would be."

"Well, I didn't want to ruin the surprise. I can still remember the first time I saw the Cathedral Church of the Holy and Undivided Trinity at Ely. It's seared into my memory forever and I wanted you to have that experience, too."

Nodding my head, I am lost for words. Perched high upon a hill and surrounded by water, the cathedral takes on the visage of a fortress. It's truly magnificent. Against the turquoise sky, it shines like a mirror, the sun reflecting off its myriad of windows. Even from this distance, I can clearly see the roofs of different levels, the pillars of uneven sizes and the crenelated turrets. All are sitting beneath the two mighty towers.

Oxherd addresses us proudly, "Your smiles tell me of your astonishment. If you will allow me, I would like to tell you a little about this most holy site." Everyone draws close to listen. "The cathedral church that stands before you was once a monastery. It was founded in the year 672 by St Etheldreda and it has grown ever since." Oxherd's pride is obvious. "Can you see the main tower? The one with eight sides. Well, it's known as the 'Lantern Tower', a beacon calling all Christians to worship. It was built under the direction of Alan of Walsingham during the reign of Kind Edward III and I'm proud to say that Alan was a kinsman of my wife." I doubt that Oxherd could puff his chest out further, even if he wanted to. "It replaced the old tower, which collapsed during the building of the Lady Chapel."

We all cross ourselves, as the collapse must have been a terrifying thing to witness. I cannot begin to imagine all the stones and tiles thundering down. I pray that no one was hurt.

Continuing along the causeway, I am enthralled by the houses that shelter beneath the shadow of the cathedral. They cling perilously to the hillside, their gardens and orchards falling away towards the mighty river. At the lowest point, we leave the causeway and cross the mighty River Ouse. The bridge is exceptionally long and it feels strange to walk on solid stone. Leaving the bridge, we all begin to pant as the upwards climb towards the town is unexpectedly hard.

Oxherd announces, "Do not fear, for we are nearly there. The town is not too far now."

I sincerely hope that Oxherd's words are true, as my knees are rather sore. True to his word, the town is not very far. On our way, we pass a group of potters and their smoking kilns, before crossing a very large green to the cathedral.

Oxherd makes another announcement with another grand gesture, "Ah... we have arrived and before us stands the Galilee Gate."

Close up, the cathedral is even more awe-inspiring. We marvel at its size and design. The central tower is flanked on both sides by round towers, each side reflecting the other perfectly. There are arches, niches and statues in abundance. Above the Galilee Gate, there appears to be a chapel or a room. Its wall is dominated by three long narrow windows, all of which are set within stone mullions, but, alas, from such a distance, I cannot see the finer details. Directly in front of us, there are two heavy wooden doors. They are set within a pointed stone arch that is decorated with a quadrant window. The stone is dense and heavy-looking. Never could I have imagined a porch of such proportions, for it must be as large a chapel. It has solid stone uprights, a vaulted ceiling and decorated ribs.

Oxherd invites us to sit. "Feel free to rest for a while. There is no rush."

Gratefully, we take our places on a low stone wall overlooking the green. Agnes is the first to speak. "What a day. My legs are killing me. They'll be no dancing tonight." Hearing this, Ned leaps to his feet and begins to jiggle about.

Undeterred, Oxherd grapples the attention back to himself. "Did you know that there are two main pilgrim routes into the cathedral? One to the west and the main body of the cathedral, and the other to the north and the Shrine of St Etheldreda." After much discussion, we decide to go our separate ways. "Whichever route you follow, you will be safe. All I ask is that you do not leave the boundaries of the high street or the marketplace. Whatever you do, do not go back to the river and do not drink with strangers. I cannot stress this enough. Now, go and enjoy. Tonight, you will be my guests and a joyous time awaits you. We will meet here when the monastic bell rings for compline. Until then, keep safe, my friends."

With that, Oxherd and Alard depart towards the sign of The Minster Tavern, closely followed by Ned. I watch as Davy, at a discreet distance, follows Anne and Cecily. I wonder where they are going. Owain, on the other hand, remains close by and holds Ethel's arm as she walks unsteadily. There is so much to see and do, and I'm glad to say that after Newmarket, Ely feels safe and embracing. The cathedral stands like a loving father looking down upon us. Together, we are finding it hard to decide where we should go first. Looking around, it is clear to see that most pilgrims are heading towards the west of the cathedral and the Lady Chapel. Although we are all desperate to kneel before the image of the Blessed Virgin – to thank her for the protection that she has afforded us – we decide to go the other way and visit the marketplace first. Hopefully, this will allow the cathedral to empty out before our visit.

Crossing the green, we manage to avoid the majority of the pilgrims by entering the high street through a small gate known as Steeple Gate. Turning right, we walk past a variety of properties. On the left-hand side of the road, there are houses and workshops, while on the right-hand side, there are various monastic buildings – all of which back onto the cathedral.

Entering the marketplace, we are greeted with the aroma of hot mutton pies. My stomach lets out a huge groan of emptiness. A laughing Ursula suggests that we treat ourselves. To this, we are all in agreement. Having bought our pies, we sit by the Almonry Gate to eat them. Such is my hunger that I bite into it in a frenzy. It's hot and spicy with bite-size pieces of mutton. In my haste, I eat it far too quickly. I contemplate buying another one, but I decide that would be greedy.

When we are finished, we cross the road once more and re-enter the market. One stall in particular calls to me because it's selling silk necklaces of every colour under the sun. They are laid out lengthways on the cart alongside lucky charms. As I approach, I notice that the stallholder is a fat woman of about forty years. Her hands are none too clean and there is dirt beneath her nails. I withdraw instantly, but this does not seem to stop her. Coming from the back of her cart, she begins to talk to me. Her teeth are stained and her breath is foul. She is extremely pushy and overkeen to sell her goods.

"These fine silk necklaces are sold in remembrance of St Etheldreda. I make them myself." The very thought of wearing something that she has touched makes me feel sick. "Did you know that, in these parts, St Etheldreda is also known as St Audrey? No, I didn't think you would. She died from a tumour in her neck. Ha… that was her punishment for being vain in her youth."

With these words, the stallholder begins to cackle with malice. I move away quickly, upset to hear such unkind words. I will not give her any of my money and, besides, some of the necklaces are so tawdry that I will wait and buy one at St Etheldreda's tomb. No doubt it will cost me a little more, but at least the money will go to the upkeep of the shrine.

Leaving the market behind us, we proceed to the north door of the cathedral. As there is no queue, we enter quickly and make our way directly to the Lady Chapel. The roof of the cathedral is a marvel to behold. Strong flat pillars support wooden beams that criss-cross each other. I wonder how the carpenters managed to design it.

As we step inside the Lady Chapel, I stop for a moment to catch my breath – for the Lady Chapel is larger than any parish church that I have ever seen and its floor is covered entirely with bright-green glazed tiles that sparkle. Light pours in from every angle through the large stained-glass windows. There are individual stone seats along the entire length of every wall and each seat is adorned with a red velvet cushion. Some depict scenes from nature, while others have scenes from the Bible. High above the seats, there are niches of different sizes. Each has a statue set within.

Turning to my right, I can see the altar for the first time. Set high upon stone steps at the east end, with candles burning brightly around the base, I can see flowers and offerings. Looking up, my eyes are drawn to a carved stone frieze that encircles the entire chapel. It recounts the story of the Blessed Virgin's life, from the very beginning to its sad end. I can see her parents and her upbringing in the temple. The Immaculate Conception and way beyond to the life of Jesus and his crucifixion. The images before me are deeply moving and it's on these thoughts that I concentrate when kneeling before the Blessed Virgin's image. Tears fill my eyes and I have a lump in my throat.

When I attempt to stand, my knees creek and it's become painful to walk. Outside, the light begins to fade, but, if I hurry, there may just be enough time to visit the Shrine of St Etheldreda. Scuttling across the nave, I notice Owain and the others directly ahead of me. They have left the shrine and are now sitting on cushions. As I pass, Ethel blows me a kiss and Owain smiles.

On reaching the shrine, I realise that, apart from the two monks who guard it, I am completely alone. I could not have wished for more. The tomb is large and situated just beyond the high altar. Alas, my mood is sombre now and I notice very little of my surroundings apart from the golden reliquary box, which is set deep within the shrine. I sink to my knees and curl my body into one of the apertures. I long to get as close as possible to the relics of St Etheldreda. This accomplished, I slide my coif away from my forehead and push my head directly against the stone. The stone is cold and soothing. I close my eyes and concentrate hard. I long for St Etheldreda's spiritual power to enter my body.

I beg, almost silently, "Please, please, in your mercy, please cure the maladies of my eyes and let me see clearly again."

Time being of no consequence, I am unsure exactly how long I have been in this position until a kind-looking monk coughs gently to wake me. I realise that the shadows are lengthening and the time has come to leave. Had it been busy, I would not have had such luxury. I am grateful for the gift of time. Pulling my coif forward, I stand and prepare to join the others in the nave. Before leaving, we all stop to buy blue and white silk necklaces in remembrance of the Blessed Virgin Mary. Outside, we stand and listen as the cathedral's bells announce the imminent service of compline. Monks scuttle past at a severe trot. Another day is nearing its end, although I suspect that we have a splendid night ahead of us. Retracing our footsteps, we are reunited with the others just outside the Galilee Gate.

Oxherd, satisfied that we are all present, proudly announces that we are ready to leave the town behind us. "We are set for the Waterside and an evening of true hospitality. Adieu, Ely." At this, he throws his head back and laughs a deep, hearty laugh.

Retracing our footsteps, we walk back along the high street before descending a steep hill to the Waterside. The evening sun has begun to set and a deep-orange glow now bathes the fields below us. I can just about see the causeway snaking away into the distance. Strangely, it feels like we have been here for an eternity and that time has stood still. Below us, the streets and wharfs appear to randomly cross over one another and they cast their reflections onto the river.

Once at the bottom of the hill, Oxherd cries out, "Please take care and watch your footings. The ground around here can be very slippery. Ladies, if you do not mind, I would like to suggest that each of you is accompanied to avoid any accidents."

Everyone nods in agreement, although I am deeply embarrassed when Oxherd asks if I would allow him to guide me. Colouring deeply, I reluctantly pass to the front of the party to join him. As he takes my arm, I realise just how old he is. His face, which I presumed to be smooth, is covered in fine lines and wrinkles.

Walking once more, Oxherd leads us across Broad Street into an area called Le Storyerd. "Well, what can I say about this fine area, apart from the fact that it generates a great deal of wealth and that it's a highly prized asset? Plots rarely become available and when they do, there's always a rush to purchase them. Few are owned by lay people, but the ones that are can treble their owners' fortunes overnight."

Continuing, we pass through a confusing maze of lanes before we reach the water's edge and the boats that are moored there. The boats all sit within three channels, which are slightly set apart from the river. "I can see that you are interested in the vessels, Mistress Bethany. They are the finest that money can buy and not one of them is over three years old. Tomorrow, before we set sail from here, everyone will meet my barge master, Mortimer. Ah… I see the recognition in your eyes. Yes, Mortimer is indeed related to our lord and yourself. His knowledge is superb and his skills are unequalled. With him, we will cross the Fens in comfort."

I notice that Oxherd's eyes appear tired. I wonder just how many years he has seen. I wonder, too, if he has served abroad with our lord – in France or in Ireland, maybe. There is so much that I long to ask, but any questions will have to wait for now as we have arrived. All of us gasp with delight.

"Welcome to my home," Oxherd announces proudly, with his chest puffed out once more. "It was built by my father when he returned from Agincourt. He served under both Humphrey, Duke of Gloucester, and Edward, Duke of York. His bravery bought him great wealth, but with it came tales of evil. Some of his stories still haunt me, but let's not dwell on the past. An evening of feasting awaits."

Oxherd's home has the appearance of a small castle, with a crenelated central tower and a water-filled ditch. It stands alone upon an island and is entered via a sturdy wooden bridge. As we cross, I realise that the bridge can be drawn up should the need arise. Beyond a long, winding gravel path, there are raised flower beds and neatly clipped hedges.

Oxherd, noting the pleasure upon my face, comments, "I must admit to having a vain pride in my garden. It brings me such pleasure."

Ahead of us, by the threshold, stands a slender young woman. Oxherd bows low and announces her to our party. "Please come and meet my beautiful daughter, Bessie."

After a flurry of greetings, we enter the house. If I thought that the garden was amazing, the inside of the house surpasses everything outside. "Now, make yourselves at home. There's more than enough seats for everyone." Oxherd is met with a stunned silence. "Oh, yes, I agree; our home is beautiful beyond words, but that's because it mirrors the design of Ludlow Castle, our lord's home in the Welsh Marches. Tomorrow, before we leave for Brandon, we will show you around."

I turn my attention to Bessie. She is about my height and has kind brown eyes. Her face is a picture of innocence. Taking both of my hands, she welcomes me as a long-lost friend. "I am so happy to meet you, Bethany. My father has asked me to prepare a special seat for you. Please come with me and mind the hearth. It's such a terrible pain being stuck in the centre of the room and it's so behind the times. I keep begging my father to move it to the side of the hall and build a chimney. That is the latest fashion, or so I'm told, but he says that these things take time and there's no arguing with him."

My seat is topped with a dark-blue cushion, similar to those in the Lady Chapel, and I feel like the May Queen all over again. The others now join me. On my right-hand side is an empty seat for Oxherd to sit and then there's Alard, Owain, Ned and Davy. To my left-hand side, there is another empty seat. This one's for Bessie and then there's Ethel, Agnes, Ursula and Bernadette. Cecily and Anne have chosen to sit alone and have moved their seats closer to the hearth. How rude – although, in a way, I'm glad they are sitting apart from us, as I do not like Cecily and Anne makes me nervous.

Turning my attention to the others, I sit and listen as everyone speaks about the day. I notice that a harpist sits patiently at the other end of the long aisled hall and that she seems to be waiting for her cue to start playing. To her left are two doors to the kitchen, while above is a gallery. It is draped in pale-blue fabric and adorned with fresh flowers. Oxherd and Bessie return and take their seats. This must have been her cue, as she begins to play softly.

The kitchen doors swing open and male servers emerge through them. They are dressed in the same pale-blue fabric as the gallery and they are carrying large pewter platters in their hands. I have never seen so much food. Meats, cheeses and pastries sit alongside honeyed buns and fritters. Wine is offered to each of us in turn, before fine pandemain trenchers are handed out. I just cannot understand this, as pandemain trenchers are made of the highest quality white flour and are usually reserved for the lord, not pilgrims.

Standing once more, Oxherd makes sure that everyone has been taken care of and, within seconds, a youth of no more than fifteen years approaches him. "Father, everyone has wine now, please may I take my seat?"

"Yes, Morland, you have carried out your duties excellently – as have the rest of the household. Please go and ask them to join us. Together, we will feast."

It takes just a few minutes for everyone to join us and once they are seated, Oxherd stands yet again. I wonder if he ever sits still. "Before we eat, let's join together and say grace." We all bow our heads. "Dear Lord, thank you for the food and drink that sits before us. Make us your obedient servants and keep us safe from harm. Amen. Before we start, I would also like to toast our lord, who – by his protection and generosity

– has brought us together." This toast brings hearty smiles and mighty cheers all round, for it seems that Duke Richard has touched each of our lives with good governance, loyalty and kindness. Oxherd ends his speech by bidding us to, "Eat, drink and be merry."

Once everything has been eaten and cleared away, it's far easier to see the hall in all its glory. There are full-length tapestries adorning each wall and a movable altar just beyond the harpist. The altar has the appearance of one from the Holy Land. Upon it stands a figure of the Blessed Virgin and a vase of white roses. In the farthest corner, there is an inordinate amount of armour, accompanied by baskets full of arrows and a barrel full of long bows. A random thought begins to race through my mind: I wonder if this hall has a dual purpose. Could it be used for both fine dining, but also as a place of refuge? Although, I suspect that, in truth, the latter is most probably its main use as each window has an arrow slit, a shutter and a bench beneath it. Under each bench, there is a rolled-up sheepskin and a saddle. I wonder just how close war is.

These thoughts are quickly dispelled though by the chants of 'Wassail' and 'Drink hail' that fill the hall. A steaming bowl of lambswool has just been carried in. How I love hot spiced cider with cream – it smells absolutely delicious and I just can't wait to taste it. As we pass the wassail bowl between us, I notice how very fine it is. It has a large flat brim and is decorated with bands of red, brown and yellow clay. The handles make me smile as they are made from grimacing gargoyles. I must be careful not to drop it.

Nearly falling off my seat with exhaustion, I am shocked when I see that the hall has been prepared for dancing. I lean over to Bessie. "Bessie, please excuse me, but I doubt that I have enough energy to dance. Would it be possible for me to retire early?"

"Of course, Bethany. Anne also wishes to retire. She would like to spend some time in prayer and contemplation. Come, I'll accompany you both."

The hall to the bedchamber is narrow and lit by lanterns, and the stone walls on either side are as thick as those in the cathedral. When Bessie opens the door, the rooms smells fresh and clean. Fresh reeds have been scattered over the floor and I can smell rosemary. There are five small beds, all of which have been dressed with fine linen.

"I will leave you now, but if you need anything, just ring the small handbell and someone will come straightaway."

I kiss Bessie's cheek and thank her once again for such a lovely evening. Choosing the bed closest to the window, I sit down to remove my boots. The mattress is soft and packed tightly with feathers. Removing my outer clothes, I climb into bed and pull the linen sheet right up to my chin. I clutch my satchel to my stomach and relax. A small fire crackles in the hearth and I feel myself begin to drift away. With thoughts of tomorrow's journey floating around my head, I drift off into a deep sleep.

***

"Heave hard. Heave hard and roll. Quickly, I said roll. Now, shove it hard and move those ropes. How many times do I need to tell you? Robin, I said move those ropes now. If they become tangled, you'll feel the back of my hand."

"Yes, sir. Sorry, sir."

Anne and myself both wake with a start, run to the shutters and open them with trepidation. My mind is racing in terror. Hearing those words has frightened me, especially, as they were delivered with a mixture of annoyance and anger. Questions enter my head, thick and fast. Who does the booming voice belong to? What is happening? Who is the quietly spoken boy?

Upon opening the shutters, I feel a flood of relief. There is no sign of impending danger, just a vision of pure chaos. It's at this point that I realise Oxherd's house has its very own quayside and a great many warehouses behind it. Men and boys are scurrying around, loading and unloading goods, while cargo is being taken away for storage. Scanning the area outside our window, I locate the man with the booming voice. He is standing upright, with his hands resting firmly upon his hips. A giant of a man, the likes of which I have never seen before. His wild red hair and bushy red beard appear to merge into one, giving the impression that his whole face consists entirely of hair and eyes. Even his mouth is completely covered.

"Robin, how many times do I need to tell you? Move the ropes now."

It's at this moment that I notice the quietly spoken boy. He appears to be a timid willowy child with red puffed-out cheeks. He, too, has a mop of red bushy hair. His name seems rather appropriate, as he has the look of a robin, especially as he darts from side to side on his spindly legs. No, oh, no. I can't believe what I'm seeing. I was so engrossed with watching Robin tug the flat-bottomed boat that I never saw the man's hand move until it was too late. Raising one of his shovel-like hands, he strikes Robin with immense force.

Robin, caught unawares, falls face down on the boat. His yelps of pain are unbearable.

Anne tugs at my arm. "Come, let's move away from the window and close the shutters. There is nothing we can do. The best course of action is to remain tight-lipped. Let's agree not to tell anyone what we have just witnessed. If and when an opportunity arises, we can act, but until then let's keep this between ourselves."

My heart pains me and I am confused about what to do. I remember my father scolding me and saying, "If you don't obey me now and learn to heed my words, what will you do if our manor is ever attacked? You need to learn to act on my commands or everything that we hold dear may be lost." In hindsight, he was completely right to teach me the importance of doing as I was told. I wonder if Robin and the man with the booming voice are related. Could it be possible that they are father and son?

Returning to my bed, it seems that Agnes and Ethel have not heard the commotion for they are sitting up and talking excitedly. Cecily, on the other hand, is leaving the room in search of breakfast. In the hall, our belongings are neatly stacked along the furthest wall. Alarmingly, so are partially sheathed swords and daggers.

"Good morrow," Oxherd greets us each with a hearty handshake and a beaming smile, as enthusiastic as ever. He then proceeds to address us in what seems to be a foreign language. For although I hear his words, they are muddled. In truth, I am finding it impossible to concentrate on anything this morning, apart from the bacon sizzling on the skillet. Oh, how I love bacon. I could dine upon it every day and never get bored. Laughter fills the air and I wonder what I've missed, but my thoughts soon return to food, for on the table are platters of fried bread and sausages. "Dig in. There's more where that came from."

Taking a plateful, I savour each mouthful. Everything is divine. Butter drips from the fried bread, so I decide to tuck a piece of old linen into the neck of my kirtle. This should protect me. I laugh inwardly as I notice that Alard has butter on his chin, nose and fingers.

Noting our enjoyment, Oxherd launches into a long story, "The pig was mine own, you know. We called it Old Soapy. He would roll around in the wet mud for hours on end. He would always be foaming from some part of his body, hence his name." Oxherd laughed at his remembrances.

I'm not too sure that I really wanted to hear the story of Old Soapy, but I inwardly say thank you to the animal for feeding me.

After a flurry of goodbyes, we walk away in a long line towards the quayside and the waiting boats. Along the river's edge, I notice a great many eel traps. These are made from willow and must be a great age, as they have developed a deep bronze sheen. Each one is beautifully woven and a work of art, with a long neck and oval bowl. I expect that the eels provide Oxherd with a vast income, especially as he has so many traps.

Once more, I hear the booming voice that woke me this morning. The man who it belongs to is standing on the side of the wharf, surrounded by a small group of men and three flat-bottomed boats. Again, he's issuing orders. "The bows and arrows must be kept flat and dry at all times. Do you understand me?"

"Yes, Master, we will take good care to load them as you say."

"Good lad."

Oxherd, who has worked his way through the line, now stands before us. His chest is puffed out once more. "These boats, my dear friends, will take you to Brandon. They will be manned by my wharf man, Jim, and his son, Robin."

Both smile and disclose missing teeth as they do so. Jim's are by far the worst, with Robin following closely behind. Looking around, I notice that Anne appears nervous. I expect that she's worried about lowering her large body into the boat. Luckily, I do not have that problem and I find it easy to climb aboard with the help of Robin. His small hands are cold and calloused. As kindly as he appears, his eyes are lifeless. They shine like the sun, but something seems amiss. I just cannot not put my finger on what's wrong. Only now do I understand a little of Jim's frustration. I suspect that Jim's instructions go in one ear and out of the other, with very little being retained for long. Anne, on this occasion, was right. I had judged this morning's situation incorrectly and now I'm glad that I said nothing.

As we set sail, I notice that Robin has begun to mutter to himself, over and over again. In truth, it's rather alarming.

Ely fades into the distance and I take one last look at the cathedral. Today, it appears grey and menacing. I cannot help but wonder if its mood is reflective of our journey. There is no doubt that war clouds are looming overhead, as is the morning mist that stubbornly refuses to lift.

"Bethany, come close." Agnes leans over and gently whispers in my ear. "I'm frightened. Robin continuously wrenches his hands and says, 'I must light a fire to call for help.' Bethany, I can't help but wonder what's happening."

"Oh, Agnes, neither can I, but perhaps you could tell

us a Bible story – something to take our minds of Robin's mumbling. You tell the stories with such feeling."

Ethel and Owain brighten considerably on hearing this. For myself, I just cannot help but observe the other boats on the horizon, especially as the oarsmen appear to be on the lookout, too. The hours pass and the day has brightened, and Ned is even livelier than usual. Once more, he produces his shawm and is blowing it enthusiastically. Raucous, high-pitched notes fill the once empty air. We clap in time and sing along.

The boats rock in time to the beat of the music until Jim shouts abruptly, "Stop! Eyes right. Towards the spire. I can see flashing metal – armour, I fear."

Weeting Castle

It takes but a split second for our boats to lurch towards the riverbank. The long reeds make excellent cover. Jim signals to Robin and the oarsmen. His hands are making shapes that I do not understand, but it matters not, as they are obviously a code intended for silent messages. Robin quietly creeps from soul to soul, gesturing for us to keep our heads down. He silently instructs us to raise our hoods. It seems an age before we move again and when we do, a shocked silence is kept by all. Slowly, our boat begins to move through the reeds, as we all work together to pull ourselves along. To use the oars would be foolhardy, as any swell in the water could be detected from the shore. A castle comes into view and I can see a beacon of fire flickering close by.

Moments later, Oxherd announces from the furthest boat, "I think we are safe. We have arrived at Weeting and the monks are waiting for us on the wharf."

My heartbeat steadily returns to normal. When it is my turn to leave the boat, a kind-looking monk holds his hand out to steady me.

"Welcome to Weeting Castle. Please come this way. My name is Brother Pandimonia."

"Thank you, Brother, my name is Bethany."

As we hurry from the boat, we pass a small church with a round tower. It's very beautiful and it shines in the sunlight, but there's no time to waste. We must get inside the castle as soon as possible.

Once inside, Brother Pandimonia explains that the castle is not really used to having visitors these days. "The only people who ever visit are close friends of the Duke of Norfolk. It's a welcome change to host a group of pilgrims on their way to Walsingham. Alas, I have not visited the Holy Shrine for many years." With these words, Brother Pandimonia looks wistfully down to his feet. How could I not have noticed that his left foot is deformed? "Well, that's as it may, but fortunately life goes on. If you would excuse me, I have to prepare the kitchen for the forthcoming supplies. Brother Prior has sent word to our neighbouring Priory of Bromehill asking them for food and drink."

Resting now in the great hall, I wait for the others to join me. Even when they do, it's deadly quiet until Oxherd returns. His outward appearance may have returned to normal, but I detect a sense of concern that was missing before. "Let's pray, dear friends. Brother Prior, would you be so kind as to lead?"

"Yes, of course. Please lower your heads and reflect on the Lord. Let's begin by praying as Jesus did by saying the Lord's Prayer." After this is said together, Brother Prior continues, "Children of the Lord, please do not be tempted to let fear enter your hearts. Stay pure and trust in the Lord as you go forth to Walsingham. Soon, we will eat together and then we will rest. The very nature of your arrival has caused you shock and you need time to recover. Sleep is the best way to heal and I urge you to take advantage of this time. Even if you are unable to sleep fully, I ask that you close your eyes and relax. Tomorrow, we will cross the fields to Bromehill Priory to the Augustine House, which has a small community of Gilbertines attached. You will enjoy it there. It's a fine place to visit. Abbot Combe has many fish ponds and Almoner Geoffrey, ever one to save money, has a full store of food. You will not go hungry or thirsty. Then, when you are fully recovered, you will resume your most holy pilgrimage. May God bless you all."

Oxherd responds by thanking Brother Prior, before turning to us, "Now, my dear friends, I feel the need to apologise for the fear that you have suffered. Please let me explain what happened earlier. Jim, ever alert and mindful of the terrain, noticed men on foot. These men were carrying weapons. So, a silent message was conveyed from Jim to myself. I had to think quickly and act decisively. My mind was set and I acted on impulse. In these times of increasing conflict and mindful that we cross manors that are loyal to Lancastrian Lords, I decided that the best course of action was to take cover. I'm sorry that I could not tell you what was happening. We are still unsure of the livery that the men wore. All we know for certain is that they were not loyal to the House of York."

Worried faces cannot be hidden – in particular, Bernadette, who begins to sob gently.

Oxherd, noticing this, continues, but in a very measured way, "In conclusion, I think it would be wise to bypass Brandon completely and head directly to Bromehill Priory. What do you think, Brother?"

"I agreed wholeheartedly. Brandon is a fine trading port where river and road converge, but danger is ever present. Recently, I have received reports, almost on a daily basis, of violence erupting. I also hear that extra patrols have been put in place as men fight and blaspheme regularly. I fear that the Cousins' War creeps ever nearer, but let's not dwell on such things. I hear that supplies have reached us and that food is being prepared as we speak. May I suggest that you make up your beds before we eat?"

After the meal has been eaten and everything cleared away, the mood in the hall becomes ever more relaxed. Brother Prior was wise to ask us to make up our beds when we did. Now, it's just a case of lying down. The doors are firmly secured with large oak timbers and sleep is calling. Beeswax candles flicker gently and the log fire crackles. My fleece is deep and warm. In such an environment, it's easy to drift off into a peaceful slumber.

We wake to a beautiful morning. The sunlight floods into the hall and is making patterns on the floor. Brothers shuffle in and out, laden with meat and ale. I must admit to being very content. After breaking our fast together, Oxherd requests that we prepare to leave as quickly as possible, as if unknown armed men are still in the area, there's not a moment to lose. Just beyond the drawbridge, we are met by four retainers and a messenger from Duke Richard's household.

"Alard, my friend. The duke has sent us to accompany you to Bromehill. We doubt that there will be any trouble, but four strong retainers in tow should be enough to scare anyone off."

A pensive-looking Alard seems relieved. "Thank you,

Edmund. Yes, I agree, it's wise to travel in numbers and we are grateful for your presence."

Turning to Brother Prior, Alard requests that he leads the way. I am left wondering how Duke Richard found out about our troubles so quickly.

Now that there are so many of us, it is inevitable that we are strung out as we walk, although everyone is careful to remain as close as possible. We are led by two retainers and four brothers and followed by a similar number. Happily, Owain is by my side once more. We have been told that we must come together when we reach the stone cross.

On arrival, Brother Prior invites us to form a circle. "Now, come close, my children, I have instructions to impart. From here on, we will leave the pilgrim's path, but please be careful as the bank is peppered with rabbit holes and it's easy to lose your footing and fall. Once we have left the path, we will turn left and follow the field boundary until the field dips down towards the River Wissey and the warrens of Weeting Hill. We are blessed in this area as the rabbits feed us with their bodies, cloth us with their skins and keep us warm with their fur, but they do churn up the fields. When we reach Otheringhyte, we will turn left and begin the short climb to the priory. Here, the fields are full of sheep. Please can I ask that you do not make any loud noises as it may frighten the sheep, who will, in turn, abandon their lambs."

Fortunately, the track becomes more visible after Warren Hill and it's easier to follow. The emptiness of the Fens has been left behind and we now walk beneath a canopy of trees on a carpet of leaves. White butterflies dance from plant to plant and small birds dart from tree to tree. Again, we are invited to come together, but this time with no warning. A tall, muscular man has appeared from nowhere. His long brown woollen cloak trails upon the ground. It is fastened with two large wooden toggles and he wears an oval broach over his heart. It depicts a heron and the words 'Hviosic No Crene'. I consider the significance of the broach. I know that herons are wiser than all other birds and they have few resting places. They fear the rain and in order to miss any storms, they fly high above the clouds. Thus, when a heron takes flight, it is to either eat, drink or as a warning of an impending storm. I fear that this is why Heron Man is here. To defend us against a storm, as if we were his own offspring.

In a rough voice, almost unrecognisable, Heron Man introduces himself as Pip. "I am the Duke of York's man. I am loyal to him and him only. From now on, I will lead your party."

It is obvious that the retainers know Pip, as they acknowledge him respectfully with a collective bow. Oxherd, Brother Prior and the remaining brothers step back as requested.

"I thank you for delivering this party into my protection, but please do not see this as an insult for I have a letter of direct instruction. Here, please inspect it." As Pip opens his cloak, I noticed a seal hanging from his belt. This, too, depicts a heron.

Retreating slightly from our group to examine the letter in depth, Oxherd, the prior and Alard nod when they are finished. Oxherd breaks the silence.

"Pip, we thank you for your presence and for your protection. We are most grateful to deliver ourselves into your leadership."

Pip speaks with a mixture of humbleness and firmness as he begins to lead us forward. "Thank you for accepting me. I am most grateful."

As we walk, it appears that nothing has really changed as Oxherd is as loud as ever and Brother Prior continues to point out places of interest. "Over there, to our right, is the priory's charcoal camp. We have one of the largest camps in the area and it is looked after by just one man, Jim the Burner. Alas, he's a solitary soul, so I doubt that we will see him as we pass." I cannot help but cough, as the smoke is quite dense.

Looking around, I notice a small, crooked man. Our eyes connect for a split second before he darts off into the undergrowth. I think that I must have just seen Jim the Burner, but Pip, who has also noticed the figure, appears agitated and halts the group. "Stop. Wait here. Keep close." In a second, he has drawn his dagger from his belt. "Come out and show yourself immediately." Pip's voice is rough and his command is chilling.

The small, crooked man returns from the undergrowth and stands, quaking before us.

Turning to Brother Prior, Pip asks, "Is this Jim the Burner?"

"Yes, Pip, that's Jim."

"Thank you, Jim, you may go now, but I ask you not to skulk about in future. These are dangerous times."

Pip returns his dagger back into its sheath and we walk on, leaving a nervous Jim behind. Next, we reach a butchery site. The aroma is gut-wrenching. Tables are laden with carcasses and wooden barrels appear to be full of blood. I know that this is a necessary part of life and that the blood will be made into delicious puddings, but I sigh with relief when we reach the priory's fish ponds, as the air is fresh and clear.

"We have arrived." Brother Prior's words are delivered with a sense of relief and I notice for the first time that his brow is covered in sweat. I quickly turn my attention to the priory with its magnificent thatched roof and stained-glass window. We enter via the south door and pass through the cloisters on our way to the hall. We are met by another brother.

"Welcome, children of God. Welcome to our house. You will be safe here. Rest and enjoy. Please do not worry about a thing. Our house is dedicated to the Blessed Virgin and St Thomas the Martyr, and they will maintain you. In truth, it's a blessing that God has bought you here on this very day, as we are preparing to honour St Thomas. We therefore invite you to join us and although we have no relics of the Blessed Martyr here, we have borrowed one from Castle Acre Priory. Many hands will make light work and we would be grateful of your assistance, as we need to clean and decorate the hall, prepare the food and pray solemnly."

A ripple of excitement is palpable. Pip graciously instructs that we are all free to explore the priory and to help, as long as we do not leave the priory. I long to sit in silence and soak up the atmosphere before the preparations begin, so I head off towards the cloisters. In front, by the far wall, I notice a seat. Yes, that's the one for me.

It's slightly sheltered and surrounded by rosemary. What a fine garden this is. It consists of four beds, each of which is surrounded by tiny white pebbles. In the middle stands a statue of Jesus, feeding the five thousand with loaves and fishes. As I cross the white pebbles, they crunch gently beneath my feet. I decide to explore each bed before I sit. The first one is abundant with herbs for cooking and I can see sage, rosemary and thyme. The second has mallow, camomile and madder. I have used the latter for dyeing cloth. The third sends my mind racing as it's full of edible flowers. With this, my stomach begins to rumble as I daydream about sweet custards decorated with marigolds and rich puddings laced with rose petals. The fourth is empty and is being nourished for future planting. I notice that the soil is a completely different colour to that of the Fens. I'd describe it as an amber clay.

After sitting for a while, my curiosity is ignited when I notice a large wooden door partially hidden in the furthest corner. As I approach, I can hear voices in the distance. The temptation to investigate is just too strong to resist. On passing through the doorway, I am confronted by a completely different landscape to the one that I just arrived by. I can see three wooden outbuildings and four fish ponds. This must be where the brothers prepare their food. As I pass, they are all very pleasant and greet me as 'Sister'.

I wander from building to building. The first is quite small and has fish hooks and sheathed knives hanging from the walls. The second has quern stones and a great number of bags of corn ready to be ground into flour. The third is lined with shelves full of pots and bowls, but the most interesting is the brewing shed. As I pass by, I notice a brother within. His black robe is entirely covered with grain and his sleeves are rolled up to just above his elbows. He is unlike any brother that I have ever seen before, as he has a big bushy moustache and a thick mop of dark brown hair. He nods in recognition, but continues to stir the steaming vat in front of him. From deep within the cloisters, I hear a solitary bell ring out. I expect that it's announcing that the evening meal is ready to be served, so I head back to the hall in search of the others.

When I arrive, I am greeted by happy faces all around, apart from Alard and Pip, who are sitting slightly apart from the others and looking nervous. I decide to sit next to Davy, who is cleaning his boots.

"I don't know about you, but I'm famished."

"Oh, yes, it was such a difficult walk today."

We are joined almost immediately by Brother Prior, who is obviously preparing to make an announcement. After clearing his throat, he kindly announces, albeit quietly, that the warming room and washing troughs are open to all. "Our brothers have made alternative arrangements and you are most welcome to refresh yourselves. If you would like to go now, everything is ready."

With that, we are led away by a thin wiry brother whose body language betrays the fact that he's unhappy with the arrangements. Agnes is the first to enter the warming room and, by the look on her face, I expect that she will be the last to leave. Once inside, I realise why. The warming room has thick stone walls, which are painted a deep earthy colour. It's sumptuous beyond belief and more suited to a private residence than a priory. A roaring fire burns in the hearth, and bowls of hot water and herbs have been placed all around. Taking a fine linen towel from the basket, I wash my hands and face before retiring to a seat to wait for the others. Once everyone has washed, we reluctantly leave the warming room behind.

Outside, we are met by the same brother, who escorts us back to the hall. When we enter, we are directed to our seats at the long table, which is groaning with vegetable dishes and fritters. Before eating, I survey the company. I am pleased to be sitting next to Alard. It seems an age since we last spoke.

"Have you had a good day?" I ask.

"Yes, Bethany, I'm pleased to say that I have. I joined Ned and Brother Alassi hunting for rabbits. Neither of us were very good, but Brother Alassi caught at least twenty. We dropped them off at the kitchen on the way back. They have been made into pottage and will be served next."

Our conversation is cut short by Ned, who has risen to his feet and started singing at the top of his voice. I suspect that the ale is far too strong. I do hope that he will keep his songs clean and not embarrass us tonight.

***

My suspicions were correct – the ale was far too strong and now my head is spinning. Oh, how I wish I could go back to sleep, but there's no chance of that as the Gilbertine nuns are passing among us, offering prayers for the new morning. By the look of Ned, he will need more than prayers. He was far too loud last night and collapsed into a drunken heap in the middle of the hall. Owain and Pip had to help him to his bed.

Sitting up, he looks less than pleased as the sisters are seeking volunteers to help prepare the feast. "Good morrow, my name's Sister Lucy and I'm joined by Sisters Jane and Constance. Now, let's arrange ourselves into groups of four. Many hands make light work and we don't want to waste the day, do we?"

After much shuffling, the groups are formed. Only Pip withdraws to the side of the hall.

"The jobs are to stoke the hearth and keep the ash even. To heat the wax in the caldron. To cut the cords for the wicks and to build a stock to hang the candles from. Lastly, we need dippers, to dip the candles."

Anne and I look at each other in surprise, as Robin has come alive. "Please, Sister, I would like to volunteer to heat the wax. I do this at home and I have the knack." Robin smiles from ear to ear.

The hours pass and a feeling of relaxed calm is enhanced by Sister Agatha, who is sitting in the corner, under the wooden canopy of the gallery, gently plucking her lute. The gallery is finer than most with intricate carvings adorned by gold leaf. It's like everything else in this priory – ostentatious and designed to impress. I decide to join the dippers. Sitting quietly next to Robin is a pleasure as his face radiates happiness. Now that the preparations are well under way, I'm so excited! I just can't wait to see the hall and the chapel tomorrow, when the bowers are hung and the windows are decorated with fruit and candles. I have heard that tonight we will pass the evening solemnly in prayers, in preparation for tomorrow's feast. In keeping with this contemplative mood, our food and drink will be plain and simple. Bread and watered ale will be eaten in silence.

As the sun rises, so does the excitement. Even Ned, having regained his cheerful outlook, is helping with the final touches. On completion, the chapel looks beautiful. Candles dance and the greenery sparkles. Brothers now stand side by side along each wall, while the sisters are seated at the front. Most of us sit on the floor, apart from Agnes, who has cheekily occupied a stool in the corner.

Once we are all settled, Brother Prior takes his place at the front. "Brothers, sisters and pilgrims, today we are feasting in the memory of the Blessed Martyr, St Thomas Becket. A man of deep principles, he fought for justice, truth and love. Alas, he was martyred for his beliefs. His body may have been broken, but his spirit joined the Lord. Since then, he has delivered a series of miracles. With this in mind, let us join together and keep our silence. During this time, I invite you to contemplate on your imperfections and those things that you seek to change."

Brother Prior's words resonate with me. For a while, I have been thinking about my old life at home. No matter how much I miss my family and friends, I do not wish to go back. This pilgrimage has opened my eyes. The people that I have met have all been so different. Their differences intrigue me. I have almost, but not quite, decided that I would like to devote my life to being a pilgrim's guide. My eyes may be a little dim, but my heart is bright and devoted to the Lord. I could support others. Maybe people like myself or those who are old and frail. I could accompany them on their journeys, or I could even carry out pilgrimages on behalf of others.

"Children, please finish your contemplation and stand. Our brothers will now sing a *Te Deum*. We will remember those who have departed this life."

The singing begins and I find it impossible to stand still. My body sways in time to the rhythm. After the *Te Deum*, the communion begins. The breaking of the bread and the taking of the wine feels intense today and far more meaningful than ever before. Afterwards, the mood in the chapel is elevated from one of sombreness to one of joy and celebration. The rest of the day will be spent celebrating the holy miracles.

The hall is every bit as beautiful as the chapel. It must have been decorated while we were in the service, as bowers now hang at each end of the hall and three very long tables take pride of place. Each has been dressed with white linen and decorated with greenery and white roses. Even the roof timbers have been bound with greenery and white rosebuds. What a lovely surprise! Among the greenery and the timbers hangs an elaborate lamp, which burns brightly.

Once everyone is seated, Brother Prior begins, "Children of the Lord, please celebrate this day. First, we will feast, then we will sing and, lastly, we will all join hands and dance around the hearth before the brothers and sisters retire. You are most welcome to continue the revelries without us and yes, Ned, you are welcome to play the shawm."

Everyone laughs. The feast is magnificent! My favourite dish is a large gingerbread, which has been cleverly crafted into the shape of a checkerboard. Honey, cinnamon and black pepper have all been carefully combined to imitate the taste of ginger, as the fresh root is unavailable at the moment, especially with Brandon being out of bounds. How strange; I had forgotten the outside world completely until this moment.

Once every crumb has been eaten and the tables cleared away, the dancing begins. Surprisingly, Brother Prior is the first to his feet. "Let's join in a circle and hold hands. Yes, that right. Now we will all move seven steps to the left and clap. Then, we will move seven steps to the right and clap."

I notice that the flames dance with us. It's funny how something so simple can cause so much laughter. Agnes, not knowing her left from her right, is now clasping her arms to her body and pointing both ways. Confusion spreads and, before long, no one is quite sure which way to go. This is the first time I have seen Pip smile. It's also the first time I have noticed that he wears a pendant. My thoughts are dragged back to Agnes, who is now singing a song associated to the harvest. She is also making hand signals to signify the falling rain. Everyone laughs heartily, while Alard and Oxherd join in.

After the singing, we are invited outside to watch as a huge ceremonial bonfire is lit. The fire represents life and rebirth – a beacon of God's presence. I am sure that all our hearts are alight at this very moment and that we shine as brightly as the beacon. As the wood burns to a cinder, we return to the hall where a wassail bowl has been prepared. We pass it among ourselves and honour our friendship.

Afterwards, the brothers and sisters depart, almost unnoticed. My, oh my, what a feast day. I will never forget it for as long as I live. I am now consumed by sleep, but not wanting to spoil the celebrations for the others, I retreat to the furthest corner of the hall and sink into a fleece. It's warm and comfortable, so I remove my boots and settle down for the night. The music washes over me and I drift off.

***

When I wake, I realise that some are nursing sore heads, while others are nursing sore feet, but no one is complaining – far from it. Everyone has a spring in their step, for today we travel to Bodney to the manor of Sir William Oldhall, our lord's chamberlain. Unfortunately, the weather does not match our mood as a thick mist has descended. It shrouds both the trees and the land. With it comes a dampness, which chills me to the bone. The sky is foreboding and marbled with dark-grey clouds. It seems an age before the clouds part and the sun peeps through.

On our way, we pass field after field of cows. Never before have I seen so many all in one place. They must surely belong to a priory or a manor. Sitting on the ground, with their legs wrapped beneath them, the scene is one of contentment, but I fear that is all about to change.

"Look, Bethany, over there." Owain points towards a very small cow, who is obviously in a playful mood. We laugh, as the little grey and brown cow runs, jumps and frolics.

"Owain, I think that we should name him Smudge. What do you think?"

"Yes, that seems an appropriate name."

Owain smiles as Smudge, not content to play on his own, is now running at full speed toward a rather large bull, which he eventually barges into. Oh, how we laugh as the bull majestically rises and walks away, leaving Smudge confused.

Owain says, with a wry smile, "I think that instead of Smudge, he should be called Ned." We both chuckle and nod in agreement.

The last leg of the walk to Bodney is across flat fields, which have been sectioned off with wattle fences. As we pass, I notice that there are pigs of all ages. They squeal for our attention as they roll in the wet ground next to the feeding troughs. On the horizon, I can see a long single-storey church, which stands proudly on the rising ground. To the east runs a small rivulet and to the west is the manor house. As we approach the west gable of the church, I notice that there is a small stone arch under the thatch, which houses a bell. It appears to be concealed. How strange!

At the porch, we are met by a rather rotund man, who is dressed in fine robes. He announces in a ringing tone, "Hello, I am Father Denning. Please let me welcome you to St Mary's church and the manor of Bodney. Brother Prior, how lovely of you to visit us. It has been an age since we last saw each other. I am looking forward to hearing all the news, but, for now, let's walk together. I have been asked to show you the way to the great hall within Sir William's house."

As we walk, I notice that poor Father Denning's back is so bent that it's impossible for him to straighten up. Upon entering, I realise that the hall is by far the grandest I have ever seen. The most striking feature is the great window at the farthest end. Its very size dictates that it's designed for decoration and not for defence. Sir William's crest takes centre stage. It depicts a white rampant lion standing proud against a background of red and blue. Above the lion's head is a sparkling silver helm, decorated with plumes of red and grey feathers, while below there is a motto, '*Parle bien ou parle rien*'. Owain explains that this is French for 'Speak well or speak nothing', which means 'If you don't have anything good to say, then don't speak at all'.

At the bottom of the window, as far left as possible, there is a small coloured pane, which looks completely out of place. It depicts a wolf's head. This image needs no explanation, as I know this to be a sign of someone who gives good service to its master through wit and dexterity. It also depicts strength and valour. I know this because it's a rarely used device of the Mortimer family.

By a strange coincidence, Pip approaches me as I gaze upon the wolf's head. "Bethany, please may I speak to you in private?"

"Yes, of course."

Pip leads me from the hall, out across the gravel and back in the direction of the church. We enter through a small doorway and, as we do, I manage to catch a closer glimpse of his pendant. To my surprise, it's an enamelled wolf's head.

"Bethany, please do not be alarmed by what I am going to tell you. Very shortly, we will be entering the presence of Sir William Oldhall and one other. I cannot stress enough how confidential this meeting is and how it's never to be spoken about. You can tell no one. Nothing must ever be divulged. Lives hang in the balance. Do you vouch to remain silent? I must know before we proceed. Please tell me now?"

"Yes, Pip, I vouch my allegiance with a whole heart and I promise to never mention a word of it to anyone, ever." Then, I remember what I'm carrying and I wonder if it holds any significance. "Pip, there is something I would like to show you. My mother gave it to me just before she died." Fumbling in my satchel, I locate my leather purse and pull it out, before emptying the contents into Pip's hand.

Pip smiles as he examines the matching wolf pendant. "Thank you, Bethany, I had hoped that you would recognise mine and realise the significance. Now I can tell you who the other person is." Pip coughs to clear his throat and says with pride, "The other person is Richard, Duke of York."

Shock courses through my body and immediately my legs begin to buckle.

Pip catches me as I fall. "Bethany, are you alright?"

"Yes, I'm just a little frightened, as I really don't understand what's happening. All I know for certain is that we wear the same pendant and that we share the same allegiances. I have always been told that one day the pendant may save my life. Are our lives in danger? Is Duke Richard's life in danger?"

Pip's face goes ashen as he replies, "Unfortunately, yes. Duke Richard's position is perilous."

I manage to recover a little before we walk in silence towards the chancel. It's at this point where we leave the church through a concealed doorway. Before us stands a tiny cottage. At the threshold, we knock and are greeted by Father Denning, who ushers us in quickly before locking the door behind us. "Come, please follow me."

Inside, a hearty fire burns in the hearth. To the left of the hearth is a large table and three chairs and to the right is a wooden trunk. The trunk causes me to stop, as we have one exactly the same at home. It was my mothers. We keep it covered with a blue linen cloth and a variety of caskets. I have never looked inside, but I believe that it contains a collection of parchment rolls. I only know this much as I spied on my father one night when he was depositing a roll.

Father Denning's words wake me from my thoughts. "Bethany, please be seated."

I do so immediately, grateful to rest my shaking legs. At this point, Pip retreats to the doorway, unsheathes his dagger and stands on guard. Ahead of me, the tapestry curtains open and in walks a tall, sturdy figure. He's wearing an emerald-green brocade gown with a matching French-style head covering. Both items are finely pleated and lined with ermine. At his waist, he wears a thick brown leather belt and on his feet are sturdy brown riding boots. His face is plump and he has deep worry lines around his eyes.

"Good day, Mistress Bethany."

I rise immediately and curtsey as low as possible out of respect. He takes both of my hands and holds them tightly. Deep down, I feel as if I know him.

"Do you recognise me, Bethany?"

"I think so, but I must be wrong." I shake my head and try to make sense of the situation.

"Who do you think I am?"

"Well, you look like my uncle William?"

For the first time, he smiles. "You are right and I am touched that you have remembered me, for it was a very long time ago when we met. You were only a child. Your mother, my youngest sister, moved away when she married your father. We kept in touch right up to the very end of her life, but your father, although loyal, has never been friendly towards me. He asked that I stay away from you. He was concerned that you would become a pawn in my world, where allegiances change almost daily. Reluctantly, I did as he asked, but I have kept a close eye on you ever since. It was I who made sure that you were taught to read and write. I also forbid him to marry you off without my permission." At this moment, Alard steps through the curtain. My mind begins to spin. I do not understand. "Bethany, please do not be alarmed. Alard is my man."

Alard bows before joining Pip by the door. He also unsheathes his dagger. "Bethany, please be seated." As Sir William pulls his hands away, I notice that the sleeves of his gown are inlaid with blue silk. I take my seat and wait. The curtain draws back once more and a man that I recognise as Roger walks in. Roger is not overly tall and he is very slender, with short blond hair and blue eyes. I am very confused. My eyes dart back and forth uncontrollably. I try to stand but I am asked to remain seated by Sir William.

Father Denning enters and the curtain closes once more, but, as it does, I notice that there are two armed guards on the other side of the curtain. I wonder where Duke Richard is.

Sir William is the first to speak. "Oh, Bethany. You melt my heart, for in your eyes I can see my sister. I can also see disappointment and confusion. You are searching the room for Duke Richard and you cannot find him. Well, search no longer. Please let me introduce you."

"Sorry, but I do not understand."

The man I know as Roger steps forward and takes my hand. "Bethany, please accept my sincere apologies. I am so sorry for deceiving you in the past, but my name's not Roger. That was my grandfather's name. I am Richard, Duke of York."

I rise and try to curtsey, but the shock makes me wobble and I sway back and forth.

In an instance, the duke steps forward and wraps his arms around me. "Bethany, please sit and do not worry about such formalities." With these words, he gently lowers me to my seat. "I already know that your heart is true and that you have an unfaltering loyalty to me. I am truly sorry for such deceptions, especially as your mother was so kind and welcoming. She allowed me to use your home as a safe haven and refuge for many years, even though your father was unfriendly and never wanted me. Now, trouble rises once more, but this time shelter is harder to find. I am travelling north to my castle at Sandal. King Henry's physicians have openly proclaimed that his mind is free from the malady that has plagued him and now Queen Margaret is on the warpath once more. She has seized power – power that is not hers to seize." The duke's eyes now darken with anger. "She has incited the Lord Egremond and my own son-in-law, Lord

Exeter, to rise up. Exeter is foolish, easily led and cannot discern the truth. I have tried to reason with him, but he has gone too far this time. If something's not done soon, these traitorous lords and our vengeful queen will tear this country apart. If she gains full power, she will be unstoppable. As it is, the king is at risk of death. She is obsessed and will stop at nothing. Her only desire is that her child, Edward, Prince of Wales, sits upon the throne."

I lean forward. "Please, may I ask… is your life in danger?"

"Yes, Bethany, but I owe a debt of allegiance to my country and my ancestors to do the right thing. Where others refuse to act, I will not."

I sit back as I try to make sense of what I have just been told. I am saddened by the news, but not surprised.

Sir William breaks the silence. "Bethany, are you alright?"

"Yes, yes, please forgive me. I was just trying to regain my calm. I am angry that false lords should prey and assist the queen."

"Bethany, will you serve us? We will make sure that you are kept safe."

"Of course, you need not ask me. I volunteer to assist in any way that I can. I will gladly serve."

The duke's eyes change once more. This time, they are filled with compassion. "Thank you, Bethany, I am eternally grateful."

My heart skips a beat as the duke walks towards me. I just cannot help myself; I stand automatically. To my surprise, he gently grasps both of my hands and looks into my eyes. "I will see you again when I return south, but for now I must say farewell. Sir William will go through the details with you.

Time is precious and I must be gone." With that, he kisses my hands and leaves.

Sitting once more, Sir William joins me. In his left hand, he holds a letter that is sealed with wax and imprinted with the duke's device. It's almost as long as my hand and tied with a pale-blue velvet ribbon. "This letter needs to be delivered into the hands of Brother James Longhorn, who resides at the House of the Friars Minor in Little Walsingham. No one outside of this room must ever know of its existence and no one must ever see you pass it over to him. We suspect that one, maybe two or even more, of your group are members of the Stanley Household."

I gasp at the very thought of treachery. Who could it be? Have I spoken ill-thought words to anyone? Previous conversations run through my head.

Sir William, seeing the shock on my face, allows me a few moments of silence to rest before continuing, "This very household have attempted to trap the duke on his return from Ireland. Now we fear that they are planning another ambush. We must act first and we must act fast."

The letter weighs heavy in my hand. With concealment at the front of my mind, I decide to hide the letter inside one of my old leather boots and then pack the boot at the bottom of my leather satchel. I place everything else on top. This way, I will be able to remove the items I need without arousing suspicion. Lastly, I replace my wolf pendant in its leather pouch and tuck it safely inside a small pocket. Sensing that it's time to leave, I stand once more.

"Farewell, dear niece. Take care and I look forward to seeing you when your pilgrimage and mission has been completed." Instinctively, he holds me tightly in his arms and, for a moment, the world stops. Our goodbye is painful. Thoughts of my mother flood over me. Once Sir William and Alard depart through the curtain, Pip and I say farewell to Father Denning and retrace our footsteps to the church. Once inside, we sit in silence. That way, anyone seeing us will simply assume that we had been in the depths of meditation and prayer. We do not have to wait very long as we are soon joined by Ned.

"Here you both are. We were beginning to think that you had disappeared. Is everything well?"

"We have been praying for a safe journey." Pip's words are warm and soothing. They hold no hint of deception. All the while, I keep a steady gaze upon the altar. "Refreshments are ready in the hall; we should make a move."

Pip leads the way and I follow. The evening passes pleasantly and the conversations are joyful, but I cannot help but wonder who the traitors may be.

***

When the morning sun breaks through the heavy clouds, I decide to explore the grounds on my own before breaking my fast. I need to clear my head before rejoining the others. On my return, I am pleased to learn that we are being treated to duck eggs fried in butter. They are very fresh and their yokes ooze all over my fried bread. For extra taste, I use a little coarse salt.

Nearing the end of breakfast, Sir William enters the hall. He is dressed immaculately and needs no introduction. Owain is the first to stand and bow, and it's the fanciest bow that I've ever seen – right down to the floor and back again. Sir William acknowledges his gesture with an amused smile before saying, "Good health and happiness to you all. I hear from Brother Prior that you will be on your way today. Walsingham awaits and I believe that you have many stops ahead of you. Most of these will be in hostels or religious establishments. Therefore, please make sure that you have your letter of pilgrimage ready for inspection. From here, each place will affix a wax seal to your letter. It's a formality, nothing more, but it will provide you with an everlasting keepsake of your pilgrimage."

A thought springs to mind. The seals, although beautiful, will certainly provide providence, but they will also change the very nature of the letters. They will become powerful documents, depicting our route and stopping places. And what if the seals are being added for another reason? They may be a clever ruse – a way of checking everyone's identity, identifying not only your name but your manor.

Sir William bids farewell and departs. He is obviously very skilled at showing no emotion, for he does so without a flicker of recognition as he passes me.

Mundford and Beyond

As we prepare for the day ahead, we are joined by another. He is introduced to us as Charlemain, a local guide, who will accompany us to Walsingham. I like the look of Charlemain. He has a kind face, a bright smile, and a warm and friendly way about him, although I do wonder how he will manage to walk such a long way as he appears to be very old. I ponder on his appearance and how it brings to mind Chaucer's pardoner. Like the pardoner, his height makes him stoop and he walks with the aid of a staff. His withered hands are swollen at the knuckles and his cheeks are red and weather-beaten. While inspecting him further, I notice that his boots are a patchwork of different coloured leathers. Most are faded, but a couple appear to be new. His soles appear to be reinforced with three layers of leather. This is an obvious sign that he walks a great deal and that the roads may be constructed of clay – a material that is well known for damaging leather soles. The peat of the Fens was soft and cushioning; I do hope that the last leg of the journey is not as painful as the gravel at Barkway.

Before leaving, Charlemain explains, "From now on, everywhere we visit will be of religious or historic significance.

We will visit elaborately decorated churches and encounter a variety of Doom paintings. There will be mysterious symbols and relics, too, and if you will allow me, I'll endeavour to explain their meanings. So, for those of you who wish to hear about such things, please stay at the front with me, and for those who seek peace and seclusion, please travel at the back of our party. I am well aware that each person has their own reasons for going on a pilgrimage and I would not like to interfere."

After much shuffling back and forth, we are ready to leave. In a scene reminiscent of Noah's Ark, we leave Sir William's manor in a long line, travelling in pairs, via a beautiful hollow way peppered with wildflowers. As we depart, I notice a member of Sir William's household hurl a wooden barrel into the moat. How strange; it sunk without trace. I wonder what was in it.

"Now, dear friends, we are approaching the first mystical place on our journey. It's an ancient cemetery comprising of three burial mounds. People have lived here ever since the time of the Roman invasion, hundreds of years ago. If you look carefully in the soil, you may be fortunate enough to find items that they left behind. Whenever the fields are ploughed, more items appear. Last year, I found a gold coin and a broach in this very field."

It seems to me that Charlemain is very well versed in this story, as he has just produced both items from his pocket. I hold the broach and marvel at the workmanship. Continuing, we pass the location of a Roman villa, before joining what Charlemain explains to be a Roman road.

It feels as though Charlemain is reading my mind when he says, "Not only are we walking on a Roman road, but it's a settlement boundary. Over there lies the settlement of Threxton and far away, in the distance, is Thetford. Have any of you been to Thetford?" It seems not, as there is a flurry of shaking heads. Charlemain continues, "That's a pity, as Thetford is a fine town with a wealthy priory and hundreds of thriving pottery kilns. Thetford ware is very popular in London and Colchester, and you will see plenty of it on your journey. In fact, Thetford is a very busy town for many different reasons. Pilgrims use it as a gateway not only to Walsingham, but to Bishops' Lynn in the west."

I am enthralled by Charlemain's commentary, as there's so much to learn, but I doubt the same can be said for Cecily and Anne, as they keep whispering and giggling. It's all very embarrassing and I suspect that they have lost interest already. I do hope that Charlemain is not offended. Again, it seems that Charlemain has read my mind.

"I am not offended, mistress. It's rare nowadays that I find anyone who is interested in my ramblings."

"Oh, Charlemain, please do not say such a thing. Your knowledge is enlightening and brings the landscape to life."

We walk on in the knowledge that the others will soon fade away. I cannot say that this saddens me – in fact, it's quite the opposite. It's really rather nice to know that soon I will be the sole beneficiary of Charlemain's knowledge and I'll be able to ask as many questions as I please.

Charlemain, determined to try one last time, raises his right hand. "Friends, we are approaching Dead Morris Hill. The spirits of our ancestors roam freely at this place. If you listen carefully, you may hear them as we pass."

Silence falls as we continue. More burial mounds give way to an extremely long barrow. I cannot tell the exact length, but it must be the length of at least fifteen people laying end to end, and as many as seven or maybe eight people wide. The structure, which is mainly hidden, appears to consist of dry stones that have been laid in such a way as to make it watertight. It is draped in grass and mosses.

Charlemain breaks the silence, "Although we can only see one entrance, there are more hidden away. Sometimes there are two, sometimes there are three. These entrances lead to the burial chamber where the bodies were ceremonially deposited."

For a moment, we stop to pay our respects. I decide to leave the group and offer a silver coin to the spirits as a mark of respect. Others scoff at my actions, but I ignore them. Returning to the group, we begin to walk once more.

"Friends, it is not too many miles to Mundford where we will rest for the night." Charlemain smiles as he delivers his words, but his eyes appear empty.

Anne has disgraced herself along the way and he is rightly annoyed at her state. I am also rather fed up with her behaviour and I am starting to doubt her. How could she have drunk so much ale while breaking her fast. Or did she fill her flask and drink while walking? How can she act like this on a pilgrimage? Due to Anne's condition, it takes far longer to reach Mundford than expected. In her drunken state, she continues to sway all over the place until she finally slumps against a tree. Being such a large woman, I doubt that anyone will attempt to carry her, so we could be here for quite a while.

The light has started to fade, but at least we have made it. I was beginning to worry. Our destination for the night is a hostel located next to St Leonard's church. Looking at it,

I'm a little confused as it has the appearance of a large manor house, set within a moated enclosure. In my mind, moats are associated with castles, not hostels. On arrival, we are met by a slim young lady dressed in a dark-brown kirtle, over which she wears a tabard. I wonder to myself what she's been doing as her tabard is completely covered by a layer of fine grey dust, as is her coif and her pretty face. Her hands, however, are perfectly clean.

"Charlemain, my dearest friend, I hope that you are well?"

"Hello, Lucy. I am very well and pleased to see you. Unfortunately, you were not here when I passed through last time."

Lucy explains to Charlemain that she had been living in her workshop recently and that she rarely ventures out nowadays. A few weeks ago, she received an urgent missive from Sir William requesting that she produce one thousand pewter livery badges, two of which are to be enamelled, and a fine silver bracelet, as quickly as possible. While they are talking, I notice that her eyes are bloodshot and tired.

"Please let me take you to my mother. She is within and has prepared a meal for you all."

"Thank you, Lucy, you are so kind."

The hostel is warm and welcoming, and is obviously used to catering for large numbers of pilgrims, as a great many dishes are laid out in readiness. I can see parsley bread, cheese and salted eggs, and two large jugs of ale. I do hope that Anne refrains from drinking any more. After helping myself to a large chunk of parsley bread and noticing that Lucy is sitting in the corner on her own, I decide to go over and say hello.

"Mistress Lucy, I am Bethany. Please may I join you?"

Lucy smiles broadly, her red eyes sparkling. "How lovely, of course you can. It will be wonderful to have some company. I have been on my own for so many days now and I get very lonely."

"Your work sounds fascinating. I have always wondered how livery badges are made. Please could you tell me?"

"Of course, but please let me know if I bore you. I'm so proud of my work that I tend to go on a little."

"Oh, you could never bore me, I love to learn."

"Well, the first thing I have to do is make the moulds. I do this by carving the design into some soapstone. It's very soft and produces a lot of dust, which I then need to wipe away with a damp piece of linen. I use a selection of knives for the carving – it all depends on how fine the detail is to be. The design I'm working on at the moment is a five-leaf rose sitting inside a fetterlock. The rose has one large section, one small section and five leaves. The fetterlock is closed and is decorated with dots and binding. There are cut-outs, too. This makes the rose stand proud. Even though I say so myself, the design is beautiful. Then, to make sure that the moulds work, I make a wax impression. To do this, I pour melted beeswax into the mould. When the wax has cooled and hardened, I ease the badge out to inspect it. Sometimes things go perfectly and I can keep the mould, but other times I have to throw it away and start again. My work is governed by the Pewterers Guild, you see, and if I were to produce shoddy work, I would be heavily fined and our lord would be most displeased with me."

From everything that Lucy has said, it is clear that she is also loyal to our lord as the badge she is making is his device.

Lucy continues, "When I am ready to make the real badges, I have to mix the powdered lead, copper and tin to make the pewter. Then, I heat it gently in my large cauldron. This is the trickiest part, as I have to stir it constantly and make sure that there are no lumps. I also have to make sure that I don't overheat it, otherwise the pewter will turn brown and be ruined. Once the mixture is ready, I use a ladle to pour it into the mould. Then, finally, I push a pin into the pewter and leave the pin to harden. I try to make sure that all the badges are left for as long as possible before I remove them, just to make sure that they are as hard as possible. Then, all I have to do is polish them and pack them in linen bags."

"Oh, Lucy, that's such a lot of work, especially on your own. You must be shattered all the time."

"Yes, I am, but our lord is in great need and all his men need to be clearly identified when the time comes." We look at each other with fear on our faces. "But for now, Bethany, let's enjoy this evening." We quickly change the conversation and spend the rest of the evening talking and laughing until sleep becomes impossible to avoid.

***

When I wake in the morning, Lucy has gone – I presume to her workshop. By my side is a small linen bag, which has been tied with pale-blue laces. Inside, there is a fine silver bracelet and a note, which reads, 'My dearest Bethany, please take this with you as a reminder of me and our lord. He wishes that you wear it always.'

My heart leaps with joy and sadness. Sadness that I may never see Lucy again and joy that our lord has given me such a beautiful gift. I secure it on my wrist, before turning it this way and that. As I move it, I notice that a small falcon motif has been carved into the clasp. I vow never to remove it. I am bought back to the present by Charlemain's words.

"My friends, it's time for us to leave. Today, we are set for Ickburgh. It's a gentle walk and very beautiful one."

Indeed, the walk proves to be an extremely pleasant one, which is punctuated with tales from Charlemain. I am glad to say that I now have him all to myself. I know that certain members of our party mock us both, but let them do as they please. Far from being deterred, I take delight in being able to ask even more questions. I'm engaged in something far deeper than a religious pilgrimage; I'm on a quest for knowledge, a quest to know myself and, ever since Bodney, a quest to protect my lord from his enemies.

"Ickburgh is a most splendid town, Bethany. It belongs to the Honour of Clare and has passed through the Mortimer and de Bohun families for hundreds of years. It's a delightful place to visit and there are so many sights of interest that I would like to point out along the way. To be honest, I'm rather excited at the prospect of sharing them with you. It's so nice to have someone to travel with who is actually interested. Most who travel this way don't seem to care. They just want to have time away from their manors to eat, drink and dice."

I nod my head in agreement, as I have suspected this all along.

Almost immediately, Charlemain raises his hand and points towards a flint wall. "I expect that you have seen a great deal of flint since leaving Weeting. It's such a marvellous material. When it comes out of the ground, it's just a dull lump of brown stone and to those with no knowledge it can quite easily be overlooked. Only when it's broken open does its beauty become visible to the naked eye. It's very hard-wearing and it can be used in so many different ways. Mainly in the construction of buildings, but – this is the interesting part – it can also be used to create mosaics. Small decorations that can be imbued with secret meanings and codes. I doubt that we understand all of the meanings nowadays, as many will have been lost in the mists of time, but the ones that remain speak louder than words."

"Do you mean they can act like livery badges?"

"Yes, they can show allegiances, but they can also be used to signpost the way, to offer guidance and, most importantly, to warn of danger."

My mind begins to race and excitement rushes through me, as I have never heard of mosaics before. "Charlemain, please do tell, where do I look for these signs?"

"Everywhere, my dearest, although they are mainly found on churches and inns. I will point them out as I see them."

When we arrive at Ickburgh, the first buildings that we see are those belonging to the Lepers House. Slightly set back from the road, they appear dark and desolate. My eyes scour the horizon for lost souls, but I can see none. I wonder how many live there? In my mind, I imagine the inflicted to be shuffling around in the manner of ghosts, clad in dying skin, which is melting and falling off. I cross myself while remembering the Doom painting in the church at home. It shows people with broken bodies and mouths gaping. They are trapped in purgatory, with the fires of hell burning all around them. I wonder if that's how it feels to be a leper? I drag my mind from such thoughts, as they are just too terrible for words.

Charlemain, calling everyone together, makes an announcement, "Friends, please heed my words. Very shortly we are to walk through a flood plain. I have been informed that it's mainly dry at the moment and that the sinking pits of winter are no longer a problem, but please keep an eye out for the springs that bubble up through the surface, as these can make the ground heavy. Once we have crossed the flood plain, we will then cross the river. This can be done in two ways and the decision is yours for the making. The old bridge is rickety but free, whereas the new bridge will cost you a coin. Unfortunately, I do not know exactly how much it will cost as it's kept by a hermit belonging to the House of Lepers, but I can ask when we arrive."

Charlemain's words ring true, for as we cross the flood plain, springs bubble forth and make the mud slippery – so much so that I can feel my feet sinking into the sticky clay. The two bridges come into sight and not a moment too soon. I, for one, will be glad of the respite. On viewing the two bridges, I decide that it's well worth parting with a coin to arrive in one piece. So, it seems, does Pip and Charlemain. The others decide to take their chances with the old bridge. They stream over it, one after the other. Suddenly, I hear a noise.

"Oh no, what's that loud creaking I can hear?" Looking to my left, I can see large beams of wood falling from the old bridge into the river.

Pip begins to shout, "Get off the bridge quickly. Get off! There are too many of you on it. Why, oh why, did you all choose to cross at the same time? Charlemain warned you that it was rickety." Exasperated, he turns to Charlemain, "All this, for the sake of saving a coin."

The creaking suddenly becomes an explosion. Bodies fall into the water. Manic screams and cries of despair fill the air. The scene is just too chaotic to comprehend.

"How many are in the water?" Ned's call is distinctive.

Frustratingly, I cannot hear the answer. Neither can I see clearly enough to count for myself. There are so many clinging to each other that it's almost impossible for me to distinguish who's who, but – praise the Lord – I can see Alard dragging Ethel onto the riverbank. She's crying, but I decide that's a good sign, as it means that her lungs are clear of water. It's often the silent ones who need the most attention. I can also see Cecily, but there is no sign of Anne. We run to their aid.

Among the sobbing I can hear someone say, "Why didn't we cross the new bridge?" I ponder on this and conclude that all would have been well if it hadn't been for the other group that tried to cross at the same time.

Pip calls to me, "Bethany, please be still. It's extremely slippery and I fear that you may fall. Please wait for me and I will help you."

I do as Pip asks. While waiting, I watch as Anne's lifeless body is hauled from the water. Cecily begins to sob, crying, "She's dead. She's dead!" before falling to the ground in despair. Ned immediately drops to his knees and holds his head close to hers, so close that he can feel for her breath on his cheek. "No, she lives."

In all the commotion I had not noticed the arrival of the hermit. He has with him a wooden sledge. Immediately, Anne's lifeless body is heaved onto its wooden slats. I do not know whether the main problem is her water-filled garments or her weighty body. Either way, the task appears cumbersome and affords her little dignity. When we begin to move again, I notice that the men are finding it hard to shift the sledge.

"Pip, where are we going?"

"To the chapel of St Mary at Newbrigge. Once I am content that Anne is safe and that Ethel is fully recovered, we will be on our way again. I have no desire for us to spend a night here."

On our arrival, many nuns are on hand to care for everyone, but in particularly Anne, who appears grey and waxen. As we enter the gloom of the chapel, Cecily becomes hysterical again. "Tell me, will she live? Will she live?"

These words appear to anger the head nun. "Please do not speak such words. She may wake and hear you. The shock could cause her heart to stop beating. Now, please calm yourself and do not fret. We will take good care of your friend. Sister Annette and myself will sit with her until she regains consciousness, then we will call for the apothecary who will tend to her. Afterwards, she will be transported to a safe house within the grounds. She will come to no harm, as the lepers do not roam the grounds."

Looking on the scene before me, I am surprised to feel such detachment. I certainly wish Anne no harm, but I sense that something is amiss. Turning towards the doorway, I notice that Pip has returned and is holding Anne's bedraggled possessions. He must have collected them from the riverbank. From the look on his face, I have the feeling that he's found something that displeases him.

Charlemain, also noting Pip's presence, shifts his weight from side to side. "Well, everyone, I think that the time has come for us to leave. We are all present and correct, are we not? Ethel, I can see that you have new clothes, courtesy of the nuns, and the colour in your face has returned. If we make a move now, the shock will disperse quicker than if we wait. Aches and pains will slow our progress enough as it is."

Cecily begins to scream and stamp her feet.

"Cecily, please calm yourself. I know that you are distressed, but we must go. Anne is safe and the nuns have assured us that they will keep us informed of her condition."

Not wishing to witness another scene, I take my leave. I just cannot understand why Cecily is acting the way she is. Outside, I join the rest of our party and wait for those inside to emerge. When they do, I notice that Cecily's face is a deep shade of red and her eyes are black. I cannot determine whether this is anger or sadness. My mind begins to race. What on earth could have caused her to become so hysterical? Is there more to this than meets the eye? Could Anne and Cecily be the traitors among us? Do they threaten our lord's life? If so, who is the main perpetrator, Anne or Cecily? Or is someone else involved? Somehow, through my confusion, inspiration hits me and the way forward becomes clear. I know what I'll do. In future, instead of watching everyone from afar, I will befriend them each evening and see if I can learn their secrets. I will trust no one but Pip and, to a certain extent, Charlemain.

As we begin to walk away, my thoughts return to Ethel. Accompanied by Ned, she walks closely behind. Her spirit has returned, but she appears frail. I hear that she is chilled to the bone and that she fears the river has entered her body. Even as we walk, Ned attentively wraps lambs' fleeces about her person, while silently signalling to Pip.

On seeing this, Pip requests that we turn around immediately and return to the chapel. "I am sorry, Ethel, but I think it would be wiser for you to stay here with Anne. I can tell from the look on your face how disappointed you are, but it's for the best, believe me. When you have fully recovered, you can rejoin us. I will leave instructions stating that you are to be put on a cart and carried the rest of the way."

Sister Louisa, realising that we have returned, now joins us.

Pip addresses her, "Sister, I would like Ethel to remain here until she is better. Please can you see that that she is attended to by the apothecary? No expense is to be spared – our lord will reimburse your house."

"Of course. We will happily tend to Ethel and restore her to health, have no fear."

Gratefully, Ethel takes Sister Louisa's arm. She lifts her hand to wave goodbye, tears rolling down her cheeks. "I will miss you all. God Bless."

Leaving Ethel is heartbreaking, but it's for the best. We walk away in silence. Tonight, we are to lodge at a strange-looking inn, just off the main road, in the village of Cockley Cley.

"Charlemain, please can you tell me more about this place? It intrigues me."

"Ah, yes. Well, where do I begin? This village is not really a village, after all. It's made up of two settlements – one old and one new. The oldest part is Cley St Peter, which is just beyond those trees in the distance over there. It has a fine church and is the manor of Thomas Oldhall, a distant relative of Sir William. Whereas where we stand now is the new boundary and all the land to our right is known as Cockley Cley."

"Cockley Cley? What a strange name. Whatever does it mean?"

"Cley refers to the soil and Cockley refers to a wood that is frequented by birds."

"Oh dear… that sounds ominous." In my mind's eye, I envisage clouds of birds circling high above me. Some are swooping down to earth, attacking anyone who gets in their way, while the others perch high in the trees, waiting for their prey.

"Do not fret, some of the locals are prone to exaggeration. They are trying to persuade everyone to move to this side of the trees. In reality, they fear the leper hospital, which stands just beyond St Peter's, and will stop at nothing to get their way. They have even built a new church, All Saints, to try and tempt people away from St Peter's, although I doubt it will work. Not all folk are superstitious."

Bang! Bang! Bang! Alard knocks loudly on the inn's large oak door, but before it can open a terrifying silence descends over our party. A herald has appeared from nowhere and is now dismounting his horse. His dark blond hair tumbles about his face as he removes his cap and bows low.

"I am seeking Pip."

"Here I stand."

"Sir, I am Robert the Herald. I bring news of Anne."

"Thank you, Robert, let's step aside."

With that, Pip and Robert are gone. Cecily, on hearing Anne's name, begins to protest.

"No, Cecily, you will not follow Pip and the herald," says Alard. "Let's go inside and make ourselves comfortable. I'm sure that Pip will return soon and let us know the news."

"No. How dare he leave us? I have a right to know what's happening."

"And you will, but not yet. Step inside, Cecily, and stop making such a scene. Our hosts await us and your rudeness will not be tolerated. I suggest that you remember your manners and sharpish."

Shocked at Alard's temper, Cecily is one of the first to enter. Inside, it takes a while for my eyes to get used to the gloom. The hall is more akin to a barn and we are greeted by an elderly couple. Both have bent backs and they shuffle as they walk.

"Greetings. We thought that something bad must have happened, as you are much later than expected."

In Pip's absence, Charlemain steps forward. "Please accept our apologies. Today has been trying in the extreme, but I will tell you more about that later. For now, I would be grateful if you could show everyone to their rooms. Pip will be in soon and it would be nice if we could eat as soon as possible."

"Don't fear about that. Maud has the pottage ready and waiting. You'll want for nothing here."

"Thank you, Davy, you've never let me down."

Both men smile at one another and it's obvious to all that their friendship is an old one.

After Cecily's earlier hysterics, things gradually begin to return to normal and by the time Pip returns to the inn, it's full of locals merrily eating and drinking. Cecily, having noticed Pip's return, is now edging towards the door. From the look on her face, she is planning on eavesdropping. I must do something and fast.

Standing, I walk over and block her way. "Cecily, how is your room?"

"It is adequate."

I had not expected friendship, but I had not expected such bitterness. Cecily's eyes are cold and full of spite. However, a strange feeling deep within my gut tells me to carry on. "Cecily, I am sure that Anne will recover soon. I am sure that there is no need to worry."

Her reply is sharp. "Yes, Bethany, I am sure that you know better than anyone else what's happening."

Cecily's coldness is accompanied by a hard stare. Undeterred, I invite her to sit by the fire. "Shall we sit and await the news in comfort?"

"No, I do not want to sit and I certainly do not want to wait with you."

Cecily's words echo all around the hall. Silence descends. Embarrassed, I gaze down at the floor and wonder what to do next. Fortunately, Alard joins us.

"Ladies, have you heard? Our landlord is just about to bring in another large caldron of steaming hot broth."

Cecily's anger, as hot as the broth, boils over. "I am not hungry. Just go away and leave me alone."

I look up and assume that Pip has heard everything as his face is now purple with rage, but Cecily seems undeterred. In a flash, she's by his side and spoiling for a fight. "I wish to hear of Anne's condition."

Pip's words are slow and considered. "She is stable."

With that, Cecily spins about to face our group. "He will not tell me the truth. Will no one else ask after Anne's condition?"

Alard is the only one to respond. "Cecily, please calm yourself. Pip has just said that she is stable. What else is there to ask?"

"But what does stable mean? I want to know more."

Pip's face now betrays a deep anger. "Well, you will be sorely disappointed then, won't you?" With this, Pip turns and disappears into the night.

"He is so rude. I hate the way that he lords it over everyone. Who does he think he is"?

Alard, intent on calming the situation, tries once more. "Cecily, I think that you need to rest."

"I do not." With that, Cecily turns her back and heads for the door. On her way, she pushes through a group of rowdy locals playing dice. Amusingly, some of them pinch her bottom as she passes. I doubt that will improve her mood! I decide to have one last bowl of steaming hot broth before I retire to bed.

Upstairs, my room is cool and I sink down onto my mattress. The solitude of the night is a welcome relief. Today was so fraught. Tonight, there will be time to dream. Time to plan my future. I wonder where my life is going. I wonder where I will end up. Perhaps in our lord's household or maybe even Sir William's. I have heard that times are changing and that women are being valued for their writing skills and their knowledge. Perhaps I could make my mark. I think of Christine de Pisan and Margery Kempe and of their writing. Maybe I will follow their lead. My thoughts are interrupted by someone knocking on my door. Who on earth could it be? Hesitantly, I walk across the room and place my ear against the door.

"Who's there?"

"Bethany, it's me. It's Pip. Please can you open the door?"

Quickly, I unlatch the door and look both ways before inviting him inside.

"Oh, Bethany, please forgive me for visiting you in your room, but I must speak with you and what I have to say cannot wait until the morning."

"Please come in."

I watch as Pip strides over to the window and strains to look out through the shutters. I expect that this is an automatic action and one that he does without thinking. His fingers tap on the window sill as he talks. "I have news about Anne. It's as I expected. She's a spy alright and, even worse, she's from Ormskirk – a manor that belongs to Richard Molyneux. He's a nasty bit of work and he's married to the daughter of Sir Thomas Stanley." I consider that name before Pip continues, "When I went through her bag, I took the liberty of examining her papers. Not only did they identify where she was from, but they confirmed that Cecily is her daughter."

Reeling from the shock, I sit motionless until I can find the words to express my hurt. "How could she? How could she befriend me in Ely? Worse still, how could she lie to Ethel? Kind, caring Ethel, who would harm no one. Does anyone else know of this?"

"Ned has always suspected that something was amiss. Hence he has been by their side all the while, telling jokes and stories, and trying to get them to lower their guard in the hope that he could trip them up. He even tried using his musical talents to impress them."

"Where is Cecily now?"

"She has been arrested and charged with theft."

"I don't understand. What's happened?"

"After you retired, Cecily returned and, by all accounts, began drinking heavily. Then, not content to sit on her own, she went over to the group of locals who had pinched her bottom and made fun of her. According to Alard, she was all over them. Something had to be done. So, a plot was laid. Ned paid one of the men to leave the table to get her a bowl of broth and when he returned, she was gone and so were his coins. She had taken the bait. This means that we can hold her for a while. As for Anne, she will stay at the House of Lepers indefinitely. Holding them brings danger, but letting them go would bring even more. Stanley will no doubt hear of their plight and try to rescue them, but I will deal with that when it happens. I have men everywhere and they will keep me informed. Oh, Bethany, now you see why it was so important for me to come to your room. I hope that you can forgive me. I would never want to damage your reputation."

"Don't worry about such things, Pip. We know the truth and that's all that matters. Why don't you fetch your mattress and place it by the hearth? I can push mine back and make more room, if you would like?"

"You are very kind and I wish I could, but Ned and Charlemain are expecting me in the hall. We are taking it in turns to keep watch. Alard is on duty now, but it's my turn next."

"Alright, I understand, but please take my sheepskin with you. I have no need of it while I'm here and it'll keep you warm when your shift is over."

"Thank you, Bethany, now that's an offer I can accept."

***

The next day begins not only with breakfast, but with gossip. Lord forgive me for joining in, but I need to find out whatever

I can. News of Cecily's confinement has broken and Agnes is holding court.

"I always knew that she couldn't be trusted."

I smile to myself as Ned gently taunts her. "That's easy to say now, Agnes, but I cannot recall you having mentioned this earlier."

"Oh, well, you know. I thought I would give her the benefit of the doubt."

Realising that there is nothing to be gained from listening to this conversation, I sit down next to Charlemain, who is in very good spirits.

"Good morning, Bethany, did you sleep well?"

"Oh yes, did you?"

"I was a touch cold but once I got off, I slept soundly. Are you aware that today is the Feast of St Anthony of Padua?"

"Oh yes. We always celebrate his life at home. I particularly like the stories about him preaching to the fish and the half-starved mule who ignored the fresh fodder to bow before the holy sacrament."

"Well, later this morning, there will be a service held in his honour at the church of St Peter's. If it's anything like last year, it will be a joy to behold. The monks from Castle Acre always attend and chant throughout the whole service. Their voices are quite unique in both pitch and tone. I could listen to them for hours on end. Afterwards, there's always a feast of fruity buns and blue cheese."

I lick my lips in anticipation of blue cheese. I love the strong, salty taste.

"Do I take it that you will join me?"

"Of course, I would love to. I will go and fetch my belongings and meet you back here as quickly as I can."

"Excellent; while you are gone, I will extend the invitation to the rest of our party, but, to be honest, I cannot see anyone else joining us."

Gathering my belongings together takes no time at all. Ever since Bodney, I have taken great care to keep everything packed as securely as possible, especially our lord's letter. The only items that need packing are those that I use on a daily basis. My spoon, my cup and my bowl. Once everything is in order, I make my way back downstairs to the hall, where I find Charlemain addressing the group.

"The offer to join us is still open should anyone wish to change their minds."

Unsurprisingly, everyone is shaking their heads. It seems that they are loath to leave the hall, where there is food and drink aplenty, and yet even more pilgrims to talk to. I fear that the fresh conversations are more of a pull than religious devotions.

The short walk to St Peter's church is a very pretty one with lots of flowers. When we arrive, we are greeted by the sound of handbells ringing out from high up within the battlements. The outside of the porch has been decorated with white roses, while the inside has blue, gold and white ribbons accompanied by pots of wildflowers. The pathway to the church door is also lined with ribbons, which move gently as we pass. Inside the church, it's breathtaking. Painted shields adorn the walls and they sparkle in the sunshine. I gaze in wonder, as I have never seen so many all in one place before. Then, there's a finely painted screen that divides the chancel and a statue of St Anthony of Padua just in front of the altar. The statue has been decorated with flowers and matching ribbons, as has the Lady Chapel and the statue of the Blessed Virgin Mary. Her face is kind and loving. She is dressed in blue silk and her cloak is adorned with pewter pins. Many of the pins are unknown to me, but I can see that she's wearing my favourite – a double-handled jug with a single lily in it. This represents the Annunciation. The one that intrigues me, though, is a heart with a crown above it. Upon the heart is a serpent.

"Charlemain, what does that badge mean? The one with the serpent on it."

"That one, my dear, represents healing. It's very beautiful, isn't it?"

Walking towards the high altar, I gaze once more on the shields. They are closer now and I can see the decoration better. Two stand out immediately, as they are the closest to my heart. One for the Mortimers and one for the Plantagenets. The Mortimer shield is an emblem that I know well and I can read it like a book. The blue represents the sky, the yellow is the desert, and the silver is the water. It commemorates Geoffrey de Mortimer, who was a Crusader – a man with true Christian morals. The Plantagenet shield is quartered, with each section showing the arms of France and England -- golden lions on a red background and golden fleur-de-lis on a blue background. Moving on, the other shields display a variety of designs. There are castles, stags, barrels, chevrons and stars, to name but a few. I can now see the high altar in its full glory. It has been elaborately decorated in honour of St Anthony.

We decide to take our places on the floor and listen to the monks chanting. To my surprise, Pip has joined us. I am so happy and I wish that this moment could last forever. The sound is rhythmic and atmospheric, and I feel completely safe.

On our way out, we pause to light candles in memory of our loved ones. These are then taken and laid out on the flagstones by a small boy. It is obvious from his actions that he takes his role extremely seriously. All of the candles are placed with precision. Neither too close, nor too far from the others. He seems to be arranging them in the design of a flower. On closer inspection, I can see that he is using a traced design on the floor.

Outside, there is much hustle and bustle. The village appears to have woken up, so much so that I am relieved when we return to the inn and rejoin the others in the garden. It seems that the ale has been flowing since dawn and Ned is in high spirits. Owain catches my eye and rolls them at Ned's antics. Looking around, I notice that Alard and Davy are resting by the arched gate, which leads to the river. Davy looks mournful today. I wonder why.

The landlord's wife, Maud, joins us. "Hello, I hope that you are having a good day? How did you find the church?"

"Oh… it was absolutely perfect, thank you. There were handbells and chanting, and you should have seen the decorations. There were blue, gold and white ribbons everywhere. They were divine."

"Aye, they certainly go to town when it's a feast day."

While talking, I notice that Maud is dressed entirely in white linen. I would have thought it inappropriate at this time of the year. Surely people only wear white at the Pentecost. She also has a variety of linen clothes stuffed into her belt.

"Well, let's see if I can't make the rest of your day even better. Today is bathing day. The air is warm and dry, so there's no chance of anyone catching a chill. Therefore, I am inviting all of the ladies to come inside and enjoy some much-needed luxury. I know there's little comfort on the road. Agnes has just finished and is now sitting by the hearth in a clean kirtle, which I sold her. They are good value at just one coin. Would you like to do the same?"

I think about it for a few seconds before committing myself, "Yes please. I have felt sticky for days and I have a spare coin."

"It's harder for us ladies to get clean. The men can just strip down, but for us it is a major effort. Come, let's go inside."

As we pass, I notice Maud's daughters wiping down all the surfaces with steaming water and what smells like rosemary oil. Maud exclaims, "I like a good clean inn. Cleanliness is next to Godliness, after all."

As we enter the bathing room, I breath in and smell the gently fragranced steam. To my joy, a barrel has already been prepared. It is lined with heavy linen, so there's no chance of getting splinters, and rose petals have been scattered over the top of the hot water. It's very enticing and no doubt a good money-spinner for Maud and her husband. What a good idea!

Before I latch the large oak door behind me, I give Maud and Alice one coin each.

"No, my dear, its only one coin, you keep the other one for Walsingham. They'll be plenty to spend your money on there."

Latching the door behind me, I notice that my clean kirtle awaits. It has been hung on a wrought-iron peg. I undress with energy and fold my clothes neatly, before placing my satchel next to them. I don't want to get anything wet as we still have a journey to complete today. Carefully, I climb the steps and lower myself down into the barrel. My legs knock against the stool that waits for me. I sit down and enjoy the water lapping against my shoulders. I close my eyes and allow myself to relax.

Getting out is harder, but I manage to do so without slipping. Once out, I dry myself carefully with a large linen sheet, before putting on my clean kirtle. I feel good. Some people think that bathing is dangerous, but I disagree with them. My mother was an advocate of a clean body and a clean mind. She taught me to wash as often as possible, whether that be in a barrel or in a stream. Some folks in our village used to moan that washing was not for our class and frowned upon us for no good reason.

When I am ready to unlatch the door, I pull the bell handle as instructed and ring for assistance.

Alice appears. "There's no need to hurry, mistress. Charlemain has just informed us that everyone will be staying another night. Unfortunately, you will be in a different room and you will be sharing with one other. Alas, by the time we knew of the change of plans, we had already rented out most of the rooms. Would you like me to help you with your belongings?"

"No thank you, Alice, I only have my satchel."

Although I'm a little surprised to learn that we are staying another night, I'm very happy at the news. Alice leads me to my new bedchamber. It's a large room with a central hearth and two mattresses. Looking around, I can see no one else's belongings, so I choose the mattress closest to the fire. Since I am sharing this chamber tonight, my satchel will become my pillow. I will wrap it inside my cloak to make it more comfortable. I wonder who will be sharing with me. In the meantime, I decide to sit down and allow my hair to dry completely before joining the others. After a few moments, I hear a knock at the door.

"Come in." I look up. I'm surprised to hear Pip at the door.

"Bethany, it's me. Pip. Please may I enter?"

"Yes, of course,."

Once inside, Pip dances awkwardly from foot to foot. "I hope that your kind offer of sharing a room is still acceptable. If not, I can sleep in the stables with Davy."

"What? Davy is to sleep in the stables?"

"It's unfortunate, but all of the other rooms are full."

"That accounts for his mournful face earlier."

"Yes. He drew straws with Ned and Owain, and lost. Alard has been trying to cheer him up ever since, but nothing's working. When I left, Ned was trying to ply him with mead – it's good for us that he's not needed as a lookout tonight." At this, we both laugh. "I know that it's unorthodox for us to share, but I have recognised some of Stanley's men masquerading as pilgrims and I want to make sure that you are safe."

"Pip, there's no need to worry on my behalf. I am more than happy to share."

"Well, that's all sorted then. I shall have the mattress closest to the door."

"Just out of curiosity, where is Charlemain sleeping?"

"Oh, he's in the room next door. Well, I say it's a room – it's more of a cupboard really."

When we rejoin the others, it seems that Ned's plan to cheer Davy up with mead is working. I would even go so far as to say that it's working a little too well. I sit quietly and listen to the conversations. They wash over me, while I enjoy the excellent bread and cheese that has been provided. After eating, I retire early, wishing everyone a good night as I pass.

Agnes catches my hand and kisses it gently. "Sweet Bethany, I will see you in the morning."

This makes my heart sing and silently I ask myself once more how Cecily and Anne could live with themselves for deceiving Agnes and Ethel. Tonight, I feel safe. Far from being concerned about the arrangements, I relish Pip's company. He has a rough beauty about him and is rather mysterious. I avert my eyes as he removes his jerkin, although I cannot help but notice that his body is very muscular. He is every inch a solider and has the scars to prove it.

"Goodnight, Bethany, I will try not to wake you too early. Until the morning then."

"Yes, goodnight, but please don't worry about waking me. I'm a light sleeper and it's usual for me to wake before dawn."

As I drift off to sleep, I can hear the revellers returning to their beds and think on poor Davy and Alard in the stables.

***

Morning breaks far too soon for me. My sleep was unusually heavy and now the sunlight is streaming in through the shutters.

"Good morning, Bethany, you slept well then."

"Oh yes, far better than usual."

"Perhaps you benefitted from my presence." Pip, to my delight, is smiling from ear to ear, while stoking the hearth. "The day ahead promises to be a good one. The sun is getting hotter each day and there's not a cloud in the sky. Alard and Davy are up and about already. Surprisingly, neither are worse the wear for a night in the stables. Owain and Charlemain are also up and about, but I hear that Ned is still in bed nursing his head."

I stretch and yawn as I stand.

"Would you like me to leave while you get ready?"

"Oh no, there's no need for that."

"I made sure that no one saw me leave your room this morning. Thankfully, they'll be no gossip to contend with, but even if there would have been that's a small price to pay for your safety. Stanley's men are the very worst kind of thugs. I was heartened to hear from Maud and Davy that they barred the doors themselves after counting everyone in last night. Anyway, we will soon be leaving for Swaffham. Others are joining us, taking our numbers to twenty in total. Alard is anxious about this, but I feel that it's the safest option. Anyway, it'll only be for a few miles, as we are to break away from the main group and travel to the manor in North Pickenham for a day or two." My heart leaps with joy as I know this to be the manor of our lord's late stepmother. "Ah, I see you recognise the significance of this manor. Well, they'll be eight of us in total. Charlemain, Alard, Ned, Davy, Owain, Agnes and us two. Oxherd, Robin and the others have already left us and returned to Ely. They were sad to leave without saying goodbye, but Oxherd is not one for goodbyes. He did send you his warmest wishes and said that if you were ever in the area, you would be a very welcome guest at his home."

I am saddened not to have had a chance to say goodbye. I will miss Oxherd's booming voice and extravagant ways. I will also miss Robin's mumbling, as he's a kindly soul, but the memories that we have made will last a lifetime.

There is no road to North Pickenham and we must walk across the fields. However, I do not believe that we are the first to travel this way, as there appears to be a dusty track. It's lovely to be in a small group once more and it's even nicer to walk arm in arm with Agnes. We do not speak of it, but I know that she misses Ethel. Charlemain has resumed his role of guide and, as we walk, he explains the importance of the manor.

"North Pickenham is a most beautiful manor, with a very fine church. It was originally held by Ralph Neville, the first Earl of Westmoreland, our lord's guardian. It's now home to George Neville, the new Lord Latimer, and his beautiful wife, Elizabeth Beauchamp. She's a most spirited lady and always great fun to be with. In fact, it's hard to believe that she's the daughter of Richard Beauchamp, the Earl of Warwick, our lord's tutor, as she's so down to earth and welcoming. We will enjoy our time at North Pickenham, I have no doubt."

I notice that Charlemain's eyes are moist. "Oh, Charlemain, what troubles you?"

"Please forgive me. I am a foolish old man. I was just thinking about our lord and King Henry. How they were bought up together and how they learnt together, but now they are being torn apart by the dark forces that surround the king."

Unable to find the right words to comfort Charlemain, I take his arm and we all walk together, three in a line. Our mood is lightened momentarily as we pass a shepherd who is crouching over his long crook. Our first impression is that his flock is completely out of control, for they are all leaping around and running in different directions. But no, there's more to this than meets the eye. I can now see that his left hand is placed on his head in despair, while he frantically waves the other one high in the air. As we approach, it has become obvious that they are not playing, but they are running for their lives. At this distance, there is nothing that we can do but make a noise and cause a disturbance. If the fox senses that we are here, it may retreat.

Agnes is the first to call out. "Get away, you rascal!" She is now clapping her hands together and dancing from one foot to the other. Then, we all join in.

The shepherd calls out with relief, "Thank you. I am most indebted to you all. The fox has gone."

When we arrive at the manor of North Pickenham, it feels good to be in a Yorkist stronghold and to know that we have nothing to fear. Our security has been bolstered even further by breaking away from the larger group, as spies have nowhere to hide in such a small, intimate party. A beautiful orchard has now come into view to our left. The trees stand side by side in neat rows for as far as the eye can see. The fruits appear to be varied. There are berries a plenty and, in the autumn, there will be an abundance of apples. Walking on, I muse on how small the manor is. It consists of a manor house, a church, a watermill and a few small homesteads. All of the buildings are thatched with reed and most have moss on them. The manor house is set within green fields, which have been scythed expertly to make them appear as velvet. To the back of the manor house, I can see a high stone wall. I wonder if it's defensive or just decorative.

When we arrive at the front door, Charlemain firmly grasps the heavy metal knocker and knocks three times.

Immediately, the door is opened by a young lady in a fine green kirtle.

"Good day, please may I see your letter of introduction?"

"Of course, but, Brody, surely you know me by now." The parchment that he produces from his linen bag is tied with a pale-blue ribbon and is sealed with our lord's wax seal. Before he has time to close his bag, I notice that he, too, has a small fox broach pinned to the lining.

The young lady unties the ribbon and breaks open the seal. I find it strange that the seal is intact. Upon closer inspection, we are welcomed inside. "Come, please enter. My name is Brody and I will be looking after you."

"If you follow me, I will take you to the garden. Refreshments have been laid out in readiness for your arrival."

At the back door, Brody pauses to inform us that Lady Latimer is waiting for us in the arbour and that her ladies are with her. As she speaks, I realise just how young she is. Her face is round and her features are soft. Outside, the view is breathtaking. If I thought that the lawns surrounding the front of the manor were like velvet, the lawns at the back are like emeralds. Unlike monastic gardens, with their formal paths, cloisters and central gardens, this garden has random rose beds and pots of all shapes and sizes. Some of the pots are yellow, decorated with red bands, while the others are various shades of red. All appear to have been decorated with bands of grey, brown and black. The one thing that they all have in common is that they are overflowing with flowers. However, the most striking feature in the garden is the large arbour, which is laced with ivy and flowers.

Sitting within the arbour and surrounded by her ladies is Lady Latimer. It's a blissful scene of calm and serenity. The ladies have obviously been reading and playing music, as books and instruments are scattered all around. Having seen us, Lady Latimer gets to her feet and walks towards us! Her ladies follow suit and are now standing behind her.

"Welcome to my home." Her eyes shine as she smiles. She is petite and unassuming. For one of such high birth, she wears a modest yellow kirtle and a plain girdle. Only the keys, which hang from her waist, convey her status. "Please join us in the arbour. In preparation for your arrival, I have had sheepskins placed in the shade for your comfort."

It's clear from the actions of her ladies that they love her and I can understand why. Instead of asking others for help, she is the one fussing over us. Once seated, ale and a selection of cheeses are brought to us by Brody and a young lad. Lady Latimer continues.

"Once you are refreshed, Brody will show you to your rooms. I want you to feel at home during your stay. Please do not stand on ceremony. When you are settled in, you are free to do as you please. All I ask is that you do not leave the boundaries of this garden. This area is as safe as it can be, but, as you all know, war looms and quite a few of my neighbours are bent on antagonising one another. Only recently, news reached me that Sir Thomas Tuddenham and Sir John Heydon, along with men from the West Country, attempted to ambush our lord as he rode out of St Albans. He was on his way to meet with Sir Thomas Hoe. Fortunately, both are safe."

Lady Latimer looks concerned and pauses for a moment, before continuing, "Now, I'm aware that this news is shocking, but please try not to be alarmed. We are strong and extremely capable of protecting our manor. I am only seeking to forewarn you. Word has also been sent to my husband and, in the meantime, a contingent of Swaffham men are on their way here. They will camp in the west field, which has already been prepared. Barrels of water have been filled, the firepits dug, wood provided and charcoal stockpiled. Soon, the encampment will grow and encompass our lord's retinue. The Swaffham men are hardened and self-reliant. That said, they are friendly and completely loyal. Their strength is in their brotherhood. I fear nothing when they are close by and neither should you." Lady Latimer's smile returns once more. "We will not allow thugs such as Tuddenham and Heydon to ruin our life. We will continue to make merry and enjoy our days."

The mood lightens instantly as Lady Latimer and her ladies return to the arbour. One of them picks up a harp and plucks it energetically. Ned, needing no invitation, produces his shawm and begins to play along, while Agnes and Owain begin to dance.

After the refreshments, Brody shows us to our rooms as promised. My room is adorned with fresh flowers and honeysuckle. It has a four-poster bed, which is dressed with embroidered curtains, pillows and a fine coverlet. I must be in the wrong room.

"Brody, this room is beautiful beyond words, but surely it cannot be for me. I am but a pilgrim. Such a room is way beyond my status."

"No, Mistress Bethany, there is no mistake. All of our rooms are decorated as such. Lord and Lady Latimer ensure that all loyal supporters are taken care of. Their home is a haven to any that need rest and protection."

"That is so kind, Brody, thank you."

Once I am on my own, I walk over to the window and lay out my belongings along the top of a medium-sized wooden trunk. The view from my window is splendid. Just over the garden wall, I can see the west field. Men are coming and going, picking the crops and making way for the ever-growing encampment.

I eventually manage to pull myself away from the window and rejoin the others outside. Marie, one of Lady Latimer's ladies-in-waiting, is reading a tale from a large red leather-bound book. Oh, how wonderful, it's *The Cook's Tale* by Geoffrey Chaucer. It's one of my favourite tales. So much so that I can recount it from memory. How I love the story of Peterkin, the devilish kitchen hand who sings and dances with his friends to the annoyance of his master. What is this? Ned has taken to his feet and has assumed the character of Peterkin. He begins to prance around, swaying this way and that, bowing to all the men and kissing each lady in turn. Now he has fallen to his knees and is serenading Lady Latimer, who – to everyone's amusement – takes on the role as his mistress.

Rising from her seat, she raises her hand and says, "Dearest Peterkin, you are corrupt and have to go. Dance to the door and leave alone. Do not stay and lead the others astray. Let me be, to enjoy the day."

With this, Ned skips away in the direction of the kitchen, leaving Marie to finish the tale. Tranquillity resumes for a few minutes before we spot Brody approaching from the kitchen, carrying a large jug. I doubt that she is aware of Ned creeping along behind her. Charlemain calls out, but it's too late. Ned has launched into song. Surprise is plastered across her whole face as she jumps into the air.

Lady Latimer, who is laughing heartily, gently berates him, "Oh, Ned, you are a rotter. Don't just stand there, help Brody with that jug. It must be heavy."

"Of course, my lady." Immediately, Ned flings himself at Brody's feet. "Forgive me, sweet child. Please let me take that from you."

Brody, unsure of what to do, stands stock-still. Ned carefully takes the jug and, in the process of doing so, steals a kiss on her cheek. After the refreshments, we all rest for a while before I decide that it's my turn to entertain everyone. Ned had played the part of a fool. Charlemain and Alard have spoken of their travels to Calais and beyond. Agnes has sung songs from her youth. Even Pip and Davy have joined in with a dazzling display of sword-fighting. Now, it's time for me to take the stage. I stand upright and take a couple of deep breaths.

"I have composed a poem about the colours of life and the gift of sight." To my surprise, everyone is very enthusiastic. So, once they are all comfortable, I begin. To aid my memory, I close my eyes. The words flow perfectly as I describe the beauty of the world as I see it.

Even as I speak, I'm aware of the rhythm rising and falling in the manner of a sweet melody. When I reach the end, I open my eyes, only to realise that everyone is staring at me. Some have tear-stained faces. Even Lady Latimer's eyes are wet and shine like mirrors. Fear grips me. On no, what have I done? Have I said something wrong? Worry clouds my mind.

"Mistress, have I displeased you?"

"No, Bethany, far from it. You have moved my heart. You have a gift so powerful that you can paint a picture with the use of words alone."

Relief floods over me and everyone smiles. Alas, the moment is interrupted by the sound of a distant horn. Three sharp hoots and a long blast echoes on the breeze.

Lady Latimer immediately jumps to her feet. "My husband is here. That's his signal."

Now, the sound of approaching horses' hooves can be heard, along with the rumble of carts. The horn sounds again, although this time it's much closer.

"They have arrived, they are here. Lord Latimer and our Lord of York, they are here." Lady Latimer beams with joy and is gone in a flash.

She is followed closely by Pip, Davy and Alard. They rush past Lady Latimer and position themselves by the front door, unsheathing their daggers before stopping.

Pip breaks the silence and falls to one knee. "Lady Latimer, I beg your forgiveness, but we must be prudent. We live in uncertain times and the horned message could be a trap. Please move well away from the door. We'll let you know when it's safe to go out."

Pip's words are wise and his message is heeded by all. Lady Latimer moves away as Davy cautiously opens the door. At the same time, Pip and Alard take up defensive positions, ready to attack should they need to, but, to everyone's relief, Lady Latimer is right. It's not a trap, but her husband and our lord. Men in red and gold stand shoulder to shoulder with men in blue and white. Behind them stand Lord Latimer and Duke Richard.

"Brody, quick. Please go to the kitchen and request that refreshments are brought to the hall immediately. Also, please tell the kitchen to take plenty of meat to the west field. The men will be hungry." Brody nods and disappears at a pace.

Lord Latimer and Duke Richard dismount. As they do, the boys from the stables step forward and prepare to lead their horses away. Duke Richard's is a Welsh Cob – sturdy with a quick turn of foot. Lord Latimer's is a dark-grey colt – taller than me with a mane of flowing silver. I realise it's imperative that I do not give myself away. None of the ladies must know that I have met our lord before. I curtsey as low as I can without falling over. Agnes and Lady Latimer's ladies follow suit.

"My Lord, you are most welcome. Please come inside and rest. Refreshments are being prepared."

"Dear Elizabeth, you are most kind, but please do not worry about me. Please welcome your husband."

Antonia, Lady Latimer's maid, smiles alluringly at our lord as he passes by, but, to my relief, he ignores her and heads straight to the hall. I do not like Antonia. There's something about her manner that seems false.

Inside the hall, we seat ourselves to the left-hand side of the table and listen as Lord Latimer explains how our lord will not be staying for long. "My dearest wife, I hate to disappoint you, but our lord must be gone tonight. He will stay for an hour or two, but certainly no longer. Just enough time for his horse and men to rest. We have received word from our scouts that the immediate danger is over, but – just to make sure – he must ride to Bodney this evening with a handful of retainers. I will remain here with the Swaffham men until the morning and then I must depart to Fotheringhay. Life must carry on as normal for now."

"Speaking of normal, I am over-hungry today. When are we to eat?"

"Oh, Duke Richard, there's nothing new there. You're always hungry." Lady Latimer chuckles and, with excellent timing, Brody and the boy appear with a feast. I notice that the boy has changed his smock and is taking great care not to spill anything down his new one.

"On no, I expected refreshments, not a feast. I fear that my horse will be sluggish later and dislike his load." With this remark, everyone laughs.

The table groans under the weight of roast meats, green peasen, lumps of fried bacon and fresh bread rolls. To accompany the food, there is a delicious ale. It has been infused with rose petals and is very sweet. I must take care not to drink too much as it's rather moreish and may be stronger than I think.

Once everything has been eaten and cleared away, the benches and tables are removed and replaced with sheepskin rugs. Sitting down, I notice that Lady Latimer is beckoning to her most senior lady-in-waiting, Isabella. In a split second, she's by her side. I wonder if something's wrong, but I cannot make out a single word of their conversation as they are shielding their mouths. Finally, Isabella rises and strides off purposefully, stopping only to request that Ned accompany her. They disappear out of sight for a short while, before Ned returns dressed in the manner of Peterkin. The vision before us is hilarious. His short smock finishes just above his knees, while his bony white legs dangle beneath it. His face is smeared with charcoal and, in his left hand, he holds his shawm. He enthusiastically begins to pirouette around the hall before dancing out of the back door in the direction of the arbour.

He is closely followed by the younger members of the household, who mimic his actions. Finally, Brody emerges from the kitchen. She is grasping an extremely large pewter platter. We all strain to see what it holds but to no avail, as it's covered with a white linen cloth. Finally, Brody lays the platter before our lord and removes the cover. His delight is clear for all to see.

"Marchpane, my favourite. Brody, did you make this for me?"

"Yes, my Lord."

"Why, it's a work of art. You are very skilled. I just cannot imagine how many hours it took you to hammer the gold so thinly." Brody blushes at the compliment. "Gather around, everyone, I am going to break open the golden fetterlock." We all move closer and watch as he uses his eating knife to ease the sugary delight apart. "Brody, please be so kind as to cut this into pieces. I would like to share this with everyone."

Our lord's generosity is astounding. To share such a delicacy is beyond kindness. Seated, I wait for Charlemain to join me before I begin.

"Have you ever eaten marchpane before, Bethany?"

"Oh yes, but only once. My mother made it when her uncle visited us at our manor."

To this Charlemain nods and smiles. "Your uncle. Yes, he was a good man and indeed worthy of such an extravagance."

"Alas, I cannot remember him as I was very young."

"That's a shame. I will speak about him later, but, for now, let's just enjoy this treat."

As I take my first mouthful, I feel the smoothness of the almonds and sense the freshness of the rose water. Then, I notice the crunch of the sugar and the silkiness of the flattened gold. As far as I can remember, this is even better than my mother's.

As the light begins to fade, our lord sends out orders to his men to ready themselves and to bring his horse around to the front door. Turning to Lady Latimer, he smiles and says, "Elizabeth, I am sorry that I must leave tonight, but Sir William is expecting me and we have a great deal to discuss. Tomorrow, we are travelling to London together. We will gather men along the way and when we enter London, we will be a show of force to be reckoned with. I will not cower and I plan on letting everyone know that. I will fight where necessary. Latimer, I will meet you in London as agreed, but before that you need to strengthen the defences both here and at Fotheringhay."

Apprehension fills the air and I turn my face away, unable to watch our lord prepare to leave.

***

The morning breaks and it's time for us to depart. No breakfast is required as we are all still full from last night's feast. However, our bags are overflowing with food to eat along the way. Brody has provided us with bread, hard-boiled eggs and cold meat. After expressing our grateful thanks to Lord and Lady Latimer, we wave goodbye and walk away. We have not been walking for very long before Charlemain stops and turns to our party as a whole. With elaborate hand gestures, he calls everyone together. The look on his face is one of a man who has a secret to tell and can contain it no longer.

"Before we reach Saltrey and Prior Thorns Manor, I have a great surprise in store for all of you. We are to make a slight detour to the church of St Mary's at Houghton-on-the-Hill.

It's sometimes known as High-Town due to its position on rising ground. I can promise you that the views from outside are spectacular and when we go inside, even more delights await us. Every inch of wall is completely covered, from floor to ceiling, with the most magnificent paintings. They are inspirational, to say the least!"

Charlemain's excitement is infectious and has set the mood for the day to come.

As we walk, he continues, "In fact, the whole manor is ancient. Tales are often told of how it was inhabited when large mammoths roamed the earth. A time when we were joined to France and there was no sea between us."

As we approach St Mary's, it appears the same as any other church, but once inside its beauty shines brightly.

"I am heartened to note from your faces that many of you are interested. Would you like to learn more about the imagery within the church?"

Davy, animated as never before, answers before anyone else can draw breath "Yes please, Charlemain."

"Excellent, I had hoped that would be the case, especially as I have organised a storytelling session with John Ryder."

Looking around it's clear to see that, for once, everyone is enthusiastic. Strangely, the church somehow feels detached from the earth. I decide to take my cloak off as I'm warm from the climb. Others do the same. Agnes and myself now position ourselves towards the main decoration on the east wall. A thought comes to mind. The wall appears incredibly thick – thicker than I've ever seen before. They must be at least as wide as I'm tall. I also notice that there are two arches that have been hollowed out. As we chatter, John Ryder appears from nowhere. He is short and fat with puffed-out cheeks. His nose is bright red and he waddles as he walks.

"Good day, everyone. It's a pleasure to meet you all. Please draw close and get yourselves comfortable. For those of you who find it difficult to get down to the floor, I have two stools that you are welcome to use."

With this command, everyone follows John's advice. Everyone, that is, apart from Alard. I expect that this has less to do with being watchful and more to do with him not wanting to get his cloak dusty and creased. As expected, he has bagged one of the stools for himself. I smile to myself as Agnes commandeers the other. I'm not really sure that I like John Ryder. He seems rather pompous. In his left hand, he has a long willow cane, which he is now waving around to make sure that he has everyone's attention.

"Come on let's begin."

With these opening words, I decide that I really do not like him at all and, within seconds, he has launched into what I suspect is a well-rehearsed routine. His manner has certainly turned me off and I do not want to listen to him. So, I allow myself to slip off into a trance. I begin to look deeper into the paintings. Over the central arch is the Last Judgement – an image so powerful that I cannot help but review my life. Difficult questions pop into my mind. Have I always been kind and obeyed the Ten Commandments? This will take far too long to consider, so I decide that it will be the subject of my next contemplation, but, for now, I will return to the images before me and make the most of my time here.

Over the chancel arch is the Trinity. It depicts the Father, the Son and the Holy Ghost, all set within a triple mandorla. To the left are the souls waiting to be saved and to the right are the souls that have been dammed forever. How I wish to be saved. The thought of roaming around in heavy chains, among the hideously deformed, chills me to the bone. Further down the wall are the twelve apostles. From left to right, I recognise them all. Firstly, there's St Peter with his crossed keys. Then St Thomas, who's better known as Doubting Thomas, for he questioned Christ's resurrection. I scan the faces until I find my favourite, St Matthew. Somehow, he appears to be calling me. It feels as though his eyes are looking straight into mine. They appear as pools of light, reflecting images for me to decipher. I can see the image of an angel or is it a winged man? I am unable to tell for sure. I can also see God's chariot waiting to be pulled forward. There are four empty harnesses.

All of a sudden, the image is gone and I wake immediately. I realise that John Ryder has just finished talking and it's of no great surprise that he has produced a brown leather collection bag. I search for a coin and contribute readily to such a beautiful church, for I am leaving with precious memories.

At the foot of the hill, I notice a section of free-standing flint wall. It seems a little strange and does not appear to have a purpose. "Charlemain, please can you tell me about this wall?"

"Yes, of course. It's a way-marker. It's used by travellers to aid their passage. Please let me show you."

We walk over to the flint wall. "Now, mistress, if you stand in front of the wall, with your back against the flint, you will notice that the signs indicate that if you turn left, you will travel towards Castle Acre. Whereas if you turn right, you will travel towards Thetford. Ah… if only we had time to visit Thetford. It's a beautiful town. Compact, yet all encompassing. It has three friaries. One belonging to the Blackfriars, one to the Cluniacs and another to the Canons of the Holy Sepulchre. The latter is a most interesting place, as it's the starting point for pilgrimages to the Holy Land. It was endowed by William de Warenne just before he went off to the Crusades. The Lord de Warenne was a most generous benefactor as he also provided for a nearby hospital called 'God's House'. It's a little run-down now, but it's still used for its original purpose."

I take a moment to contemplate the Holy Land before returning to the here and now. "And the symbols, Charlemain, please can you explain these to me?"

"Ah yes… well, let's start with the one on the right. It's the Star of David and a symbol of hospitality. It has been used by the Knights Templar since the time of the Crusades. It indicates that all who arrive at the Priory of the Holy Sepulchre in Thetford will be provided for. They will be given food, drink and shelter. Then, on the left, we have a chalice. This is the sign of spiritual refreshment and the Last Supper, and it leads to Walsingham."

Excitement wells up inside of me.

Agnes calls to Charlemain. "Are we close then?"

"Unfortunately, not. We still have a long way to go."

"Oh dear, my poor feet. They are so sore and blistered."

"Well, at least we only have about three or four miles to go until we can rest. Luckily, the journey is all downhill and on flat ground. Prior Thorns Manor has a well-stocked apothecary, so, as soon as we arrive, I will get some foot ointment for you. This will hopefully ease your pain until someone can look at your feet."

On hearing this, Agnes nods and smiles gratefully.

Charlemain goes on to announce that by travelling directly to Prior Thorns, we will make a slight diversion and avoid Swaffham. "I hope that you will forgive me, but I think that it's wise to avoid Swaffham at the moment, as it's overly busy at the best of times with people constantly coming and going. Its market has an excellent reputation, but the town has very little else of interest and it always seems to attract the wrong sort. Our time will be better spent at Prior Thorns."

My mind immediately returns to Newmarket and to my ordeal there. I, for one, am glad to be avoiding Swaffham.

When we eventually near the large wooden gates of Prior Thorns, I notice how the torches burn brightly from within and how the brothers are standing ready to welcome us. I cannot help but wonder if they aren't expecting another party as they seem so formal. Within seconds, Davy has uncharacteristically broken from our group and is now kneeling before the prior.

"Davy, please rise. You do not need to kneel before me. I am your uncle and I love you wholeheartedly." Standing eye to eye, both men smile. "I have good news for you, Davy. I have a collection of letters from your mother. We have a great deal to catch up on."

Two holy brothers step forward to greet us. "Welcome," they chant in unison.

It's obvious that Charlemain knows them both very well. Smiling, he shakes their hands. "Please, Brother Luke and Brother Ackolyte, let me introduce you both to our party."

One by one, they shake our hands and talk at length about our travels. I soon decide that Brother Ackolyte is my favourite. He appears to be kind and gentle. His skin is the colour of olives and his almond-shaped eyes are dark brown. Brother

Luke, on the other hand, has ice-blue eyes that chill me to the bone. I swear that I can see right through them. His manner disturbs me, too. He laughs like an imbecile, but I must try not to judge him. Surely, Charlemain would not favour an idiot.

Once inside the gates, we're taken directly to the hall where refreshments have been provided. The coolness of the hall is most welcome after the heat of the day. How lovely – spiced buns are accompanied by a rich malty ale. Charlemain breaks the silence as he calls to Agnes.

"Agnes, I have not forgotten my promise to you. Brother Luke will collect you in a short while and accompany you to the apothecary. Brother Ackolyte will see to your feet while we are at evening prayers."

"The Lord be praised; I knew you wouldn't forget me." Agnes giggles.

After prayers, everyone apart from Davy returns to the hall and settles down for the night. The hall is very well lit with beeswax candles. The smell is delightful. Agnes returns after what seems an age with her feet bound with strips of fresh white linen. Pointing down to them, she proudly announces that she's been healed.

Charlemain, supressing a smile, explains that the brothers here take great pride in their preparations and that feet are their speciality. "They wash the feet of travellers before anointing them with hot oil. It's reminiscent of Jesus washing his disciples' feet. They offer this service to all who enter. If anyone else would like to partake, please do tell and I'll make the necessary arrangements."

This offer is far too good to turn down, so, after a brief discussion, we all decide that the best course of action is to stay for one more night.

"It's agreed then. Tomorrow, I will ask the brothers to treat us all. They will anoint our feet and we, in turn, will dedicate all our thoughts and prayers to St Thomas and St Philip. Indeed, this cleansing process seems fitting as when we leave here, we are to visit two holy shrines. The first being West Acre Priory and then Castle Acre Priory."

The thought of the priories excites me. I watch as Davy enters the hall. He has an air of confidence about him that I have never seen before. Crouching down next to Charlemain, I can see that Davy is pleased to hear of our extended stay.

The Holy Shrines of West Acre
and Castle Acre Priory

The morning begins with a great deal of hustle and bustle. The brothers certainly have their work cut out anointing all of us today, alongside all of their other tasks. So much so that Agnes and myself are enrolled in preparing strips of linen, while the rest of our group help to prepare the bread and the pottage. It would seem that pilgrims arrive at all hours of the day and night, and that most only rest for a short period. I try to focus on tonight's vigil, but I'm distracted by another group of pilgrims who have just arrived.

Something about their appearance intrigues me. They look so different to us. There are eight of them in total. Six men and two boys. Their clothes are heavily worn and faded. I wonder how the cloth was originally dyed green, as I can think no flower or herb that would produce such a shade of green. All of the pilgrims are tanned and have dark hair. The men wear traditional large-brimmed pilgrim hats, but the boys wear skullcaps. In my mind, I question why they wear such heavy woollen coats on such a beautiful day.

Brother Prior appears and is closely followed by Davy and a welcoming party. He extends his hand in friendship to one of the elders. "*Hola querido amigo.*"

I wonder what he's saying. In return, the elder smiles and utters the words, "*Gracias hermano, estamos muy agradecidos por su hospitalidad.*"

"Charlemain, I'm confused. I do not understand what are they saying."

Charlemain's face displays great awe. "Mistress, these pilgrims are from Santiago de Compostela in Galicia. They have walked through scorching heat, sailed stormy seas and travelled through foreign lands to reach here. Can you see their pilgrim sticks? Each has a scallop shell, marked with a cross, and a small leather bag attached. The shell represents St James."

"Charlemain, why do they wear such heavy cloaks?"

"I expect that it's cold here compared to Galicia."

From the look on Pip's face, he does not seem to be as enthralled by their presence. "Charlemain, I do not mean to be disrespectful, but I think that we should leave immediately after breaking our fast. This party disturbs me. How easy it would be for them to hide weapons beneath their cloaks and attack us."

"Yes, but the anointing and the vigil?"

"Both can be undertaken at West Acre Priory. I will ask Brother Prior to arrange it."

Charlemain's face becomes crumpled with sadness. "Very well, I agree. Our safety must come first."

"Charlemain, I am truly sorry. I do not mean to upset you and I expect that they are probably as they seem – pilgrims from Galicia – but as Brother Prior was not expecting them, they could be imposters."

Charlemain nods and takes his leave to tell the others about the changes. Then, before we leave, we break our fast together.

While doing so, a more cheerful Charlemain relays the story of St Thomas Becket's life. "He was quite a remarkable man. Both saint and antagonist. During our stay at West Acre, we will see their most sacred relic. His finger! We will also have the honour of lodging within their guest apartments."

Agnes and myself gasp with delight. I do not know if it's just in my mind, but today I feel lighter. I also have a bounce to my step that's been missing for quite a while. I also have no aches or pains. To our great surprise, Brother Prior announces that he is to accompany us on the next part of the journey, along with Brother Ackolyte and Brother Kenneth. Brother Kenneth is rather short and rotund, with short blond hair and dazzling green eyes. I notice that he does not have a tonsure and therefore has not been fully inducted into holy orders.

Walking together in a small group allows Brother Kenneth the chance to speak to me. "Mistress Bethany, how joyous to see such a spring in your step."

"Oh, Brother Kenneth, I'm so excited. I just can't wait to see the holy relic at West Acre."

"Indeed, I feel the same."

Sensing my chance, I decide to ask Brother Kenneth about his calling.

"As you can see, I'm still finding my feet. At present, I'm neither one thing nor another. Neither soldier nor clergy. For many years, I fought under the banner of Humphrey, Duke of Gloucester. He was a good soul and a generous patron. His death shook me to the very core and ever since I have been trying to find a place where I belong. All I know for certain is that I do not wish to fight again. But equally, I do not know if the holy life suits me. The brothers understand this and are immensely kind to me. They provide me with food and shelter. In turn, I carry out protection duties for, as you know, travel is never safe, not even for Brother Prior, so I accompany him everywhere. The relics also need protection. Most recognise them as being sacred objects, but others see them as a means of easy money."

I am fascinated by Brother Kenneth. His knowledge is really quite amazing.

"You see that wooden shack over there? That is one of many scattered across this region. If you keep your eyes open, you may be able to spot them, although most are camouflaged extremely well. Some are set on stilts, while others are hidden in trees. They are used as lookouts. For it's a wise precaution to see who's coming and going. Patterns come to light. People travelling on the same days of the week, at the same times, may be harmless, but you never know. Most journeys tend to be just regular visits to the market, but they can also be preparations for insurrections and war."

Not wanting to think about insurrections and war, I decide to change the conversation. "Brother Kenneth, my father also fought under the banner of Humphrey, Duke of Gloucester."

With a knowing smile, he replies, "I know."

With these two words, I realise that nothing about my life is a secret.

Our first stopping point is a crossroad where three trackways converge. Straight ahead, flanked by trees, is the track to Castle Acre. In the distance, I can just about see the castle standing proud and to the left is a track to the villages of South and West Acre. Unlike the one to Castle Acre, this track crosses open fields and appears quite flat. So, we are in for a pleasant walk. Shortly, we turn left once more and divert to South Acre. As we turn, I notice a small clump of trees. In their shadow is a small wooden shed. It stands on sturdy wooden legs and has a hatch, which is slightly open. From this distance, I am unable to see if anyone is within. I also notice that there are men tending the surrounding fields and that they appear to be watching us. It all seems so obvious now, but I still wonder how I did not see these sheds before Brother Kenneth pointed them out to me. This train of thought continues along the entire section of this walk. I wonder what else is right in front of my eyes that I'm not seeing.

The meadows here are beautiful and they gently slope down towards the bottom of the valley. To enter the priory, I realise it will be necessary to cross a small wooden bridge and a dry moat before entering the stone gatehouse. The gatehouse appears very grand and has three large shields above the entrance. I recognise the middle one to be that of the Earl of Warwick's, but I do not recognise the others.

"Brother Kenneth, I do not recognise the two outer shields. Who do they belong to?"

"Ah yes, they belong to the de Toni family. They founded the Augustine Priory just after the Norman Conquest. It's officially known as the Priory of St Mary and All Saints."

Brother Prior steps forward to greet the brothers who are now standing proudly on the steps. "Brothers Leon and Brother Theodore, how lovely to see you. Are you both well?"

Both smile and bow low.

Brother Theodore is the first to speak. "God be praised, there have been no incidents in your absence and the rhythm of life has continued as normal."

Brother Prior seems both pleased and relieved.

Once inside, the priory appears to be a self-contained village. It has its own church and an assortment of buildings. I think that there must be a north gate as pilgrims seem to be coming and going via that end of the complex. One group, who are preparing to leave, are barefoot, their boots hanging about their waists on long pieces of rope. I wondered how long it would be before I saw this. I already feel connected to these pilgrims and I wonder if bare feet would enhance my spirituality? I am pretty sure that Alard does not agree with barefoot pilgrims as he's shaking his head and muttering, "Madness, sheer madness."

I turn my attention back to Brother Theodore as he announces that the priory's main guest rooms have been prepared for us and that they are now ready to use. "Please follow me and I'll lead the way."

On opening my door, I am greeted by limewashed walls, which are the colour of wet sand. The colour is very comforting and made even more so by the hazy sunlight streaming through the part-opened shutters. A large bed sits in the middle of the room and, to my delight, it's adorned with fine white linen and plump cushions. Underneath the window is a large wooden box with a runner on it. The runner has been decorated with pale-blue flowers and golden crosses. Sitting on the runner is a large wooden crucifix, an illuminated manuscript and a carved wooden icon. The icon is beautiful. It consists of two oil paintings facing each other. One is of the Virgin Mary and the other is of Joseph. It is hinged in the middle with golden hinges and on the outside, there is gold leaf. I know that icons are used as an aid when praying, but surely this one is far too decorative to hold for very long. I would hate to damage it. The illuminated manuscript is also an aid to prayer. I hold it up and realise that it's the Lord's Prayer. This collection makes me think about my nightly prayers. Tonight, more than any other, I am looking forward to being on my own. The new candles in the wall sconces will provide a subtle scent and gentle light. For now, though, I must rejoin the others.

Downstairs in the panelled room, I find everyone apart from Agnes. Concerned, I ask after her welfare. Alard has a worried look upon his face. Weeks of travelling together has taught me the signs to look out for. When worried, he fiddles with his fringe. Brushing it from one side to the other and then back again. Suddenly, the door creaks open and, to everyone's delight, Agnes enters. She is accompanied on one side by Brother Prior and on the other by Brother Kenneth. Determined to make prayers and view the relic, she smiles as the brothers help her walk.

Inside the chapel, the air is hot and heavily scented. A mixture of rosemary and myrrh, I think. Brother Theodore shuffles past everyone with a stool and a cushion. He carefully places the stool as close to the altar as possible before indicating that it's safe for Agnes to sit. Then, he places the cushion on top of the altar. Even at this distance, I can see that it's heavily embroidered with three swords and the same amount of silver crosses. I believe that these represent the martyrdom of St Thomas.

Once we are all settled, Brother Theodore and Father Prior take their leave to collect the relic. The anticipation in the room is palpable. When they reappear, they are sombre with downcast eyes. Accompanied by brothers who are chanting rhythmically, they walk in line. Brother Prior is carefully holding a beautifully enamelled casket in his hands. It is shaped in the image of a tomb and is about two-hands long, one-hand wide and one-hand deep. It is obvious that none of us have ever seen the likes of this before by the collective gasps and, in one case, an expletive. God, please forgive Ned for his indiscretion, as from the colour of his cheeks, I can tell that he's mightily embarrassed.

When Brother Prior reaches the altar, he places the casket upon the cushion. All of a sudden, I understand. The casket must be a replica of St Thomas's tomb. How stupid of me not to realise.

Before speaking, Brother Prior bows low and crosses himself. "Children, please behold a holy relic of our Blessed St Thomas of Canterbury."

Looking around in awe, I try to gauge the others' emotions. It is only at this point that I realise that Owain and Davy are guarding the door to the chapel. They must have closed it silently when the brothers entered. Pip is now turning a very large iron key in the lock. We have now entered a world of silent contemplation, secure from any outside influence.

Brother Prior is now positioned directly in front of us and requests that we all stand in prayerful contemplation – that is, apart from Agnes, who he motions to with both hands.

"No, not you, my dear. Please remain seated. Just bow your head a little."

Brother Theodore is now weaving his way among us, inviting us to wash our hands with holy water as he passes.

Brother Kenneth is following closely behind with linen cloths for us to dry our hands. Once we have all been washed and dried, the brothers silently return to their places and Brother Prior begins again.

"My dear children, for special pilgrims, such as yourselves, I have gained dispensation from the archdeacon to open the casket and let you touch the bones of St Thomas. Brother Kenneth will proceed with the cushion and Brother Theodore will guide you in what to do, while I will intercede with special prayers. Mistress Bethany, I will pray that your impending blindness recedes and that your vision returns. Agnes, I will pray that your heart will regain its strength and that your health will return. I will also pray for those who are not here. I pray that Anne and Cecily's minds are freed from treachery and that they learn to judge situations better. For Ethel, that her recovery is speedy, so she can complete her pilgrimage to Walsingham and, last but not least, I will pray for all the men of your party. I ask that they remain strong of both body and mind and that God guides them as they carry out their duties."

A collective "Amen" is spoken. Brother Prior then carefully removes a long golden pin, which holds the jewelled top of the casket together. This allows both side panels to open downwards. Ceremonially, he removes a long oblong piece of bone. It's almost white and very porous at each end. Looking at it, I realise that this is very real, unlike those touted by the pardoners we have met along the way. Most of those are just charlatans, out to make a living from any old bones they can get their hands on.

To my surprise, I am the first person invited to hold the relic. Carefully, I cup both of my hands together to make sure that I do not drop it. Once in my hands, it begins to vibrate.

The sensation is so strong that I feel waves of pressure creeping up my arms. Closing my eyes tightly, I pray that my sight is restored. "Please, St Thomas, please heal my eyes, I beg of you. Please let me see clearly, if that is your will?"

Although, in truth, I hold the relic for just a few minutes, it feels much longer. When I open my eyes, Brother Theodore smiles at me and carefully removes the finger. I decide to screw my eyes up tightly and pray once more. When I have finished, I cover my eyes with both hands. Hopefully, any power that remains will seep through and my prayers will be answered. When I eventually open my eyes, I realise I have missed everyone else holding the relic and that the casket has been closed. The door is being unlocked and the brothers are departing. Somehow, I feel different now. Light-headed and whole. My vision appears to be much clearer and I can see a bright white light in the distance. Not wanting to draw attention to this, I sit and listen to Ned and Agnes talk. It would seem that they both enjoyed the experience. Now, Agnes is rubbing her foot in an attempt to heal it further.

When the time comes to leave, Charlemain appears by my side. "Shall we take some fresh air?"

"Oh yes, what a good idea."

As we leave, Brother Leon steps forward and hands us both a beautiful pilgrims badge of St Thomas. "Please accept this as a reminder of your visit."

I reach inside my satchel for a coin, only for Brother Leon to say, "That's very kind of you, but there's really no need." I decide to give the coin anyway.

Outside, evening has fallen and we cross the green to the hall. Inside, bread and turnip pottage awaits us. Charlemain and I recall the relic.

"You must have seen it many times, Charlemain?"

"Oh no, I have never seen it before. I have heard others describe it, but today was the first time that I witnessed the casket being opened in all my years and I doubt I will ever see it again."

As I eat the pottage, I cannot help but look around the hall. I am sure that I can see far more detail than before.

"I wonder why it was opened today then?"

"Who can say!"

We eat our evening meal in quiet companionship before retiring.

Returning to my room, I sit on the edge of the bed and recall the events that have just taken place. I attempt to understand how I feel. Such amazing experiences are always hoped for, but rarely ever happen, and I certainly never believed that they would happen to me. Sleep comes too soon. I had hoped to pray for a great deal longer, but my body is weary and my mind will not keep still. So, I remove my outer kirtle and slip between the sheets. I wonder if the relic has affected me as my mind is muddled. Memories of the day come back to haunt me. I question where the bright golden light that covered my face came from, and why my eye sockets are hot and tender to the touch. In a fit of panic, I clutch my satchel to my chest and ask God, "What's happening to me?" I cannot breath. I sit up and gasp.

A knock at my door makes me jump. "Who is it?"

"It's Pip, is everything alright?"

"Yes. No. Well, I don't really know. Please come in, I'm frightened."

Once inside, Pip closes the door. His face is taut with fear. "What's wrong? Are you ill?"

"No, I don't think so. I just feel very strange."

"I have some ale in my flask. Let's share it?"

I nod gladly, happy to have Pip's company once more.

After finishing the ale, Pip suggests that it's time for him to leave. "Alas, it's very late and the candles are close to burning out. I really must go now, but I'm only next door if you need me." With that, Pip bends down and kisses my forehead before leaving.

A Miracle Happens

The morning breaks in spectacular style. The birds are singing loudly, their joyful tunes complementing one another. To my surprise, the sunlight appears brighter than ever before and my eyes are unusually moist. I use my under-kirtle to gently dab them dry. In doing so, I notice that the sockets feel cool to the touch and that the heat of last night has vanished. I begin to sob uncontrollably. Not tears of sadness, but tears of joy. My lashes and cheeks are soaked within minutes. There is no other answer for it; a miracle has happened. I can see. I can see! For the first time in my life, everything is in focus. Nothing is smudged or distorted and the milky white mist that has always been there is gone. I resist the urge to scream and instead pace back and forth with speed. I begin to question myself. What if I'm wrong? What if this is just temporary? Surely it's not wise to mention anything yet. I rock my head gently from side to side before going over to the window. I need to clear my head before I join the others. I need to calm myself.

When I eventually enter the hall, I find myself on my own. Fortunately, there is still plenty of food for me to break my fast on. After a short while, Brother Palmer enters to clear the last of the remnants away. On seeing me, he turns and stares directly at me.

"Mistress, you startled me. I had not realised you were here. Are you happy for me to carry on clearing?"

"Oh yes, Brother, please ignore me. I'm nearly finished. I'll be gone in a couple of minutes." Something about Brother Palmer's manner unsettles me.

"I did not knock and wake you earlier, mistress, as I noticed that a light burnt in your room well into the early hours." His eyes question me. No doubt he wonders if I was on my own or if someone was with me. Smiling, I choose to ignore him and leave. Being able to see this clearly will certainly be a great help in the future. No doubt I will see many things that I did not see before and that includes people's suspicions.

Returning to my room, I quickly pack my belongings and return to the hall to meet everyone. How different they all appear today. I try desperately hard not to stare. As Charlemain approaches me, I realise that he is much older than I had first thought.

"Bethany, I have a favour to ask. Will you accompany me?"

"Of course, Charlemain, is there a problem?"

"No, my dear, not a problem, but I need to speak to you in private about a request."

As we walk, curiosity gets the better of me. "Where are we going?"

"To the infirmary, my dear, but please do not worry. In fact, I have relatively good news. At last, Agnes has given in and agreed to rest for a day or two in the infirmary. She is very tired, but her spirits are high. She has befriended a dear old soul already. Her name is Clarise and she must be at least eighty years of age, if not older. She was also on pilgrimage to Walsingham, but exhaustion overtook her. Alas, she is in a bad way and has lost all movement from the waist down. The infirmarer thinks that Clarise will live, but is at a loss over how to treat her. Next week she will be transferred to a local nunnery, where she will be well looked after. She will be comfortable there." Charlemain, noting the worry on my face, seeks to allay my fears. "Please, my dear, do not worry. Her future, likes ours, is dictated by the lord and he will call her home when the time is right. Until then, her life will be spent resting. She will have food, drink and a comfortable bed. The nuns are used to looking after pilgrims, especially those who are old and frail. They include them as much as possible in the life of the nunnery and, more importantly, they are kind and friendly. Clarise will be engaged in a life of offering up prayers. This is where you come in. Clarise has requested that someone complete her pilgrimage for her and, on hearing this, Agnes immediately mentioned your name. Clarise would dearly like to meet you."

This request warms my heart and I nod in agreement.

The infirmary is much larger than I expected and once inside, I realise that it is separated into two parts. Immediately to the left is the infirmarer's room where herbs hang from the wooden joists. The smell is magnificent. Rosemary is the dominant fragrance, although I can detect the presence of sage, thyme and fennel. In the middle of the room is a large wooden table, which is partially hidden under a mountain of linen bags. Pots of all different shapes and sizes are also scattered about. To my right is a finely panelled door, which Charlemain steps forward and opens. The atmosphere inside is tranquil. Truckle beds line the walls, while a roaring fire burns in the central hearth. The air is moist and beautifully scented with flowers.

"Yoo-hoo! Bethany, we're over here." Agnes and Clarise wave to get my attention.

I walk over and drop to my knees besides Agnes' bed. I notice immediately how her skin appears greatly improved and how her eyes have begun to sparkle again. She is cocooned within a sheepskin-lined truckle and covered with a linen sheet. Her hair gleams and her cheeks are pink.

"Well, what do you make of all this then? I'm so lucky to be here, don't you think? I'm warm and comfortable and I can rest in peace. In a couple of days' time, I'll be back on my feet and a pilgrim once more, although I have been persuaded to travel the last leg of the journey in a cart. I am in two minds about this, but – on balance – I think it's for the best. I'm determined to complete my pilgrimage and, for once in my life, I have decided to accept help. I'm sure that I will enjoy Walsingham far more when I'm refreshed." Hardly stopping to draw breath, Agnes begins once more. "Now, Bethany, please meet my new friend, Clarise."

Clarise raises her hand to shake mine, but her arm falls back to her side before I can reach it. Clarise's cheeks redden. "I'm so sorry, my dear, but I'm unable to control my body nowadays. Nothing seems to work in the same way as it did before, apart from my mind and my mouth – that's it. Thank the Lord I'm still blessed with these gifts."

Agnes indicates that she would like me to move closer to Clarise.

"Mistress Bethany, I hear good things about you and this warms my heart. I have been told that you are pious, gentle and kind. Good of heart and generous beyond measure. Therefore, I ask for your assistance. I am in dire need of your help. My time on earth is running out and I still have things that I need to do. I'm in no state to finish my pilgrimage, so please, I beg of you, could you finish it for me?" Tears erupt from Clarise's eyes and begin to spill down her cheeks.

Immediately, I take her hands in mine and lay a kiss upon them. "Of course, it will be an honour to finish your pilgrimage for you."

With a smile and a nod, Clarise visibly relaxes. "Thank you, Bethany, you will never know how much this means to me. Now, let me tell you what I need you to do. Time is running out even as we speak. When you arrive at Walsingham, please offer up my prayers at the Shrine of the Blessed Virgin and then light four candles. As you light each candle, please recite these words: 'Clarise remembers the days that have gone before and all those who have touched her life with love and joy. She thanks the Lord for keeping her safe and for guiding her along the way'. The candles are for my mother, my father, my husband and my child. After lighting the candles, please leave my donation."

I recite the words over and over again in my head, just to make sure that I can remember them.

"Now, Bethany, please can you get my purse for me? It's over there, on my belt."

Clarise's purse is well-worn and made from dark-brown leather. It has two large belt loops and a long leather strap for fastening it to her belt. On the top flap, a white rose has been added. The stitching that holds it in place is very neat. Whoever made it certainly had an eye for detail.

"Now, Bethany, please remove all the coins and count them carefully."

On opening Clarise's purse, I am surprised by just how many coins there are. Once counted, I have twenty shillings, but I count them once again just to make sure.

"Excellent. Now, Bethany, can you get my cloak? I need you to cut the bottom hem of it for me."

"Surely, I cannot cut your cloak?"

"Oh, but you must. You will understand why when you do so."

Lifting it, I am surprised by the weight – so much so that I am relieved to sit down and drape it across my lap. Cutting the hem with my little scissors, I try as hard as possible not to damage it too much, but the weight from within causes the lining to unravel and tear. All of a sudden, a great many coins begin to drop to the floor. Charlemain kindly stoops down and helps me collect them. To my surprise, Clarise's hem has yielded another twenty shillings. I just cannot believe how much money Clarise has been carrying around with her. Forty shillings! That amount could buy at least two horses.

"Now, Bethany, I need you to separate the coins into four piles. Please can you put fourteen shillings aside for the infirmarer and fifteen shillings for the nunnery. Ten shillings for the shrine at Walsingham and one shilling for you."

Shocked at such kindness, I hesitate. "No, Clarise, I cannot accept money for finishing your pilgrimage."

"Oh yes, you can, my dear. Agnes warned me that you would say as much, but it is my wish."

I look at the coin in my hand and accept it with grace and humility. "Thank you, Clarise. I don't know what to say. It's so kind of you."

"Bethany, you do not need to say anything. I am just grateful for your help."

With this, Clarise smiles before closing her eyes and drifting off to sleep. Agnes appears overjoyed.

"Bethany, you are a good soul and you have done a good deed today. See how Clarise sleeps. You have given her a great deal of comfort. Now, I would like to speak of my journey. As you know, I will meet you at Walsingham. I long for us to be together again, as I will miss you with all my heart." Agnes pats my head gently.

I can no longer hold in my news. "Agnes, before I go, I must tell you something. Now, promise not to shout loudly when I tell you."

"I shall try to remain quiet, but that all depends on how excited I get."

"Well, I believe that a miracle has taken place. After touching St Thomas's finger, I felt a strange sensation and then, after waking, I can see clearly. The milkiness has gone and everything is clear. I have told no one else as I am still in shock myself, but I wanted you to know before I leave. Now, I can read and write and see people's faces as never before."

Agnes places both hands over her mouth. I can see that she is desperately trying not to yelp with excitement. Her body begins to rock from side to side. Unsurprisingly, it takes quite a while for Agnes to still herself and let her hands drop to her side. Her face is beaming.

"That is indeed a miracle and one that I have prayed for ever since we first met. Purity radiates from you, my dear, and it touches the hearts of all those who come into contact with you."

Rising, I place a kiss on Agnes' forehead before she, too, falls asleep.

Charlemain, as kind as ever, touches my shoulder. "It's time that we leave; the others will be waiting for us."

As we approach the north gate, I can see Pip and the others sitting on a low wall. Before we reach them, Charlemain stops, places his hand on my arm and asks, "Are you alright, Bethany?"

"Oh yes, I was just thinking about Clarise and Agnes."

"Please do not fret, Bethany. They're in the best place. Agnes will rejoin us at Walsingham, God willing, and Clarise is at peace now, safe in the knowledge that you will complete her pilgrimage for her."

My mood begins to lift when Pip smiles at me.

"Are we ready to go Charlemain?" he asks.

"Yes, Pip. I'm sorry to have kept everyone waiting for so long."

"Ah… do not worry about that. Did all go well in the infirmary?"

"Yes, very well indeed."

"Excellent, let's go then."

Hearing this, everyone picks up their belongings and we file out through the open doorway. As we move away, we can hear the gates shut behind us and the heavy iron bolts being drawn across. West Acre is secure once more. It is unfortunate that I never got to say goodbye to Brother Kenneth or Brother Prior, but I understand that they had urgent business to return to and that they could not wait for us to return from the infirmary.

To take my mind off Agnes and Clarise, I decide to ask about the day ahead. "Well, Charlemain, where do we travel to today?"

Charlemain's excitement is clear for all to see. "Today is the easiest day of the journey so far, my dear. This track will take us directly to South Acre and then onto Castle Acre. It's only a short walk, but one that I love with all my heart. Today, we are free to stroll and enjoy this beautiful area."

As has become tradition, I accompany Charlemain – although, in reality, we all walk together, as our numbers have diminished even further. Now, there are only seven of us in total: Charlemain, myself, Pip, Owain, Davy, Alard and Ned. I am the only female remaining and I am acutely aware that I am being protected. I wonder if the letter in my satchel has become ever more important.

Towards South Acre

The walk to South Acre is as beautiful as Charlemain described. The small winding track is now edged with beautiful flowers that sway as we pass. Just in front of us is a large copse of trees and further on is a little wooden bridge, which crosses over the River Nar. As we walk through the dense undergrowth, I become a little frightened, as I can hear creatures scurrying about under the leaves, but luckily it's not too long until we emerge from beneath the canopy of trees. Once more in the sunshine, we are greeted by field after field of long grass. Each is peppered with pretty blue cornflowers and butterflies that dance from flower to flower. I can hear the bees gently buzzing as they dart around, collecting honey.

"Bethany, is it not as beautiful as I said?"

"Oh yes, Charlemain, it's quite breathtaking."

"I know that you will enjoy our visit to South Acre. There is so much to see and do, and the history in these parts is as diverse as anywhere else I have ever known. The very place where we stand now was a burial place many hundreds of years ago and although no one knows why this place was chosen in particular, it could be that the revered burials took place in the barrows and cairns to the west on the higher ground, and those of base parentage were buried down here on the lower ground."

"Charlemain, I have heard that the monks of Norwich hold a great many rolls relating to this area. I have often thought that I would love to see them. Just to gaze upon the intricately painted illuminations would be a dream come true."

"Bethany, once this pilgrimage is over, why don't you write a journal? Many noble women do so. I have heard that it's very fashionable nowadays."

"But Charlemain, I am not a noblewoman."

To this, Charlemain makes no comment and walks on. Little does he know that I have been thinking along the same lines. A journal is an excellent idea!

Charlemain continues enthusiastically, "Over there, by that large copse of trees, a magnificent fair is held each year on the Feast of St Bartholomew. Sellers from all over the country flock here to sell their goods. The fair raises much-needed funds for the poor souls of the local leper hospital."

I ponder on those pour souls. How awful it must be to be afflicted in such a terrible way. Then, even worse, to be shunned by society. Charlemain appears to read my mind.

"Yes, leprosy is a vile disease, but those who are afflicted must be isolated as it's highly infectious."

"I wonder, Charlemain, do you think that the monks are afforded protection from the disease by God?"

"Indeed, they must be, as it's rare for them to catch it."

Soon after crossing the River Nar, we reach the most handsome range of buildings that I have ever seen in my life. They are surrounded by a moat, which is even grander than the one at Bodney.

Charlemain proudly announces, "We are now officially in the manor of the Harsyck family. Have you heard of them?"

"No, I don't think that I have ever heard of that name."

"Well, they're an ancient family who have served this country since the time of glorious King Edward III – first as sheriffs of the county and then, much later, as trusted retainers in the retinue of King Henry V. Sir Roger Harsyck, who was the bravest of soldiers, served across the sea in France many times." Thoughts of Agincourt come to mind, as does good Duke Humphrey. "Today, we are going to observe prayers in the Harsyck's private chapel. The chapel is dedicated to the Assumption of the Blessed Virgin and is very fine indeed. It was built when the Harsycks became the local sheriffs and it's a great privilege to be invited inside, especially for the saying of prayers. Prayers are usually offered up for the locals and pilgrims alike in the parish church of St George. St George's is a most beautiful building in its own right. I'll take you there before we leave. It houses a sturdy Norman font, a finely carved rood screen, an unknown wooden effigy and a newly commissioned stained-glass window in the western wall. This sits above an effigy of Sir Eudo Harsyck, who lies atop a stone slab coffin. Sir Eudo was a member of the Knights Templar and he fought in the Crusades."

As we pass the church of St George, I notice that it stands proud. The old and new parts of the building complement each other perfectly. The north face is a vision of older grandeur, while the south face is newer, with freshly carved stone. No doubt it will begin to mellow in a few years and they will blend together perfectly.

Charlemain, noticing that my eyes rest on the tower, continues to tell me that the church houses a full-size brass of Sir John Harsyck and his wife, Katherine. "They are portrayed holding hands – something they will do for evermore. It would seem that they wanted everyone to know they loved each other so much that their love could never be broken, not even by death." With this, Charlemain goes silent for a moment. "Sadly, there is another effigy being carved at the moment, but I'll tell you about that later."

As we near the manor house, Pip takes the lead. He obviously knows the Harsyck retainers extremely well, for they embrace him as a long-lost brother. Once over the moat, I notice how the buildings have been arranged into two long lines with an entrance building joining them. Above the entrance, the family crest is carved into the stone. It consists of a plume of feathers, sitting within a hoop, attached to a helm. I am certain that I have seen this crest somewhere before, but I just cannot place it. To the left is an oriel window and to the right is the chapel. Behind me, I can see a kitchen block with smoke billowing from its roof, a collection of wooden sheds and a fine stable block. I am beginning to suspect that the Harsyck family may be the leaders of fashion in this area.

A nearby commotion wakes me and we all turn around to look. About ten paces away, a group of kitchen staff are crowding around the well.

"I told you, didn't I"?

"Yeah, Walter, that you did."

Our suspicions raised, we join the staff. A large man steps forward and bows low. "Please, I beg your pardon. We are overly animated I know, but one of our number, the cook's new assistant, young Hal, has infuriated us all. He is always playing practical jokes, but this time he's gone way too far. Earlier this morning, he took some of Jack's tools.

Not stolen, you see, just taken – to play a jape on him. Jack has now fallen behind with his work and is rightly furious. To make matters worse, Hal, in a state of panic, has thrown them down the well. Luckily, the cook observed the incident, so the tools can be retrieved, but I fear that poor Hal will pay a heavy price for his mischief this time."

Charlemain nods before taking my arm and leading me away towards the chapel.

"Oh dear… what do you think Hal's punishment will be?"

"I dread to think. Probably a stint of hard labour, but maybe that's what he needs. Perhaps turning a spit for hours on end over the hottest fire will make him think twice in future."

The chapel is cool and refreshing. Its walls are painted a very pale-blue and stencilled with white roses and golden feathers. Each wooden seat is capped with an embroidered cushion, the design mirroring that on the walls. Charlemain leads me towards the front and bids that I am seated to the right of the altar. The seats on the left are obviously reserved for the Harsyck family as they are intricately carved and have cushions portraying their crest. After a few minutes, two women and a man enter. We immediately stand out of respect. They walk towards us at quite a pace. The elder woman is wearing a dark-grey kirtle and a thick grey veil. Her skin is the palest that I have ever seen and her eyes are bright red. Realising this to be Lady Harsyck, I bow my head and curtsey as low as possible.

"Welcome to my home, Mistress Bethany."

Shocked at such recognition, words stumble from my mouth. "Thank you, Lady Harsyck."

"I see your shock, Bethany. You wonder how I know your name?" With this, a smile crosses her face and she indicates that I should sit down beside her. Leaving Charlemain, I sit to Lady Harsyck's left. "I have heard good things about you from a very reliable source. I know that you are loyal and extremely trustworthy, and that you hold confidences and are faithful."

"Sorry, mistress, but I am confused. I do not understand; how do you know so much about me?"

Lady Harsyck's focus shifts over my shoulder to Pip and Alard, who are now entering the chapel, kneeling as they do so to make the sign of the cross. "I know all this, my dear, as you are my son's friend."

Lady Harsyck's eyes suddenly grow moist as she beams with pride. Still confused, my eyes dart back and forth between Pip and Alard. Again, noticing my confusion, Lady Harsyck lays her hand upon my arm, before Pip approaches and embraces his mother. I smile with delight!

Everyone is seated before prayers begin. Lady Harsyck's attendants take their places alongside Charlemain, while Pip sits between his mother and myself. Still reeling from the shock, I find it hard to regain my focus, so I decide to concentrate on the family priest who has just entered the chapel from behind the altar. He is a rather rotund man with pink chubby cheeks. I know that my thoughts are a little unkind, but I am surprised to see that he can squeeze through such a small door. All of a sudden, the chapel has become warm from the heat of the bodies. I feel safe and secure. Prayers begin by remembering Sir Roger.

"Holy Father, we humbly remember before you Sir Roger Harsyck, our liege lord, a most generous and admirable man. A dearly loved husband and father. One who gave his life in service of our country. A man of honour and loyalty. Let us in Your mercy light candles in remembrance of him."

Calling us forward one by one, we are all invited to attend the altar. Lady Harsyck, assisted by Pip, is the first to do so, then Charlemain and each of us in turn. The heat from the candles intensifies the heat in the chapel further and I feel beads of sweat form on my brow. Embarrassed, I dab them away with a piece of linen that I keep up my sleeve. The service ends with the priest bowing first to the altar, then to a statute of the Blessed Virgin and finally to Lady Harsyck.

"Thank you, Father. We would be most grateful if you would join us in the hall, where we will dine early."

"I am most honoured, Lady Harsyck, thank you."

"Bethany, I would like you to join us, too."

Once again, the shock returns. A worried Lady Harsyck takes both of my hands.

"Why, Bethany, you look troubled. What's wrong?"

"Oh, Lady Harsyck, nothing's wrong. Please forgive me. I am just wondering if Charlemain and the rest of our party are also invited. I should not like to leave them."

"Of course Charlemain and the rest of your party are invited." Then, she pauses before wiping away her tears and replacing them with a smile. "Charlemain, my dear brother, has his own seat in the hall. Did no one tell you we are related? You must forgive my family. They are terribly forgetful and rather shy at introducing who they are. The only one who ever advanced himself was my husband."

The hall is dominated by a long slender oak table, darkened by many years of use. It has been finely decorated with a pale-blue linen runner, which is embroidered with the same white roses and golden feathers as the cushions in the church. Each place has been set with a pewter plate and an elaborately enamelled glass. At the head of the table, beneath a canopy of pale-blue silk, sit two large chairs. The canopy is very elaborate and edged with golden tassels. Unlike other halls that I have visited, each person has their own wooden chair and there are no benches in sight. Before we are seated, Lady Harsyck takes her place. She is accompanied by Pip. Father Robert sits immediately to Pip's left and Charlemain takes his seat next to Lady Harsyck. Charlemain beckons for me to join him, while Alard, Davy, Owain and Ned all take their seats alongside the other household retainers.

Charlemain is the first to speak, but in very hushed tones. "Bethany, I do hope that you can forgive me for not mentioning my family connections. I do not like to boast. I longed to mention it at West Acre, but Pip asked me not to. He was worried that it would change our friendship. He's a proud lad, you see. Kind and loyal. You'll never find another so passionate and protective. He's a superb soldier, too, and he's never been beaten in combat, but he's rather shy and unassuming at the same time. He's not one to push himself or his family forward. I understand that our lord also requested that no one was told of the family ties until we arrived at South Acre. He feared that if this information was overheard, we would become targets for abduction or maybe worse. Recently, my dearest brother-in-law, Roger, died in France. Killed by an enemy, but not a French one. He died at the hands of the Duke of Somerset."

My head begins to spin as I think of the treachery, so much so that I am glad to be distracted from my thoughts by a petite lady of a very great age, who is approaching us with a large jug of wine.

Charlemain smiles. "Thank you, Lily. Once you've finished serving everyone, please take your seat and enjoy your meal with the rest of us. By the way, where is Arthur?"

"As we have guests today, he's helping John serve the food. It reminds him of his youth and it gives him the chance to dress up. He enjoys passing on the customs he learnt in his youth."

"Very well. I just didn't want him missing out."

Realising that everyone is seated, Pip stands and strides purposefully towards the far end of the hall. Disappearing through the door on the left, he reappears a short while later through the door on the right. This time, he is accompanied by two men – one young and the other ancient. I think that the ancient one must be Arthur. He's dressed in a fine brown linen tabard and bright yellow hose. Across his left forearm is draped a piece of snow-white linen. His face displays a look of pride. Leaving them, Pip returns to his seat and requests that Father Robert says grace.

"Of course, my Lord. Without Thy presence, nought, O Lord, is sweet. No pleasure to our lips can ought supply. Whether 'tis wine we drink or food we eat. Till grace divine and faith shall sanctify. We ask for your dearest blessings."

At the end, Lady Harsyck stands. "Thank you, Father. Now, before we begin, I have an announcement to make. This feast, although small and intimate, is of great importance. Befitting of Pip's personality, I thought that he would appreciate a fine meal shared by his close family and friends. A large impersonal gathering would not suit him at all."

Pip nods and smiles before Lady Harsyck begins once more.

"Since the death of my dearest husband, I have been in consultation with our lawyers, planning for the next stage of my life. I am sure that you will all be relieved to know that I have no plans to remarry. I have no need of money and I require no protection. I have been blessed with an amazing son and our lord is most generous."

Pausing to wipe her eyes with a silk handkerchief and to look at Pip, she takes a deep breath before continuing, "My plans are really quite simple. I will continue to live here and everything will remain the same. No one should worry about anything. Pip is very happy with his life and he wishes to remain active in the service of our lord. His dedication knows no bounds; even at this most dangerous time, when war looms, he still wishes to serve. To this, I wholeheartedly agree. Although, as a mother, I fear for his safety, but I am aware that we must all do our bit. His career is progressing nicely and he reminds me so much of his father." Looking around the room, I can see a mixture of relief, tears and smiles. "Now, I must be formal for a while. Pip, please stand."

Standing shoulder to shoulder, the look of unconditional love between Pip and his mother is undeniable.

"Philip Harsyck of South Acre, I am extremely proud to announce to one and all that, as heir to Sir Roger, you are now the lord of this manor."

Immediately, a great roar erupts, which is accompanied by thunderous clapping. Pip's eyes meet mine and I can see immediately how uncomfortable he is. He looks sad and hesitant, but slowly he finds his voice. "All I can say to such a rapturous reception is that I promise to be a good lord, to care for you all, protect you all and continue to serve our lord and patron, Richard Duke of York."

Charlemain, noticing Pip's deep embarrassment, nods towards the back wall where Arthur is waiting for his orders. Standing, Charlemain announces that it's now time to eat.

"Arthur, if you would be so kind, I would like you to start serving, but first, please can I ask everyone to stand and raise their glass to the new Lord Harsyck?"

Another hurrah sounds.

After the toast, Arthur ushers in four kitchen maids. They are all carrying great platters of food. Today, there will be no distinction – everyone will eat the same. I notice how Lily refills the wine glasses before the cook, who is wearing a clean apron, joins the celebrations. Charlemain, noticing that Hal is missing, asks of his whereabouts.

The cook replies with a cheeky grin, "Oh, he's on his way," before bellowing out, "Come on, lad... don't keep us all waiting. We haven't got all day."

The door slowly opens and Hal enters the hall, wearing a particoloured outfit and a jester's hat. He has bells tied to his legs, arms and neck. Oh, how we all roar with laughter as he walks into the hall. What a sight to see!

"That'll serve you right, my boy. If you keep playing tricks on people, you'll stay in those clothes forever and a day, and always be seen as a fool. Now, sit, eat, drink and be merry."

Hal, who has quickly regained his sense of humour, begins to prance around. He leaps high in the air, before quickly spinning around and around. Seizing his opportunity, he cheekily kisses each lady on the cheek before sitting down.

"Oh, dear," says the cook. "This may have backfired."

Laughter sets the tone for the rest of the celebrations.

A smiling Pip leans forward. "Are you having a good time, Bethany?"

"Oh yes, Pip. What an amazing celebration."

Immediately, I put my hand to my mouth.

Pip looks concerned. "Bethany, what's wrong?"

"I'm so sorry. I should not address you like that now."

"Oh yes, you should. My title will only be used for necessary formalities, not by my close friends and family. Nothing must change between us."

Relief floods over me as I realise just how much Pip means to me.

The feasting lasts long into the evening with music, singing and dancing. Ned, always one for a party, is now free to play to his heart's content, while Owain recites stories of valiant battles. Hal, loving his new role, is also taking every opportunity to entertain. Alas, such joy cannot last forever and as darkness falls, the festivities begins to draw to a close. After everything has been cleared away the household retainers take up their nightly positions. I watch as they settle down for the night. This leads me to wonder where I can curl up to sleep. Pip, reading my mind, once more takes my hand.

"Oh no you don't, you're not sleeping in the hall. You're coming with me." Pip stoops to pick up my satchel. "Mother has had the main guest chamber prepared for you."

I gasp in amazement. "No, Pip, really, I'm perfectly happy to sleep in the hall with the others."

"We know you are, but, as a trusted family friend, it's only right that you have your privacy."

Realising that it's folly to argue with Pip, I follow behind as he leads me up a winding stone staircase. When we reach the first level, we leave the stairs and pass through an elaborately carved stone archway before passing through a narrow corridor. On our right, there are doors leading to the bedchambers, while on our left there are openings that look down onto the hall. We are nearly at the end of the corridor before Pip comes to a halt.

"This is your room. I hope you like it." By the beaming smile on his face, I imagine that he knows what my reaction will be when the door is opened. Pip steps aside. "Here you go."

As I open the door, I immediately lose my breath. After what seems an age, I begin to take it all in. "Oh, Pip, it's the most beautiful room I have ever seen in my whole life."

"I'm so glad you like it. Mother will be overjoyed when I tell her in the morning. Now, goodnight, Bethany. Sleep well and I will see you in the morning. If you wake early, you are very welcome to go for a walk in the inner bailey. You are safe here."

As we gaze into each other's eyes, I feel a connection like never before. In my mind, I ask myself: why does this moment ever have to end?

The room is exquisite and incredibly hard to describe. In truth, I do not know where to begin. I will start by describing the walls. They are painted a vibrant shade of red. Some have gold feathers stencilled onto them, while others have the family crest. In the middle of the room, there is a large four-poster bed with rich velvet hangings. The beams above are decorated with gold leaf and there is a fireplace set against the outside wall. Its beauty is overwhelming. On closer inspection, I realise that the fireplace is surrounded by small green and blue glazed tiles, some of which have the family crest embedded into them. I turn to the window to inspect a small writing desk and a large wooden chest. Both are painted a myriad of colours and both glisten in the candlelight.

I notice a curtain in the farthest corner of the room. I walk over and draw it aside. To my delight, there is a private garderobe, a bowl of steaming hot water and some linen wipes. Keen to make the most of this experience, I remove my cloak and set my satchel down on the floor next to the chest. Even though I am tired, I wash my hair and sit by the fire until it dries. I watch as the flames dance gently. Memories of my mother flood over me, as this is something that we always did together. Before retiring, I change into a clean linen under-kirtle that has been left out for me. The cold linen makes my skin tingle. Even though I am safe, I cannot break the habit of sleeping with my satchel. I place it carefully beneath the sheets, before gently kicking it to the bottom of the bed.

***

Morning begins with a knock at my door.

"Who is it?"

"It's Lily, mistress."

"Oh, please come in, Lily."

"Good morning, mistress, I trust you had a good night's sleep?"

"Oh yes, I slept like a log."

"Well, that's music to my ears. I always worry that I've forgotten something. I've just come to let you know that it will soon be time to break your fast in the hall. A bell will ring shortly, announcing that the food is about to be served."

Lily smiles as she turns, before closing the door. When the bell rings, I throw back the covers and retrieve my satchel. I know that we are safe here, but I would still prefer to take it with me. Dressing quickly, I leave and make my way to the hall. The first person I meet is Charlemain.

"Good morning, Bethany. Did you sleep well?"

"Oh yes, Charlemain, I had a splendid night. Did you?"

"Indeed, it was lovely to sleep in my own bed for once. I fear that I'm getting too old for all this travelling, but never mind that. It's time to break our fast and, let me tell you, our cook always does us proud."

The hall looks magnificent once more. Every inch of the long slender table has been dressed in fresh white linen, which drapes down to the floor. Bunches of white roses and blue cornflowers now line the length of the table and each windowsill. The door arches have been decorated with yet more white roses and blue cornflowers, all of which have been tied together with gold and silver ribbons. The enamelled wine glasses are now joined by small individual pewter plates.

"Shall we take our seats, Bethany?"

As we pass, I gaze at the vast array of breads that have been prepared. I notice that all of the crusts have been removed to make them easier to eat. Next, there's a platter of roast meat, which has been decorated with saffron and madder jellies before a plate of salt eggs and a variety of cheeses. Some of the cheeses are soft, while others are hard, but the most succulent-looking has delicate blue veins running all the way through it. Pip is the last to enter the hall. He appears refreshed and ready for a new day. Once settled, he turns to Charlemain.

"Uncle, would you like to lead? Alas, Mother is not up to joining us this morning."

"Of course, Pip. Let's get started."

Charlemain nods towards the back of the hall in Arthur's direction and he approaches enthusiastically. Stopping directly in front of Pip, he bows as low as his old bones allow.

"Lord Harsyck, how can I be of service to you?"

"Arthur, please can I have a bowl of oats cooked in milk and topped with honey?"

Arthur, having anticipated the answer, holds his hands aloft and taps the floor with his foot. Without hesitation, the kitchen door opens and John enters, carrying a bowl, which he places on the table next to Arthur. Arthur then picks up the bowl and places it before Pip.

"Mistress Lily will be so happy that you asked for your childhood favourite."

"Well, Arthur, no one can cook it in the same way as Lily does."

Arthur now turns to me. "Mistress Bethany, what would you like?"

After thinking for a moment, I request a slice of thick white bread with some ham and a spoonful of saffron jelly.

Arthur calls forward an elderly maid. "Alice, please would you be so kind as to get Mistress Bethany's breakfast for her?" It seems a little weird to be served by someone of such a great age, but I can see that Alice is pleased to serve.

Before turning to Charlemain, Arthur seems to remember something. "Mistress, please forgive me, but I completely forgot to say that Lady Harsyck would be most grateful if you would join her in the solar once you have eaten. She asks that you do not rush. Just finish you breakfast and then call for me when you are ready and I will take you."

By the time my food arrives, Pip has finished his bowl of oats and is ordering a large plate of everything. Leaning over, he explains, "There's nothing to worry about, Bethany. In fact, very far from it. Since my father's death, my mother has been withdrawn. Her maids are constantly worried, as is Father

Robert, but since your arrival, she appears much lighter. Our visit has given her something to think about. When I was a child, my parents would love to entertain a great deal and I think that last night did her the world of good."

After breaking my fast, I am ready to visit Lady Harsyck. "Charlemain, please can you help me? How do I call for Arthur? I'm ready to visit Lady Harsyck now."

"Don't worry, Bethany, I will call Arthur for you and he will take you to the solar."

The solar is yet another magnificent room. Bright and airy with velvet drapes and sunshine pouring in through the large window. As I enter, Lady Harsyck rises from her window seat to greet me. Her outstretched arms fill me with joy.

"Thank you for agreeing to sit with me, Bethany. Did you enjoy your breakfast?"

"Oh yes, I had bread, ham and saffron jelly."

"Next time, you must try some of Lily's hot oats. They're Pip's favourite, you know, but I forget myself. Let's sit and be comfortable."

With this, Lady Harsyck points to two plump cushions. As we sit, side by side, tears begin to roll down Lady Harsyck's face once more.

"Oh, Bethany, please forgive me, but this is the worst time of the day for me. When my dear husband was alive, we would always sit together and welcome in the day. We would plan what needed to be done and then allocate the tasks. We've never been distant from our household; in fact, we have always taken pride in our closeness to everyone. We're more like a big family. After allocating the tasks, we would always potter in the garden. Oh, how we loved to change things around. We would mirror the latest fashions from France or Flanders. Then, we would plan with the gardeners how to rotate the crops to make sure that there was always plenty of fresh food to go around. We would often laugh and say that we had enough food to withhold a siege for months on end. Now there is no laughter and I am mostly on my own. I am blessed, though; Jack and Walter help me with the garden and we never go without. However, no one can help ease my heart. I sit here for hours on end and worry every day about the impending war. It's bad enough losing my husband, but I could never bear to lose any of my children. That would be too much to bear. I would have nothing to live for. I would die."

Gently, I take hold of Lady Harsyck's hand and we sit in peace. Lady Harsyck looks tired and drawn and my heart breaks for her.

In an attempt to lighten the mood, I ask, "What is your favourite task now?"

This was very clearly the right thing to ask. "Oh, I love to weed around the flowers. I find it very satisfying. When I'm finished, everything is neat and orderly. I can lose myself for hours on end. Bethany, please let me show you."

Within seconds, we are on our feet and heading out in the direction of the walled garden. When we arrive, Lady Harsyck knocks on the door and it opens promptly. Inside, I am greeted by immaculate hedges and raised flower beds, all of which are overflowing with flowers. Various scents waft gently on the breeze. I notice that in the farthest corner there is an arbour, covered with pink honeysuckle.

"Shall we go and sit? I want to enjoy your company for a little longer. I dread you all leaving, as I will be on my own once more."

A thought pops into my head. "Lady Harsyck, why don't you join us on our pilgrimage?"

She smiles for a moment, before speaking, "Alas, I cannot. I must stay here and play my part. I must prepare for war. This house is to be used as a safe refuge. It must be kept in readiness at all times."

We sit silently, drinking in the beauty of the day until Pip arrives. Without speaking, we both look at each other and know that it's time for me to go. Kneeling, Pip takes his mother's hand.

"Please forgive me, but we need to leave. I have some urgent business to attend to at Castle Acre."

With sad eyes, Lady Harsyck nods. "Very well, I knew this time would come. It has been wonderful having you at home, even for such a short while. You are my world and you mean everything to me. Take care and come home safely."

"Of that you can be assured, Mother dear." Pip kisses her hand and rises, before addressing me, "The others are ready and waiting. Have you got everything, Bethany?"

"Oh yes, I'm packed and ready."

"We must be off then."

Before we leave, I turn and face Lady Harsyck. "Thank you so much for my stay. I've had a wonderful time and I will miss you so much."

"I will miss you, too, Bethany. Now, remember, you're always welcome here. Should you ever wish to stay, there's no need to let me know, just turn up."

To hide my tears, I bow my head and check my satchel. After a moment, the tears stop and we walk away. Pip, obviously sad at departing, draws his hood firmly over his head and retreats into his own world. We wave one last time before walking on purposefully towards Castle Acre.

In just a short while, we are treated to our first view of the east end of the Cluniac Priory of Castle Acre. It rises dramatically above the town walls. Even from this distance, the stone looks to be of an excellent quality and not dissimilar to that of Ely Cathedral. The leaded windows glint in the mid-morning sun, while panes of coloured glass tantalise the senses.

Charlemain, having regained his composure, breaks the silence that has followed us ever since leaving. "It's beautiful, isn't it?"

"Why yes, but I never expected the priory to be so grand. Please do tell me some of its history."

"Well, to tell the history of the priory, I need to tell the story of the De Warrenne family, and to do so, I must wait until we arrive."

With my mind pleasantly imagining the joys to come, we continue along the grassy path until we come to a ford. The area around the ford is very beautiful. Rushes bend this way and that in the gentle breeze, while butterflies and small birds dance from stem to stem. The water is crystal clear. So much so that I can see bright-green mosses and tiny fishes. Before I know it, a bright-blue flash passes before my eyes. Charlemain, seeing me wobble, chuckles out loud as he extends a hand to steady me.

"Ah… we are blessed today. Did you see that flash, Bethany? That was a very rare bird indeed and one that rarely comes inland. It's known by three names. Firstly, the kingfisher; secondly, the halcyon; and thirdly, the sea foam. It's a sight to behold with its magnificent blue and green plumage."

I smile with excitement and scour the area for another flash. Alard, not caring for the bird, is preoccupied.

"It's not just the kingfisher that moves fast, Charlemain. I hear that the River Nar is swollen further upstream. Some say that it is twice as deep as normal." Scratching his head, he continues, "Pip, I'm concerned. We have two options that I can think off. We can either walk through it as normal or we can turn around and take the long way."

To this, Owain gasps. "Can't we just walk through the water? Then we'll have plenty of time in Castle Acre."

Alard, sensing an alternative motive, turns to me. "Bethany, what would you prefer to do?"

I think for a few moments. "Well, I'm happy to take a risk. My feet are still sore and the water may help to soften them."

Alard nods and we all walk on. Crossing the ford, however, is much harder than I anticipated. The water tugs at my legs relentlessly and I'm surprised by just how much energy I need to stand up. Luckily, I am surrounded by strong men who can help me. Owain, being the closest, realises that I'm struggling and offers to help.

"Bethany, please, let me help you." Standing by my side, he plants his feet slightly apart. "Ready. One, two, three."

Then, with one sharp tug, I lurch towards the opposite bank and dry land. Once we are all safely across, Owain takes up the lead with all the enthusiasm of a child, before Pip clasps a hand upon his shoulder.

"Owain, we must report to the priory at once and settle ourselves in. They are expecting us."

I can see that this is not something that Owain wants to do and that he is a little frustrated. I wonder why? He's usually so happy.

We are welcomed at the priory by an extremely cheerful brother, who introduces himself as Roger.

"Welcome, friends. I hope that you enjoyed your short walk from South Acre. At this time of the year, there's so much to see. Wildlife abounds and the river is full of fish. Speaking about the river, I was not entirely sure that you would be able to cross the ford today. It can be quite difficult when the Nar is flooded. In fact, the rising water is playing havoc with everything around here, especially our outbuildings." With this, he points towards a stone building in the distance. "You see that building over there? Well, that's where the washing is done. The only trouble is that when the river is high, the dirty water has nowhere to go, so it comes directly back into the room. Brother Johnson, who is prone to complaining at the best of times, has not stopped moaning for days."

I suspect that this situation amuses Brother Roger, as he tries but fails to suppress a huge smile. Pip, stepping forward, embraces Brother Roger in an affectionate way. Both appear very emotional.

"Oh, Roger, it's been such a long time. Are you well? I had not expected you to be on door duty. Is everything alright?"

"Oh yes… well, no, not really. Things haven't been too good here since our father died. Brother Mark is constantly biting my head off and making me do the most menial tasks. He takes pleasure in embarrassing me. He is convinced that now you have been acknowledged as the new Lord Harsyck, you will pay for my advancement over his."

"Why, that's rubbish. You joined the church of your own free will. You sought the life of service and contemplation. You didn't join to become an abbot, even though you would make a very fine one."

"Every word that you say is true."

Pip's face darkens. "Well, if Brother Mark wishes to make an enemy of me, he has succeeded. I will not stand by and see you treated in this way. I do not like bullies."

"Oh, Pip, no one could wish for a better brother than you. You have always looked after me, but please try not to worry. I'm sure that you have more than enough on your plate at the moment. Overall, I'm very happy. I enjoy my life and Father Abbot has given permission that I can visit mother whenever I have any free time. I'm sure that things will improve."

"No, Roger, this situation is not right. I have always respected your calling, even if I do not understand it, but I will not stand by and let this situation carry on. You would be far better off at home, looking after mother. You have skills that others do not readily possess and people respect your judgement. The manor needs your steady hand. Please think about it for my sake. I have no alternative as lord of the manor and I cannot change my lifestyle. I am, and have always been, a soldier. Nowadays, Prince Richard needs me more than ever and I will not desert him."

"I can see that it makes sense, but I need time to think. When you return from Walsingham, I will let you know my decision. Just please don't mention it to mother, as she will get overexcited and put pressure on me to return home. This is something I need to do for myself. If I decide to go back, it will be a huge change to my lifestyle and I need to make sure that I can handle the pressures of outside life once more."

With a nod, Pip agrees to his side of the bargain.

The ensuing silence is broken by a very enthusiastic Owain. "Hello, Roger. Oh, come on, Pip. Let's get settled into our lodgings."

Pip's face becomes increasingly hard to read. "Yes, let's make a move, but, Owain, I want to be very clear. I know what you're planning. It's plastered all over your face, but remember that you are my man and that I'm now the lord of this manor. You must be above suspicion at all time. Your actions must be true and honourable. I'm aware of the dicing and the gaming that takes place in the back room of the Speckled Lamb. So, listen to me when I tell you that I strictly forbid you going anywhere near that place. Father was tolerant, but me, not so. I really don't want such an inn on my land and I intend on closing it down later today. However, this information is strictly confidential for the moment and you must mention it to no one. I'm going to see the landlord before we leave for Walsingham. No doubt he will plead poverty and beg me to change my mind, but my decision is final. I'm also going to demand that he leaves the manor immediately. I have arranged work and accommodation for him in London, in the hope that I can keep a better eye on him.

"One of my spies has been observing the inn for almost six months now and has reported that the landlord seems to be acquiring a great deal of money. This concerns me greatly, as I have also heard that since my father died, he has changed allegiances. He has plans to make the inn a safe house for supporters of our queen. I will not allow this to happen under any circumstances. I will crush him before he has the chance to destroy us. He thinks that he has been clever. He thinks that I do not know of his plans, but I do. He has been seen smuggling people in and out of the quayside at night. I am determined to stop this immediately. Therefore, I have ordered that the quaymen are to work both day and night.

They will take it in shifts to keep a lookout. They are to check every piece of paperwork thoroughly and if they have any suspicions at all, travellers are to be refused entry. I have also requested that loyal men are to be stationed along the entire length of the riverbank to make sure that no one attempts to come ashore further upstream. In addition, I have ordered that all groups of pilgrims are to travel via the main roads. I fear that groups of pilgrims can be infiltrated far too easily. They are still to be welcomed, but everyone must be visible at all times. Old Jack will take over the inn. His wife will provide good food and clean lodgings. Later today, I will also give the orders to dismantle the quay. I can also see no need for it. We have no market and the castle has fallen into ruins, so it makes sense all round."

Owain, now embarrassed by his plans, appears sheepish, although it only takes a few seconds for his smile to return. "I hear what you say and I will obey, but it's such a shame that I could not visit one last time. Ned and I could go and see how the land lies."

Pip, halfway between consternation and frustration, reluctantly agrees. "Alright, but just once, mind you. I trust you both implicitly. I always have and I always will, but you are not allowed to game. By all means partake of the ale one last time and keep an eye out. All I ask is that you gather as much information as possible and report back to me before nightfall. Be careful, though. Do not ask any questions. Just note what's happening and keep alert at all times."

Owain and Ned smile and bow respectfully to Pip. We turn and begin to walk, but before we can progress in the direction of the priory, a figure dressed all in black comes into view. He is marching at top speed, diagonally across the field, in our direction. His face is contorted with anger and his eyes are flashing with unconcealed rage. Ignoring us, he immediately launches into a blistering attack on Brother Roger.

"Can you not be trusted with even the simplest of tasks?" The severity of his words and the excruciating embarrassment is far too much for Brother Roger to bear. Tears immediately erupt from his eyes and pour down his face. "Brother, stop that now. You are weak and I will not tolerate such weakness."

Before Roger can draw breath, Pip explodes with anger. Stepping out from behind Owain and Ned, the man in black, who I presume is Brother Mark, freezes in terror. From the look on his face, it is clear that he did not see Pip before.

"Why, Lord Harsyck, please accept my apologies, but I did not see you there, otherwise I would have greeted you sooner."

Pip's face, now purple with rage, scowls. Ignoring Brother Mark, he turns and nods to us as a whole. "Come, we will proceed. Roger, please can you convey us as planned to our lodgings?"

Walking away, we leave Brother Mark alone, shaking. Our route to the lodgings is a pleasant one. Charlemain, keen to regain normality, points out the fish ponds and the vegetable beds as we pass. As we approach, I can see the stone arches of the washing building more clearly. It seems that the washing duties have been moved outside due to the flood, as brothers dance merrily in half-barrels filled with water. They appear to be pummelling the contents from one side to the other.

A laughing Charlemain asks, "Bethany, have you ever seen such a sight before?"

"No, never, but I have washed linen this way myself. When my mother was alive, she taught me how to use hot water, urine and ash to get the linen white. It was a rather smelly task and it made my feet sore, but it worked."

"Yes, it's not the most pleasant thing to do, but the ones in the tubs have it far easier than those who rinse it, don't you agree?"

To this, I look sympathetically at the brothers, who are standing in the water, some up to their waists, rinsing the linen.

"Alas, when the river is swollen, there is no other way. Thank the Lord it's not winter."

In the distance, we can hear the priory bell calling the faithful to pray. Momentarily, we stand aside to make way for the brothers of the wash house. Looking over my shoulder, I can see that Brother Mark has caught up with us.

"Brother Roger, come, you are to accompany me."

Pip, still furious, turns in confrontation. "No, Roger, you will not be joining the others at prayer today. You are to remain with us. I need your assistance. Please deliver us to our lodgings."

No further words are required and Brother Mark leaves of his own accord. The priory's lodgings are on the south side of the complex and, as such, they are bathed in the midday sun. Two storeys high, with newly carved stone mouldings, they appear very fine. At ground level, there are two small windows, while, above, stands one large window that dominates the entire wall. Each window has been glazed with a mixture of blue and green glass, before being finished off with a fine stone moulding. Gargoyles grimace down grotesquely at those standing below. Amusingly, one appears to have been carved in the image of Brother Mark!

In my mind's eye, I imagine Father Prior standing stately by the window, surveying the comings and goings of the grand north gate. I do not have to imagine him for very long, as Father Prior appears from a nearby doorway.

"Welcome, everyone, welcome. I am so glad to see you. Refreshments are waiting for you. Please come in." Then, without any warning, he lurches forward and hugs Pip enthusiastically before quickly moving backwards. "Please forgive me. I am too familiar. I forget myself and, in particular, Pip's new title, but it's hard to change the habits of a lifetime. I have known Pip for many years, you see. In my past life, I was a professional soldier. I have fought alongside both him and his father. Now though, he's the lord of the manor and I have to remember myself."

Pip beams. "Father Prior, there's absolutely no need to ask for forgiveness. In fact, I am the one who should be thanking you. I am heartened that you treat me in the same way as usual. Nowadays, with this title around my neck, it can be hard to distinguish true friends. People speak such fine words, but I find myself doubting their hearts. Whereas with you, I have no such worries. Speaking of doubts, I need to speak to you about Brother Mark."

"Yes, I thought that you might. I, too, have my doubts about him. Recently, I have noticed a change in him. He has begun to harbour grudges. In truth, I am thinking of sending him on a pilgrimage to Jerusalem. A spell of hardship will do him no harm. The rough seas and the flea-ridden ships will make him grateful for his life here."

A thoughtful Pip agrees. We carefully climb the dark, winding staircase to Father Prior's chamber where refreshments have been laid out for us. On a large oak table, bread and brie sit alongside strawberries and lettuce.

"Shall we begin? There's little time to waste. We must

eat everything before it's ruined by the heat. When we are finished, I will call for Brother Mark. He will then show you to your rooms. Afterwards, we will meet and enter the priory together, and then we will view the arm of St Philip."

On hearing Brother Mark's name, Pip immediately begins to shift from one foot to another. Agitated, his face begins to twitch.

"Why, Pip, have I said something to displease you?"

"Sorry, Father, but my blood boils as soon as I hear his name. When we arrived a short while ago, he was immensely disrespectful towards Roger. He made him cry. Sorry, but there is nothing holy about him. He's a thug and a bully. He uses his position to terrorise my brother and no doubt anyone else that he comes into contact with. I cannot forgive him this time. For once, I have managed to catch him red-handed. You should have seen the shock on his face when he saw me. His anger blinded him. He had no idea who was in the group. I hate to think of how many times he has done this before and got away with it."

Father Prior's shock is overwhelming as he steps back and lowers himself into his chair. "Lord, forgive me. I am mortified. I have failed in my duties. I knew that Brother Mark suffered from false pride and that he had developed ideas above his station, but I never guessed that he treated anyone in this manner. Why has no one told me of this before? If I had known, I would have done something. He should never have been allowed to get away with this." Looking around, Father Prior calls for his attendant. "Joseph, please go and bring Brother Mark to me at once. Tell him that it is urgent." Turning to face Roger, Father Prior asks him to step forward. "Roger, why did you not mention this to me before?"

Alas, this is too much for poor Roger and he begins to sob uncontrollably. Shaking his head, Father Prior continues, "Pip, if you will allow me to deal with this, I will ensure speedy retribution."

"You are most welcome, Father. In truth, if it were left to me, I might do something that I might regret. Holy cloth or no holy cloth, no one bullies my brother and gets away with it."

Pip's words chill me to the bone. Almost immediately, Father Prior rises and goes to the door. After checking that the landing is clear, he closes the door firmly.

"Pip, I have another problem. I was going to speak with you later, but now seems as good a time as any. To my great regret, I believe that the priory has been infiltrated by a Lancastrian spy. If you permit, I would like to deal with both issues at once. The person I suspect goes by the name of Brother Stanley. He arrived unannounced about four weeks ago. His papers were incomplete and his story seemed a little far-fetched, but as he wore the cloth of our house, I took him in and secretly sent word to the Prior of Shrewsbury, as that's where he's purported to come from. Up until now, I have not received a reply. I also suspect that Brother Stanley wears a weapon beneath his robes and this, coupled with the fact that there have been strange comings and goings in the village, worries me. In addition, he appears to have befriended Brother Mark. Only the other night, I saw them creep out of the main gate and disappear in the direction of the Speckled Lamb. My spies in the village also saw them and, on their own initiative, followed them until they disappeared into the back room of the inn. Stanley appeared much later, holding what appeared to be a roll. Sensing that he had been followed, he quickly disappeared down Pudding Lane in the direction of the church. Later, he was discovered sheltering by the porch. My spy remained out of sight and observed him lift his habit before secreting the roll in his hose. I'm sure that we all know that brothers do not normally possess hose. Cluniac rules permit that only a habit and sandals are to be worn unless dispensation is sought."

Pip seems relieved. "Father, by telling me this, you have inadvertently confirmed information I received yesterday. This matter requires urgent action. I need to act quickly. Bethany, you must go with Charlemain. Roger, take them to the main guest room. Once inside, lock the door behind you and let no one in. I will come as soon as I can." Pip's face is now grave. "Alard, you must throw away any refreshments that are now left in this room. Now, Bethany, what I am about to say will shock you, but there's no choice. From now on, you will never sleep on your own again. I will always sleep in your room with you. A wooden bed placed in front of the door will act as a barrier should anyone try to enter. If Brother Stanley is a Lancastrian spy, it's possible that we are being watched."

Quickly, we depart from Father Prior's room, but, to our dismay, as we reach the main guest room, our way is blocked. In front of us, Brother Mark is shouting at both Brother Joseph and Brother Stanley.

"No, Brother Joseph, I will not go to Father Prior immediately. I have things to do; can't you see that I'm busy? And you, Brother Stanley, why are you here? You have no duties here at present."

Brother Mark's words have stunned Roger and he is now frozen to the spot. Charlemain nudges him none too gently in the back and we attempt to move forward. If only we could get inside the main guest room and lock the door, we would be safe. Stepping aside, we attempt to avoid Brother Stanley, who is standing with a thunderous look on his face. I wonder to myself if they really are friends.

Brother Mark begins once more, "Be gone with you, Brother Stanley, and remember to only participate in the tasks that I specify. You will do as you are told or pay the price."

Brother Stanley's eyes flash with rage and, to our surprise, he quickly grasps the hem of his habit with one hand, before reaching underneath with the other. He produces a dagger, the blade of which reaches Brother Mark before any of us can move. Roger automatically lurches forward and grabs at Stanley's wrist. The shock causes Stanley to drop the blood-soaked blade. More brothers join us from seemingly nowhere and quickly restrain Stanley, tying his hands and feet together with the cords from their habits. Being a caring soul, Roger immediately falls to the floor and begins attending to Brother Mark's wounds.

"No, go away. I can look after myself, I do not need anyone."

We watch as his dark blood streams onto the floor.

Brother Mark, relenting a little, states, "Well, if you must help. Get me some clean linen and then summons Brother Apothecary. Quickly now."

Even when wounded, Brother Mark is completely despicable. I can look at him no longer. So, I turn my attention back to a now-gagged Brother Stanley, but I keep being drawn back to Brother Mark. Writhing on the floor in the manner of the devil, I conclude that he's an evil person through and through, and not one that deserves to be saved. Roger, having a pure heart, cannot help but act out his Christian values and sends word to the apothecary. Nervously, I tug at my sleeves while surveying the scene. I am increasingly confused and I sincerely hope that more help comes very soon, as I'm not too sure how long Brother Stanley's restraints will last under such force. Matters are made worse by Charlemain, who is now shouting loudly at Brother Mark. He is demanding that Brother Mark remains as still as possible to stop the flow of blood, but I fear that Brother Mark has descended into madness.

"Stop struggling, you fool. You will bleed to death."

However, Brother Mark seems blind to Charlemain's instructions. It would seem that he has revenge in his heart as he slides across the floor through the pools of sticky blood, before trying to fling his body on top of Brother Stanley.

"You have betrayed me." Then, without warning, he begins to tear violently at Brother Stanley's habit. "You do not deserve to wear the robes of this house. I will rip you to shreds for what you have done to me." His fury knows no bounds and only subsides once Stanley is naked and covered in blood.

Charlemain, in a state of shock, begins to scream, "I know who you are, you dog. I recognise your scars and that old wound in your belly. You are no brother of this house. You are Alan of Scarisbrick. May you go to hell and burn in the eternal flames when you arrive there."

Confusion descends even further when Pip, closely followed by four castle guards, rush up to the scene. Quick in their actions, they remove the naked, bound and gagged Alan of Scarisbrick, while Brother Apothecary attempts to staunch the flow of Brother Mark's blood.

"My, oh my, he's lost a great deal of blood. Brothers, please help me. He's nearing death."

A mortified Father Prior now runs to join us before falling to his knees. Clasping his hands in prayer, he screams, "God forgive me, I am a fool. I let both a bully and a known murderer make this priory their home. My foolishness allowed this to happen." Panting hard, Father Prior turns to look at us. "Please forgive me, you should never have been placed in such danger. I was a fool. I allowed a suspect to walk freely within this priory when I had suspicions. It was foolhardy to do. Pip, do you think that he is part of a network?"

"Yes, for certain, and it is now my job to track them down. I have already sent word to South Acre asking for as many healthy men as possible to join us, but the first thing that I need to do is to shut down the Speckled Lamb and flush out whatever scum resides there. Uncle, can you accompany Bethany as normal? Why should she suffer because of all this? Bethany, I would like you to continue as normal. It pains me that you had to witness such a violent incident. I want you to rest and be looked after, but not before you are treated to a private viewing of St Philip's arm. Rest assured that no one will hurt you. Brother Stanley was the only new arrival in years. Now, I must go." For a split second, Pip smiles.

Deep within the priory, the feeling of sanctuary returns. It is cool and silent. Approaching the high altar, I can feel the warmth of an inordinate number of candles. Charlemain leads me to the right, down a step and through a very small doorway. I cannot help but think of the pilgrims that have travelled this way before. Indeed, their feet have worn an indentation into the stone step. Once inside, Charlemain leads me down yet more steps.

"Bethany, are you recovered?"

"Yes, I think so."

"Are you sure?"

I nod, not wanting to speak of the incident.

"Now, let's be seated."

We take our stools, opposite Father Prior's chair. The beauty of the crypt astounds me. Charlemain nods to Brother Redbeard.

"Brother, now we are settled, please can you bring the blessed arm to us?"

Brother Redbeard bows slightly and walks towards a glass-fronted cabinet, which is located at the foot of the altar. Opening the door, he reaches inside and carefully removes the relic. My heart is pounding with anticipation. Unlike the holy finger of St Thomas, St Philip's arm is black and shrivelled. I wonder what the black part is, before it suddenly dawns on me that it is dead skin. A wave of sickness passes over me. I am glad that I am seated.

"Please let us pray before I tell you a little of St Phillip's life. God grant that our hearts are open to your love. Let us live this day without fear. Let us also pray for the newly invested Lord Harsyck. Lord, please guide him and protect him as he endeavours to rid us of murderous enemies."

At the end of the prayer, sweet music brings us back to the present. St Philip's arm is now resting directly in front of us on a white silk cushion.

"Now, Bethany, let me begin. We are in the presence of the blessed arm of St Philip the Apostle. As one of Jesus' apostles, his calling was to go out and preach. This saw him travel far and wide. He was also present at the Last Supper when Jesus was betrayed. After Jesus' crucifixion, St Philip was reluctant to join the other apostles. He preferred to travel on his own, telling everyone how Jesus fed the 5,000 with just five loaves of bread and two fishes. He converted people everywhere he went, for he carried love in his heart. His message was so powerful. Alas, his life was cut short and he was martyred in the city of Hierapolis. Crucified. A true believer to the end, he continued to preach until his dying breath. Even when others were cut down from their crosses and released, he demanded that he be left on the cross to die. When his body was eventually taken down, his skin was so burnt that it was stuck fast to his bones. Despite this, his body has never truly decayed. To this day, his nails still grow! After his death, miracles began almost immediately. The powers that be tried in vain to destroy his body and, to this end, he was beheaded before being laid to rest in Hierapolis. Many years after his death, the lord sent a message saying that St Philip's relics should be recovered and distributed across the Christian world. It was at this point that St Philip became synonymous with the sign of a basket full of bread – meaning that even in death, he has continued to spread the message of redemption through Jesus Christ."

Stunned, I sit and absorb Charlemain's words.

"Now, Bethany, you have a choice to make. Father Prior has given special permission for you to touch St Philip's arm if you desire, but think carefully before you accept. If you touch the arm, your prayers will have a greater intensity. Not just for now, but forever. Remember, miracles do happen."

After a few moments, I decide that I would like to touch the arm. The blackened flesh unnerves me, but the thought of my prayers having a greater effect outweighs any concerns that I may have. "I would be honoured to touch the arm of St Philip. I would also like to light candles around it. Not for me, but for Clarise. I would also like to leave one of her coins, if that's possible. I promised faithfully that I would complete her pilgrimage for her and I'm sure that she would have touched the arm if she could."

"Bethany, what a lovely idea. I will arrange for the candles to be bought to us."

Although I am fearful of touching St Philip's blackened skin, I shut my eyes and recall Clarise's words. I am anxious to get them in exactly the same order. Then, fumbling inside my satchel, I feel for my purse before removing one coin. When I am ready, I nod to Brother Redbeard, who begins to chant. His voice is beautifully pitched and it produces a haunting melody. St Philip's arm is now in front of me. I stretch out my hand and allow my fingers to brush against it. Immediately, I feel a rush of energy course through my entire body. The shock makes me want to move away, but I remain still. I struggle to find the right words to describe what's happening to me. A bright white light has exploded somewhere in my head and silver stars now blur my vision. As they begin to fade, another light explodes. This time, its bright blue and accompanied by small blue teardrops. These also begin to fade after a few minutes. Then, by way of a miracle, when I open my eyes, my vision is perfect and everything is in sharp focus! I cannot believe it. I close my eyes again and shake my head. Then, I close each eye in turn to check my vision. My body begins to shake. Charlemain, ever loving, holds my hands.

"Bethany, has a miracle happened? Can you see? Please tell me."

"Yes, Charlemain. I can see. It's a miracle!"

With this, we both sink to our knees and sob uncontrollably. Brother Redbeard smiles before removing the arm and carefully placing it back inside the glass-fronted cabinet. Turning to us, Brother Redbeard's speaking voice is very different to how I imagined. It is low and rough, with an accent I have never heard.

"Mistress, can you hear me? Mistress, please do tell. Has a miracle taken place?"

Through my sobbing, I manage to answer, "Why, yes, it has. I can see sharper than ever before." Then, realising I had told no one but Agnes, I turn to Charlemain. His old eyes are now red. "Please forgive me, Charlemain, for not mentioning it before, but after touching St Thomas' finger at West Acre, my sight was much improved. But now, it is even better, and I can see everything as clear as day. First there was energy, then there were stars and then there were white and blue lights. Oh, Charlemain, all of my prayers have been answered and the strangest thing is that I wasn't even asking for myself. I was concentrating on Clarise."

"Bethany, in my experience, that is so often the case. God gives us what we need, not what we ask for." With great excitement, Charlemain helps me up. "Come, we must visit Father Prior immediately. He must know about the miracle. His clerk will have to record all of the details and there are, no doubt, procedures that we will need to follow."

Outside, the light is blinding and I immediately shield my eyes. As I wobble, Charlemain catches me. "I expect that everything will seem very strange for a while, but I'm sure that you will get used to it in time."

"Oh, Charlemain... I feel like I'm walking on air. It's a wonderful problem to have."

As we enter Father Prior's lodgings, we are greeted by Alard and Davy, who are guarding the building. Happy to see them, I try not to stare. I wonder if they can guess what has just happened to me and I wonder if my eyes appear different to them. If so, nothing is mentioned. They just smile as we pass. Only now, on our way to the prior's room, do I remember the events of the day. Alan of Scarisbrick, Brother Mark. Blood and terror.

At the Abbot's door, we are met by Owain. He is standing guard and has a sulky look on his face.

"Why the long face, Owain? Has there been any further trouble?"

"No, Charlemain, I'm just disappointed, that's all. I had been looking forward to a good few games of dice and the best ale in the area for ages."

"Well, we could always arrange a game here, as long as there is no money involved. Would that help your mood?"

"Yes, that would be fun. It's not the gambling, you see. I just enjoy beating everyone." Owain's smile returns as he opens the prior's door.

Inside, Pip and Father Prior sit opposite each other across a large oak table. As we enter, they both stand. Father Prior, ever keen to make us comfortable, pours us each a large glass of red wine, while Pip draws forward two stools.

"Now, I propose that we leave the events of the day behind us. We have done what we can. I am keen to hear of Bethany's experience. Did you touch St Philip's arm?"

Charlemain, bursting with enthusiasm and unable to remain silent, begins immediately. "There has been a miracle! God, be blessed! There has been a miracle! Bethany can see! She can see clearly! Her eyes have been healed!"

Father Prior's shock is palpable. Standing, he turns this way and that, then calls loudly to Owain. "Owain, please go and fetch my clerk immediately. Alard and Davy will be protection enough."

Without another word, Owain runs off into the distance. Father Prior's shock has turned to panic. Sitting, he takes a large gulp of his wine. "My, oh my. It has been many years since a miracle has taken place at Castle Acre and I need to record every detail. I will get Johnson to prepare a document for the archbishop's delegation. By chance, they are residing at Walsingham as we speak. Archbishop Thomas must hear of this tonight."

After what seems hours of questioning, Johnson is ready to leave. All that remains is for Pip to seal the document. Going over to the fire, he melts a handful of small wax beads in a golden spoon until they bubble. Then, he carefully places a pool of hot green wax onto the end of the parchment. Before it cools, both Father Prior and Pip use their signet rings to mark it.

"Johnson, I wish you God speed. The horses and Brother Redbeard await you at the front gate. Deliver this to no one but Archbishop Thomas. Brother Redbeard will do the rest. As he witnessed the miracle, he can recount it in detail. Then rest and return tomorrow."

After Johnson departs, we all sink into our seats and let out a collective sigh before Father Prior speaks. "Today has been a good day. We have much to celebrate. I will send word to the kitchens. Tonight, we will feast on roast rabbit and pike with garlic sauce, but before that we must rest."

Charlemain, remembering his promise, announces that he has promised Owain that there will be gaming and music tonight.

A joyous Pip replies, "For once, we can let Ned loose to make as much noise as he wants."

To this, we all laugh before leaving for our individual rooms. I am glad to be escorted by Pip, but then I remember that we are to share a room from now on. As we walk, I take delight in Pip's features. Before, I found it almost impossible to see his face clearly. Now, I can see that he has a strong jawline, a sturdy nose and pronounced brow ridges. His eyes are a deep shade of brown and they shine like the sun. It crosses my mind that I have no idea what I look like. I have never used a hand mirror before. The distortion has always been too great.

Once inside our room, I ask Pip about Roger. With a worried expression, he turns to face me. "When I last saw him, he was shaking so violently that he could not stand. Fortunately, Father Prior has agreed that he can return home to the manor for a while. He will be far better off with mother and she will be glad of the company. It will give him time to think about his future. Today has been very trying, but at least it's bought events to a head. I have been worried about him for months. The last time I was here, he stubbornly refused to let me intervene, even though things had deteriorated. At least his nightmare is over now. Brother Mark is dead and I suspect that there are few, if any, who will mourn his passing. Alas, my headache continues, as my men spotted two of the queen's spies roaming behind the church this morning. They disappeared before my men could apprehend them, but let's not think about the past. Let's look to the future. I am so happy that you can see. It must be a very strange sensation. Did you ever have good sight?"

"Yes, when I was small, but the shock of my mother's death changed everything."

"Well, now you have a second chance. Have you any idea what you would like to do in the future?"

"Well, I should like to keep travelling. Maybe I could visit all the shrines in England or perhaps I could join Duke Richard's household."

To this, Pip beams. "I would say that the latter is a most worthy thing to do."

After resting, we set out for the hall. As we approach, we can hear Ned singing at the top of his voice.

Pip is the first to speak, "Ah yes... Ned is in fine form tonight. I understand that his mood was boosted even further when Owain told him about the games. I know that I shouldn't, but I felt very mean for closing the Speckled Lamb before they could play one last game of dice. I had no choice, though. I would have been negligent to ignore what my spies had reported."

In the hall, we are greeted by Owain, Davy, Charlemain and Alard. They are all seated on the floor, surrounded by dice and cups.

"Are you going to join them for a game, Pip?"

"No, that would be unwise. I will just observe from a distance. How would it look if the brothers saw their new lord of the manor dicing?"

"Oh yes... I hadn't thought of that."

I cannot say when the others retired, but Pip and myself leave the hall soon after the brothers retreat to the chapel for evening prayers.

"I fear that there will be many a sore head from tonight's entertainment, but at least they are happy," Pip says.

"Pip, do we have a long walk ahead of us tomorrow?"

"Oh Bethany, please forgive me. In all the excitement, I failed to mention my plans for tomorrow."

I can see from Pip's face that something is amiss.

"After consulting Father Prior and identifying Alan of Scarisbrick, I have decided that to carry on by foot would be unwise. Therefore, I had Johnson send a letter to Brother James Longhorn at the House of the Friars Minor. We are to travel to Little Walsingham directly. As it is still quite a distance, I have arranged for us to ride. The horses will arrive in the morning. But if you would prefer not to ride, I could arrange a cart for you?"

"Oh no, I'm more than happy to ride." Far from being disappointed, I am ecstatic!

***

The morning is dry and sunny once more, and the sunshine floods the room. I rise early, forgetting that Pip sleeps on a bed by the door. He wakes up with a start.

"Oh dear, Pip, I'm so sorry. Please forgive me. I completely forgot that you were here. I'm just so excited about the day ahead that I cannot sleep. Never in my wildest dreams could I have ever imagined that I would ride into Walsingham. To enter on a horse is beyond words!"

Pip's face glows as he rises and stretches. "That's music to my ears, for I had feared that my decision would ruin your experience entirely."

"What do you mean 'ruin it entirely'?"

"Well, when you started out, you had no idea of your family's connections or that you were being shielded. Then, when we met, I was guarded, fearful of attack and not overly friendly with anyone. Then, what with Duke Richard's letter and all, I was worried that you would dread the very sight of me."

Walking over to Pip, I cannot help but reach out and touch him. It seems the most natural thing to do. In turn, he pulls me close and holds me against his chest, so close that I can feel his beating heart. How I wish we could stay like this forever, but, alas, we must leave.

Outside, all of our things are packed and ready to go. Charlemain then leads us to the stable block where the horses are waiting for us. Most are bay with white markings, but in the end stall, I spot a grey one. I just cannot resist taking a peep. On closer inspection, I notice that his front legs are slightly darker than his body and that they are dappled. His ears are bolt upright and his eyes are inquisitive. I enter carefully and stroke the entire length of his neck. He appears to be a gentle creature. I doubt that he is likely to bite or shy away.

Charlemain approaches. "I see that you have made friends already. I think this one is called Eric."

"What a strange name for a horse."

"Yes, I agree, but it sort of suits him, don't you think?"

Laughing, I rub his ears. "Well, Eric, what do you think of your name?" To my surprise, he starts to whinny loudly, starting the others off. "Oh, Charlemain, I do hope that I can ride Eric?"

"I can't see any reason why not. Here, let me help you up."

Once aloft, I realise that Eric is far taller than I had imagined. Squeezing my legs gently against his belly, I ask him to move forward. He does this without a problem. So, I decide to see if I can stop him as easily. Again, he responds to the pressure from my legs.

"Charlemain, I think that Eric will be the perfect companion."

With that sorted, I ask Eric to walk on into the yard before dismounting. As we make our final preparations, I am alarmed to see that everyone is wearing swords.

Pip, noticing my alarm, speaks, "Danger still abounds, Bethany. Those spies I mentioned yesterday have been seen again." Unfortunately, his words are cut short as a filthy female beggar, with straggly hair and muck-stained hands, has seemingly appeared from nowhere. Now directly in front of me, the beggar raises both of her hands in a claw-like fashion before lurching straight towards me. I feel her rough nails pierce my skin and I immediately drop to the ground and curl into a ball. Fearful that she will blind me again, I hold my head as I rock around. Before I know it, the beggar has climbed on top of me. She is not overly heavy, but I cry out in pain. She begins to pound my body uncontrollably with her fists. The pain is intense and the smell of her body is putrid. I gag uncontrollably until bile fills my mouth. I roll over to release it as Owain drags her away.

Still lying on the ground, I watch in terror as a bald man dressed in dark red approaches Pip. His body moves slowly as his fat moves from side to side. He is so close now that I can see his eyes. They are black and guarded. His jowls sag and his mouth is twisted in anger. Shockingly, he changes direction with an unexpected stealth and grabs my satchel. I foolishly lurch towards it and feel the full force of his boot for doing so. My cheek burns with pain.

Then, in a split second, Pip runs him through with his blade before kicking him in the ribs. Both Davy and Alard leap forward and tie his hands securely behind his back. Pip's face is angrier than I could ever have imagined.

"Take him to his master, Alan of Scarisbrick, and find out what they know. I have seen this man before; he is one of the queen's puppets. Let's keep him as bait and see if the queen actually cares for him."

As the man is lifted from the ground, blood gushes from his thigh. Pip orders that no mercy is shown to either, only that the man's wound is staunched. "We don't want him to die as dead men can't talk – and keep that witch in a separate cell. I'll decide what to do with her later."

Kneeling by my side, Pip slides his hand around my waist. "Come on, let's get you standing. Owain, can you get a stool?"

The shock is unbearable and I struggle to comprehend what's just happened.

"Bethany, I am so sorry. I failed you. My spies should have known where those two were hiding."

Looking into Pip's eyes, I protest, "You haven't failed me. Far from it. Your quick actions saved my life."

"Yes, but if I had known, it would never have happened."

"Oh well, it has and we must move on. I don't want it to ruin Walsingham."

"You are right; we must move on. Now that those two dogs have been dispatched to the dungeons, let's rest a while as we'll soon be on the road again. Before we go, I have good news. The situation has changed once more. Others are to join us on our journey to Little Walsingham and it's my job to afford them protection."

All of a sudden, I'm confused. "Who are these people and why are you smiling? Surely if protection is needed, then that's a bad thing?"

"Not always, have a look over there."

I follow the direction of Pip's hand and I am shocked by what I see. Two carts are approaching. I strain to see inside them and I am overjoyed when I see both Ethel and Agnes sitting upright!

"Well, Bethany, I always promised you that we would enter Walsingham together and I would never lie to you. You never doubted my word, did you?"

I am unable to hold back the tears any longer. "Oh, thank you, Pip. This is the best surprise that I could ever have. Never once did I allow myself to imagine that we would all enter Walsingham together. I never thought it would be possible."

"If I'm completely honest, neither did I, but with Scarisbrick and his sidekicks under armed guard, I doubt that any of his followers will be foolish enough to attack us now. Without their leader, they will be forced to regroup and wait for another leader, meaning that we are free to ride at a gentle pace."

Ethel, now greatly recovered, is gently lifted down from her cart and placed alongside Agnes in hers. Overjoyed, they hug and kiss each other.

"God be praised! I thought that we would never see each other again."

"Neither did I. We have much to catch up on."

Walsingham Awaits

Pip, eager to leave, calls to the others. "We will journey in twos. I will take the back with Davy, while Ned and Owain will travel either side of the cart. Bethany and Charlemain will be towards the front and, Alard, would you be so kind as to lead?"

As we pass the castle, I look down from the bridge onto the quayside where men are happily dismantling the wooden struts of the quay and sorting them into piles. Pip's instructions were obviously very welcome and it would seem that peace has returned to the people of Castle Acre. A place that I will always hold dear to my heart; a place that has given me back my freedom.

The hours pass and the shock of events at Castle Acre fades. The countryside is beautiful and riding Eric is such a joy. Eventually, the Friary of the Friars Minor comes into sight. It is only now that I truly realise how much clearer my vision actually is.

As we wind our way through the narrow lanes, I gaze upon the pretty flowers that cling to the stone walls. They are small and delicate and they move gently in the breeze. As we approach the friary, my stomach leaps with excitement and it seems an age before the large wooden gates are opened and we eventually enter. Inside, the grounds are beautifully manicured and I long to explore, but I must wait patiently until the gates are shut tightly behind us.

After dismounting, I rearrange my kirtle and my coif before rubbing Eric's nose. Then I watch as Ethel and Agnes are carefully lifted to the ground by Alard and Davy. They are laughing like little children. What a pleasure to watch their joy. Shakily, they are helped into the main building and eventually to their seats in an extremely large reception room.

As I enter the room with Pip by my side, I am astonished by the number of candles. There must be at least one hundred, maybe even more, and the heat is stifling. Needless to say, this heat pleases both Ethel and Agnes, who are now basking in the glory with their shoes off. I turn this way and that to get my bearings and, as I do, I notice that a great many seats have been prepared around the hearth and that there is food a plenty. My stomach lets out an enormous growl. Mortified at this, I can feel myself beginning to blush.

"There's no need to be embarrassed, Bethany. My stomach feels the same, but before we can sate ourselves, there is one very important task that we must complete."

With this, Pip takes my arm and gently leads me away from the others and towards a long narrow passageway. At the end, there is a heavy door with strong metal fixings. Pip knocks five times in rapid succession. From within, I can hear the bolts being drawn back. I contemplate on why such security is needed, especially within a friary.

As the door opens, I feel a ripple of shock run through my entire body. In the middle of the room, there is a sturdy oak table, which is dressed in pale-blue cloth and decorated with white roses. In front of the table stands a man who I presume to be the guardian of the friary, as he is not dressed in robes.

"Bethany, my dear, you are most welcome to our house. I hear that your journey has been most eventful."

I smile cautiously and nod in agreement.

"I can see that you are most anxious. Pip, shall we conduct the business of the day and then Bethany can rest?"

"Yes, that's a most excellent idea."

With these words, the locks are secured once more before Pip walks towards me and stands by my side. Turning, I notice that Brother Guardian has approached a curtain in the far corner of the room. Purposefully, he grasps the heavy material and draws it back with one sharp tug. I immediately fall forwards, only to be saved by Pip's strong arms. I can hear my name piercing the air.

"Bethany, oh Bethany, my dear child." Before I know it, my father is standing directly in front of me. "My dear child. You are safe. I have been worried sick. I thought that I would never see you again."

Tears are streaming down his cheeks. Immediately, he lifts his hands to wipe them away. Suddenly, I notice that his wrists are cut and bruised. He has dark-red marks cut into his skin. Alarmed, I reach out for him.

"Father, what has happened to you?"

Arms outstretched, he embraces me and I feel like a child once more. "Oh, Bethany, it's a long story." Chairs are bought to us. "Let's sit a while, I need to gather myself."

As we take our seats, our eyes never leave each other and our hands remain locked together.

"Bethany, please forgive me, for I have lied to you. I never wanted you to go on a pilgrimage, but it was the only way to get you to safety. It broke my heart seeing you leave our village without so much as a kiss goodbye. However, I knew that it was the only way. I couldn't take the risk of being seen. Spies may have been watching and I didn't want them to see that I was sending you away. The signs aren't good. War fills the air and it's only a matter of time until blood is shed. Believe me when I say that I never wanted that blood to be yours. I have been trying to shield you your whole life. I know that my actions have seemed cold at times, but that is very far from the truth. I have lived in fear since your birth. For your lineage brings danger. A Mortimer by birth, you are kinswoman to the Duke of York." My father stops only to draw breath and to cross himself. "A true and valiant man, but one who is in constant danger." I sway in shock. "That letter that you carry. Please can I have it?"

Alarmed, I look at Pip.

"Yes, Bethany, please give it to your father."

Rummaging through my satchel, I pull it out.

As he takes it, my father smiles. "This letter, my dearest Bethany, is proof of your standing. It will provide you with access to the court and your rightful place in the household of Richard, Duke of York. Your safety will be assured and that, my darling child, will make me happier than anything else."

I begin to cry, but I cannot understand why.

"Your mother would have been so proud."

"But, Father, I am only a country girl. I have no money for fine clothes."

"Oh, Bethany, you have a gift far greater than money."

With these words, Pip smiles at my father. With an outstretched hand, Pip takes my satchel and, before I can protest, slits it open.

I cry out loudly. "Oh no, how could you? That was my mother's last present to me."

"Oh no it wasn't, Bethany. This is your mother's last present to you."

I fall from my seat as Pip picks up a magnificent jewel and places it in my hand. Crumpled on the floor, I clutch a huge sapphire to my heart. My father breaks the silence.

"Bethany, you are holding the Mortimer Sapphire. A stone so precious that it will ensure you a life of luxury. Richard, Duke of York, knows what to do with the stone. He will see that it is delivered safely back to Ireland, where it belongs. He will also support you financially for life. You are free to marry, or not, as the case may be. This is your dowry and your way out of servitude. All I ask is that when the time comes, you choose wisely. A husband is for life and your children will also have Mortimer blood running through them. So, you need someone who is sympathetic to their needs. Our vicious queen desires the sapphire with a murderous lust, but do not worry, Pip here knows what to do. Now, there's just one more deception to lay bare and for this one you will have to forgive both myself and Pip."

The shock is far too much for me to deal with. I shake violently as the heavy curtain draws to the side once more. To my surprise, Ethel and Agnes totter in.

This time, Pip breaks the silence, but, far from looking sad, he beams with happiness. "Please, Bethany, let me introduce you to your mother's sisters – your aunties."

Still reeling, I manage to catch my breath, but I find it hard to comprehend everything.

"We had to get them to safety, too, and it seemed like the perfect plan. I would then be able to look after you all!" Pip laughs as he takes my hand and raises me up. "Oh, Bethany, you have so many people who love you, but I'm sure that none love you more than I do."

With this, Pip falls to one knee and gazes into my eyes. "Bethany, would you do me the honour of becoming my wife?"

Never before have I felt so sure of anything. I hesitate only to get my breath. "Yes, Pip. I would be honoured to be your wife."

With these words, the room comes alive and an overjoyed Pip rises from the floor and wraps both of his arms around me. I can feel his muscles twitch with excitement. "I must be the happiest man alive. You, Bethany Mortimer, have accepted a humble man. One who will love and protect you forever."

Looking over at my father, I am ecstatic to see that he is nodding his approval. All of a sudden, I freeze.

Pip, noticing the look of alarm on my face, becomes concerned. "Bethany, what's wrong? Have I displeased you?"

"No, not at all. It's just that you never sought my father's permission before asking me."

"Oh yes, I did. I asked him this morning." Laughter fills the air. "Come on, Bethany, take my hand. We have people to see." With this, Pip almost drags me out of the room, such is his haste.

"Where are we going?"

"To see a very important lady." We rejoin everyone in the main hall where a feast has been laid out. "Come on, Bethany, our places have been prepared. Today, we are to sit at the head of the table. On the dais, no less, so that all can see the soon-to-be Lady Philip Harsyck of South Acre."

My eyes reach the dais before my legs do and, before me, I can see Pip's mother. She is standing proudly and smiling. "Welcome, Bethany. Welcome to our family."

I look from Lady Harsyck to Pip. "Bethany, of course my mother knew I had fallen in love with you. I asked for her permission to marry you just before we left South Acre."

With these words, the hall erupts into cheers.

Charlemain then steps forward and kisses my cheek. "I am so proud. I never thought I would ever see the day when Pip would be anything other than solider. Now he's to be a lord, a husband and a solider, and I know that this would have filled his father's heart with joy."

I look around and smile uncontrollably. Pip has made me the happiest woman alive. Woken from my reveries, I notice that Ned has assumed the role of court jester once more and is now tumbling toward me at great speed. Fortunately, he manages to stop at my feet, before crouching like a small child. From his inside pocket, he retrieves a small velvet box, which he hands to Pip. Giggling like a child, he then rolls away again at top speed. Standing straight and proud, Pip opens the box to display a beautiful sapphire ring. The sparkling stone is set within a golden lattice. Once more, Pip takes to his knee and lifts my hand, before slipping the ring onto my finger.

I have never heard such a noise. It's a mixture of cheering and crying, so much so that my ears are now ringing.

Upright once more, Pip addresses the room, "Father Prior, may I thank you and all of your brothers for such a fine feast. You have made this day perfect. Now, let's eat, drink and be merry, before we all walk barefoot at dusk to the Holy Shrine of Walsingham, where we will thank God for our safe deliverance and the miracle of life."